Music of the Night

Nancy Herkness

REDBURN PRESS
New Jersey

Music of the Night

MUSIC OF THE NIGHT

September 2007

For information, contact Nancy Herkness at nancy@nancyherkness.com

ISBN: 978-1-59899-102-4

Music of the Night

Acknowledgements

My heartfelt thanks to:

Peter Tiboris, maestro and musical entrepreneur, who inspired the character of Nicholas Vranos and who got me onstage at Carnegie Hall without a moment's practice.

The staff of Mid-America Productions for patiently answering my questions and guiding me around Carnegie Hall's backstage.

The Glen Ridge High School Marching Band for bringing Beethoven's Tenth Symphony to the world, or at least to New Jersey.

Chris Pappas, who helped give Nicholas that touch of Greek.

Patti Anderson for her unerring ability to pinpoint what needed fixing.

Tara Doernberg, for her painstaking proofreading that went far above and beyond the ordinary.

Barbara Bretton, Deirdre Martin, and Joanna Novins, who bring sanity to this crazy business.

Damon and Sam, the world's greatest cheerleaders.

Jeff, Rebecca, and Loukas, who keep me in touch with what's important in life.

Any errors in this book are entirely my own.

Other books by Nancy Herkness:

A Bridge to Love

Shower of Stars

To Muffy and Daddy,

the foundation on which I build

Everywhere in the world, music enhances a hall,

with one exception:

Carnegie Hall enhances the music.

--Isaac Stern

Yes, death is strong, but . . .

stronger is music than death.

--Franz Werfel

CHAPTER 1

"Who'd want to kill a French horn player?" Detective Lieutenant Anna Salazar muttered to herself as she jogged up a short flight of steps and ducked under a strip of yellow police tape.

She started to flash her badge for the young police officer posted at the door of the crime scene but he waved it aside.

"You Detective Salazar?" the officer asked, blocking the doorway.

"Yep," Anna said.

"Man, I've heard a lot about you," the cop said.

"Oh," she said, blushing as she tried to slip around him.

Caught in the throes of hero worship, he didn't move.

"You figured out the Tatoo Artist Killer from the paintings he was copying onto his vics."

"That just pointed the team in the right direction," Anna said, looking over his shoulder for rescue from her partner Kevin "Mac" McKenzie. "A lot of good people worked on that case."

"I heard you caught a bullet and took the shooter down before you called for—"

"Hey, Salazar, you ever coming to work?" Mac said, finally taking pity on her.

"Sorry," Anna said with an apologetic smile for the young officer. "Mac's getting grouchy."

"Oh, right," the young officer said. He stepped sideways but turned to watch her all the way into the room.

"Thanks," Anna murmured to Mac. "I don't know where those stories come from."

"Face it, kid, you're a role model. You prove it can be done."

Anna just shook her head.

"I'm no different than anyone else."

Mac snorted.

Of course, one of the things he liked about his partner was her lack of conceit. She didn't understand why men sometimes acted like idiots around her and she didn't use it to her advantage. She insisted on solving her cases the hard way: with her brains and guts.

Originally, Mac had bitched big time about being assigned a rookie female partner, particularly one with big brown eyes and a smile that heated men up like Angelina Jolie's. He knew she had book smarts: she was Columbia Law before she quit to become a cop. It had taken about two days before he realized she had a core integrity like steel and she never gave up on a case. That was the other thing he really liked about her.

"What have you got on him?" Anna asked, interrupting his thoughts.

She stood beside the victim, a good-looking blond man with prominent cheekbones who was slumped forward on the piano bench with the side of his head resting on the keyboard. A black-edged hole at the base of his skull offered clear evidence of what had killed him.

"Alexei Savenkov. Age 39. Born in Russia, lived in New York City since age twelve. U.S. citizen. Top shelf French horn player," Mac said. "It looks like an execution. He was shot from behind at close range."

"In Carnegie Hall?" Anna said.

"Maybe someone didn't like the way he played Bach," Mac said.

"Why not just write a bad review?"

Anna flipped her long auburn braid behind her back as she leaned over the victim. She surveyed the body closely before she shifted her gaze to the police officer guarding the door. "Has anyone touched him since you got here?"

The young cop was still lost in his awe of the dark-eyed, long-legged detective so it took him a minute to register her question.

2

"Uh, no, no one. I didn't either," he stammered. "And the guy who found the body claims he only checked for a pulse."

"Someone searched his pockets after he died," Anna said, pointing to several folds of the expensive woven silk blazer lying at odd angles. "I wonder what they found."

Anna straightened and scanned her surroundings. The man had been shot in a small interior room which was evidently used for either practicing or auditions since a Steinway baby grand piano took up most of the available space. A couple of music stands and some vinyl-upholstered chairs were the remainder of the furniture. The cream walls were freshly painted and the flooring was commercial tile. A technician was combing the area, checking for fingerprints and fiber samples. A police photographer snapped pictures of the body from all sides.

"They must have blown their decorating budget on the concert hall," Anna said.

"And buying pianos," Mac said. A decade older than Anna, his ethnic heritage was evident in his sandy hair, ruddy complexion, and blue eyes. "They've got these pricey suckers scattered around like folding chairs."

"They buy new ones every couple of years, too. My piano teacher used to get the old ones at a discount," Anna said.

"You play piano?" Mac said, his eyebrows rising.

"Not in a long time."

"How long did you take lessons?"

"Ten years, give or take. I never got to be any good because I skimped on practicing."

"Every kid does," Mac said. "But I hereby officially declare you the music expert on this team."

Anna laughed.

"We have any witnesses?"

"Two." Anna and Mac turned in surprise as the young cop interjected himself into the conversation. "They're in the dressing rooms across the hall. One's the guy who found the

3

body. He's the one who identified the vic. The other's a woman who bumped into someone she thinks was an electrician just before the body was found."

"Thanks," Anna said with another smile. The officer almost saluted.

Mac rolled his eyes and flipped open his notebook to read from his notes.

"Witness one: Nicholas Vranos. He was meeting the victim here. He's a conductor. World class, evidently. Junior here says he's seen him on TV. Witness two: Jessica Strauss. She's a violinist who had an audition on the same floor. There's a cop in with each of them."

"Okay, details," Anna said, prompting Mac to list names, ages, residences, and whatever information the young officer had gotten from his first contact with the witnesses.

"You want to lead with the man or the woman?" Anna asked when he finished.

"I'll take the woman. I do avuncular real well," Mac said. "But we'll visit with Vranos first."

Opening the door the officer pointed to, Anna and Mac nodded to the policeman seated inside who quickly rose and left. The witness stood with his back to them, facing a window which looked out onto 56th Street.

Anna took in thick dark hair that grew over his collar, a black leather jacket outlining broad shoulders, and long, jeans-clad legs. When he turned at the sound of the closing door, she nearly gasped out loud. Anna had seen a lot of unusual people in her career with the NYPD but never had she seen such weirdly brilliant blue eyes. They were almost aquamarine, and she wondered if he wore tinted contact lenses. For a long moment, she couldn't focus on anything but those eyes. Nor did his gaze waver from her face. Mac moved a chair and the scraping sound brought her back to the task at hand.

"Nicholas Vranos? I'm Lieutenant Salazar with the NYPD and this is my colleague Lieutenant McKenzie. May we ask you some questions?"

"Of course," he said in an authoritative baritone. He had registered something that looked like surprise when he first turned but now his face was impassive. She sensed he was exerting a fair amount of effort to keep it that way.

"Shall we sit?" she asked, waving to the ubiquitous metal and vinyl chairs. This room lacked a Steinway, containing instead a Formica vanity and a large mirror surrounded by light bulbs.

"Certainly," he said, covering the distance to the chair in two strides. She found her gaze riveted on the fluid motion of his walk. To say he was magnetic was understating the truth; the rest of the room simply faded into insignificance around him.

When he sat, he stretched his long legs out in front of him and crossed them at the ankles, displaying a pair of black leather boots Anna suspected would cost her a week's salary. He crossed his arms as well and raised one of his dark eyebrows at her.

His body language was closed so Anna tried a softening approach.

"I understand you were friends with Mr. Savenkov," she said gently. "My condolences on your loss."

"Thank you, Lieutenant."

No sign of softening so far.

"I'm sorry to make you relive a distressing experience but would you tell me what happened today beginning at about three P.M.?"

The conductor glanced toward the window for a moment, and Anna heard the faint creak of his leather jacket as his weight shifted on the chair. He seemed to have forgotten Mac completely, turning his hypnotic blue gaze directly back to her without a glance in the other man's direction.

"I was bringing in my ex-wife's harp to hand it over to its new owner. While I was wrestling it out of the elevator, I saw a young woman walking down the corridor toward me, carrying a violin case. We said hello, a mere courtesy between strangers, and she continued down the hall past the elevator. I rolled the harp to the Maestro's Suite and locked it in. Then I checked my watch and realized it was time to meet Lexi . . . Mr. Savenkov . . . in the practice room. He had called me the night before, saying he had recently returned from Vienna and had something he wanted me to look at."

"And he wanted to show it to you here?"

"He said he needed to have a piano handy."

"Did he hint at what he had brought with him?"

"No." Vranos' lips curved in a faint smile. "Lexi likes to surprise people."

Anna could hear Mac's pen scratching on his pad of paper as the conductor paused, evidently lost in a memory of his friend.

"Please go on with what happened," she said quietly.

His smile vanished, leaving nothing but bleakness in its wake.

"I walked down the same corridor the young woman had taken, turned right, walked up a half flight of stairs. These hallways don't make a lot of sense since this back-stage space is made up of three buildings. Then I turned right again and walked to the room across the hall. The door was closed but not locked."

He stopped.

"I'm sorry to ask you to do this," Anna said.

At last he moved, waving his right hand in a gesture accepting the necessity of her question. She was surprised by the grace and eloquence of his motion until she remembered he was a conductor and regularly used his hands as a means of communication. His movement sent a thick strand of dark hair curving onto his temple. Anna fought a strange and unwelcome urge to lean forward and brush it back.

"I walked in and saw Lexi with his head on the piano and his eyes wide open," he said. "The angle of his neck and body was unnatural so I knew something was wrong. I was afraid he might have had a heart attack and dialed 9-1-1 on my cell phone as I walked toward him. Then I saw the bullet hole in the back of his head."

He pulled his legs in under the chair and leaned toward Anna. The blue of his eyes darkened as grief and anger vibrated through him.

"Lieutenant Salazar, Lexi was my closest friend. I want to know who murdered him and why."

"So do I, Mr. Vranos," Anna said. "That's why I'm a detective."

"What made you become a detective?" he asked in an odd tangent.

Anna considered his question and whether she should answer it. She decided trading a little personal information might persuade Vranos to loosen his control somewhat.

"I was going to be a lawyer but I had a problem with defending someone I knew was guilty. I decided I really wanted to catch the criminals and make sure they went to jail."

"So you believe in justice?"

"Yes."

"And innocence until proven guilty?"

"Well, I tend to work from the other direction."

"A cop through and through." His brief smile was fierce but approving. "You'll do fine, Lieutenant."

"Thanks," Anna said with some irony. "After you saw that Mr. Savenkov had been shot, what did you do?"

She wanted to put the interview back on course. Nicholas Vranos was getting to her. When he focused his blue eyes on her, she felt like a butterfly pinned to a board while the lepidopterist examined every vein in her wings. She found it more unnerving than unpleasant which bothered her even more.

"I finished my call to 9-1-1 except I told them there had been a murder, not a heart attack. Then I sat down in the chair by the piano until the police officer arrived."

"You stayed in the room with the body?"

"I didn't want to leave Lexi alone."

His look dared her to point out the absurdity of that; it was the first chink in his armor.

"I feel that way myself," Anna said, hoping to widen the crack. "The dead become my clients. I work for them."

Vranos leaned back and crossed his arms with another subtle sigh of expensive leather. Anna wanted to swear; she'd thought he was starting to open up to her.

"So you saw no one alive between the time you entered the corridor to the room and the time the police officer arrived?" she said, going back to policespeak.

"That's correct."

"Did you see any sign of a struggle in the room when you entered it?"

"These rooms are often messy. Music stands and chairs are left haphazardly when the musicians are finished with them. However, nothing was knocked over or broken. I was careful not to touch anything except the chair where I sat. And Lexi's neck. I did check for a pulse."

Anna nodded her approval of his restraint.

"Thank you for being so careful. Mr. Vranos, can you think of any reason why someone would want to kill Mr. Savenkov?"

"No." His response was instant. "He left his women laughing. He has enough money to be comfortable but not to kill for. He treated his colleagues with respect and they generally returned the sentiment. The music world is very competitive but Lexi is at the top; he has . . . *had* no need to play politics and he simply ignored the people whose envy made them dislike him."

"So he had no enemies professionally?"

"Not the murdering sort." His gaze turned inward and he muttered, "It must have been whatever it was he brought back with him. Have you found anything in his coat pockets?"

They had found a set of keys, a PDA whose contents looked unrevealing, although that would be checked more thoroughly later, sunglasses, and Savenkov's wallet with identification, money, and credit cards, apparently undisturbed. Nothing was hidden in the piano or elsewhere in the room. Whatever Lexi had wanted to show Nicholas Vranos was gone.

"Only the usual things. His wallet wasn't stolen or emptied."

Vranos stood and paced over to the window, giving her an excellent view of muscles moving under snug denim.

"If they got what they wanted, why did he have to be killed?"

"We'll find out, Mr. Vranos. Trust me on that," Anna said, shoving herself out of her chair. "And we'll make sure the killer is punished."

"So Lexi is *your* client now," he said, turning back toward her. He gave her a look so long and intense Anna thought her skin might have scorch marks. "I believe I do trust you, Lieutenant. So what do we do next?"

Anna sighed. She had guessed he would want to be involved.

"You stay where we can reach you and let us know if you think of anything else that might help our investigation," she said, handing him a business card with all her contact information on it. She made sure their fingers did not touch. She was afraid of the heat she felt surging between them. "We'll take care of the rest."

His brows snapped down in an angry line and for a moment she thought his control would slip. She underestimated him, however.

"In other words, let the police do their jobs without bumbling civilians in the way," he said. "Here's my offer: I promise you full access to Lexi's friends, relatives, and fellow musicians. In return, you keep me apprised of any developments in the case."

"Sorry, Mr. Vranos, I can't make that deal. Right now you're as likely a suspect as anyone so I obviously can't share details of the case with you."

"A suspect?" He laughed, a harsh sound that set Anna's teeth on edge. "Don't waste your time trying to prove me guilty, Lieutenant, because you can't do it. Are we finished here? I have work to do."

"At seven in the evening?" Anna asked, glancing at her stainless steel Timex.

"Yes."

"Please don't leave town unless we okay it."

He looked down his nose at her from almost a foot above her head and she could easily imagine him dominating a concert hall.

"Fortunately, my next two performances are in New York City so I can comply with your . . . request."

"Thank you," Anna said, locking eyes with him to make sure he knew it was more than a request. "Since you're offering to cooperate with us, could we send a team over to search your apartment?"

"I don't see what good that would do. Obviously, I couldn't have hidden the murder weapon there."

"It would look good for you," Anna said.

"Go ahead then, Lieutenant," he said with a ghost of a smile.

"Thanks for your cooperation."

He nodded.

"By the way," he said, looking directly at the bulge of the shoulder holster beneath her suede jacket, "I like a woman who wears a gun."

Anna watched him walk out the door without being able to think of a word to say.

"What kind of exit line was that?" she said, turning to Mac.

Her partner shrugged.

"Maybe the guy has a firearms fetish," he said. "A lot of men do. I know that's why I became a cop."

"Yeah, right," Anna said. "Did you notice how weird his eyes are? Once you look at them, you can't stop."

"The feeling was mutual. You could have lit a whole skyscraper with the electricity crackling between you two. I was invisible."

"What are you talking about? I was conducting the interview so he answered my questions."

"Watch yourself, Anna," Mac said. "Vranos took one look at you and decided there was something there he wanted. I get the feeling he's used to getting what he goes after."

Anna hunched a shoulder and started toward the door. She wasn't going to let even Mac believe she might be rattled by a suspect.

"He just has strange eyes. And he's not in the habit of taking orders."

Mac shook his head and followed his partner. He knew what he saw and he was worried.

"Ms. Strauss, I'm Detective Lieutenant McKenzie and this is—"

The young red-haired woman leapt out of her seat and threw herself into Mac's arms.

"Oh, thank you for coming!" she sobbed, clutching the lapels of his sports jacket in a death grip. "I blew the audition but he'll find me and kill me. He'll kill me so the audition doesn't matter. How could I screw up that audition?"

The female officer stationed by the door rolled her eyes at Anna and exited at high speed.

Mac, however, stood stoically as he waited for a break in the hysteria. Anna looked a question at him but he shook his head before taking the young woman's wrists and gently pulling her hands away from his collar.

"Ms. Strauss, please sit down," he said, finding a package of Kleenex in his pocket and handing it to her as he guided her to a chair. "No one will kill you. We'll make sure of that. But to keep you safe we need you to answer some questions."

Jessica Strauss held the packet of tissues as though it were spun gold.

"Thank you," she said with a slight hiccup. "Thank you so much. You're so incredibly kind."

Since she didn't seem to get the idea, Mac pulled a tissue out of the package and handed it to her. Anna sat down outside of Jessica's view and flipped open her notebook, waiting for the interview to begin.

"I needed that job," the violinist said as tears dripped onto the Kleenex still resting on her open palm.

Mac sat down in a chair across from her and leaned forward.

"What audition did you have?" he asked in calm, sympathetic tones.

"F-f-for the Manhattan Strings. W-w-with Claude St. Albans. I couldn't get through the piece. I kept missing the triplets. Oh God, how could I be so incompetent?" The sobs started again and she crumpled the tissue in her hand without using it.

Despite the tears coursing down the violinist's cheeks, Jessica's nose showed no signs of running and her green eyes were only slightly reddened around the rims. Anna envied her ability to cry without looking repulsive. Although the woman was almost as tall as Mac's five foot eleven, she had an ethereal pre-Raphaelite look with her long red ringlets and pale skin stretched over delicate bones. She was dressed in a long, floating purple dress with ruffled sleeves which looked as though they'd snag on the violin's strings.

"Was it just you and Mr. St. Albans in the room?" Mac asked.

"Oh no, the first violinist Maureen Fitzpatrick was there and also Stephen Beck, the orchestra manager. Mr. St. Albans was being really nice to listen to me at all. He could have left the audition to Maureen and Mr. Beck. Now I wish he had."

"What time was your audition?" Mac asked, before taking the neglected tissue package out of her hand.

"Three o'clock," Jessica said. "But Mr. St. Albans was late so we didn't get started until about 3:15."

"How long did it last?"

That brought on another burst of tears. Mac put a fresh tissue in her hand.

"N-n-not very long when I couldn't finish the piece," she wailed.

"Who left the room first, you or Mr. St. Albans?"

"I did. I was too humiliated to talk to him. I took my violin and went into a practice room down the hall."

Her violin case had already been searched so Mac didn't pursue that line of questioning.

"What did you do there?"

"I cried for awhile. Then I pulled myself together."

Anna found the latter hard to picture.

"I went out into the hall and ran into the *murderer*," Jessica said with great emphasis on the last word.

"Why do you think he's the murderer?" Mac asked in the same rational tone of voice.

"Well, he must be since he was here when Alexei Savenkov was killed. And he looked . . . murderous. He was carrying a big tool kit where he could hide the gun."

"He looked 'murderous'?" Mac prodded.

Jessica's shoulders sagged and Mac handed her another tissue.

"He . . . he . . . well, I ran into him because I wasn't watching where I was going. I was still upset about the audition. He grabbed me hard on my left arm and stared into my face with this cold, mean look in his eyes. I started to apologize when he sort of threw me out of his way." She sobbed harder. "Now I know he was memorizing my face so he could find me and kill me because I'm a witness."

"Can you tell me what he looked like?"

"He had really dark brown eyes, almost black, but with a weird light rim that made them scarier. He was wearing a baseball cap so I couldn't see his hair but he had a brown mustache."

Anna noted down the description, thinking the mustache might be a fake.

"Can you estimate how tall he was?"

A hard number was more than the violinist could come up with.

"Where would you say your nose came to compared with him?" Mac prompted.

"Um, well, about the top button of his shirt. It was green and had some writing on the pocket. I think he was an electrician because it looked like that kind of workman's uniform."

"They have security cameras here," Mac said. "Would you be willing to take a look at the videos and see if he's on one of them?"

"They have cameras in here?" Jessica said.

"They're also on the stages and in a few other places," Mac said. "One of them might have caught him."

She buried her face in her hands.

"I don't want to see his face ever again," she said through her fingers.

"I understand," Mac said. "But if we catch him, you won't have to worry about him any longer."

She raised her head and squared her shoulders, making her ruffles flutter.

"All right. I'll do it," she said.

"Thank you. You're a brave woman," Mac said.

Anna somehow kept a straight face.

"Before we go to the security office, tell me what happened after you ran into the electrician?" Mac asked.

"He upset me again so I went back into the practice room to get away from him and to calm down. When I was sure he was gone, I started toward the stairs. I saw Mr. Vranos, you know, the famous conductor, in the hallway with a harp case. He had just come off the elevator so I decided to take that down to the stage door. But the elevator doors had already closed so I had to wait for it to come back. That took awhile because it's slow and not many people can fit into it at one time. By the time I got to street level, the security guard had blocked the exit so no one could leave. That's when I found out Alexei Savenkov had been murdered."

After a few more questions, Mac got Jessica on her feet for the journey down to the security office. She threaded her hand through Mac's arm and leaned heavily on him, her head practically resting on his shoulder. Anna was left to carry the violin case. When the elevator door opened to reveal a miniscule space, Anna wheeled toward the stairs. Mac threw her an imploring look, so she wedged herself and the instrument case into the claustrophobic car, earning a huffy sigh from Jessica.

The guard had the relevant tapes ready for them and it wasn't long before Jessica pointed at the black-and-white screen, saying, "There, that's him behind the two women. I recognize his hat."

The guard froze the image and they all examined it. However, all that was visible was the baseball cap and one shoulder. The two women he was following hid his features. The guard restarted the tape but the electrician stayed well concealed, although as he walked Anna could see a black tool box in his hand.

Jessica spotted the man on two additional cameras and Anna caught him on a third. In each case, he had his head turned away or he walked behind a group of people. The man had marked the cameras and had deliberately avoided being recorded.

Anna met Mac's look and mouthed the word, "Pro." Mac nodded, his mouth tightening.

When Mac had handed Jessica over to the female police officer again, he turned back to Anna.

"That tool box was plenty big enough for a handgun and silencer."

"Yeah, not to mention all the musical instrument cases that came and went," Anna said. "The weapon could have been in any of them."

"Let's look at the tapes one more time," Mac said.

"I'm thinking the mustache might be a fake," Anna said. "And that he wore contact lenses."

"I'm thinking the same. That would explain the light rims around his irises," Mac agreed, as they scanned the video recordings.

They froze the best image and enlarged it.

"You remember this guy?" Mac asked the guard.

The man looked closely.

"No, but I think I recognize the symbol on his shirt pocket."

Anna and Mac leaned over his shoulder to squint at the image.

"It's a contractor we use sometimes: Hayes Electric. I'll look up the contact information for you," he said, trotting into the next office.

"He stole the uniform," Anna said under her breath.

"Yeah, but we gotta check it out anyway," Mac said, thanking the guard when he came back with the information. "This isn't going to be an easy one."

Anna thought of being locked in the blue gaze of Nicholas Vranos' eyes and nodded.

"I guess I'd better brush up on my Beethoven."

CHAPTER 2

"It's your turn to do it, Mac," Anna said as she took another sip of her double mocha chip frappuccino. She always bought herself a comfort beverage when they had to notify the next of kin that a presumably beloved relative had died violently. Mac waited until he got home to have a shot of single malt. "I told the last one and I still have nightmares about it. Take this exit."

Mac grunted and swung the dark sedan onto the exit ramp. "So what do we know about Savenkov's sister?" he asked.

Anna put down her cup to flip through her notebook.

"Age: thirty-two. U.S. citizen. Divorced a year ago. Two children, ages four and two. She's an accountant. Lived at this address in Queens for six years. Seven years younger than Savenkov. That's about it."

Mac grunted again and their conversation went back to the dead ends they had encountered at Carnegie Hall: no murder weapon, two questionable witnesses, no face for the electrician in the security tapes.

"At least we can take St. Albans and his bunch out of the equation, unless all three of them committed the murder together like one of those Agatha Christie books," Mac said. "The video tapes show them entering and exiting the building in one group and they swear they were with each other the whole time in that one room."

"You know, if I decide to commit a murder, I'm doing it at Carnegie Hall," Anna said. "That place is a rabbit warren. Doorways and corridors that make no sense. All those little interconnected rooms."

"Instrument cases in all sizes for the weapon," Mac agreed. "Whoever did this knew they could easily carry the gun in and out."

They pulled up in front of a stucco house with brown trim and shutters. The small front yard needed mowing but sported two circular beds of geraniums that glowed red in the reflected light of the streetlamps. Mac rang the doorbell and the pale blur of a woman's face appeared in one of the sidelight windows by the door. Anna held her badge up against the glass and the face nodded and vanished before two locks clicked open.

A barefoot woman wearing a wrinkled pink man-tailored blouse and straight black skirt swung the door wide and gestured the two detectives inside without saying a word. She had blond hair twisted into a knot at the back of her head, bloodshot blue eyes and red-rimmed nostrils, as well as the same high cheekbones as the dead man.

"Ms. Gromyko?" Mac asked.

The woman nodded.

"I'm afraid we have some bad news—"

Ekaterina Gromyko waved a hand to stop him as tears welled up in her eyes.

"Lexi's dead. I already know. Nicholas told me." She choked on a sob. "Come in, please."

Anna and Mac exchanged a glance as they followed her into the living room. Nicholas Vranos had blatantly ignored their instructions not to discuss the case. Lexi's sister sank into a wing chair by the fireplace and then bolted back to her feet.

"Would you like something to drink?" she asked.

"No, thank you," Anna said, seating herself in the matching wing chair. "We're very sorry to intrude on your grief but may we ask you a few questions?"

"If it will help find Lexi's . . . the person who did this to him, yes." Ekaterina collapsed into the chair again.

"Your children can't hear us, can they?" Anna asked. "I don't want to upset them."

"No, they're at a neighbor's house. I haven't told them yet. They adore their Uncle Lexi."

They ran through some easy questions to give Kathy, as she asked them to call her, time to get used to their presence. Anna decided to throw a tougher one at her.

"Can you think of anyone who held a grudge against your brother? We're not asking you to accuse anyone of murder but sometimes grudges fester."

Kathy shook her head, swallowed, and shook her head again.

"My ex-husband hated Lexi." She took a deep breath. "But I don't know . . . George was abusive when he drank but just hitting me and throwing things. It wasn't planned or . . . or organized like getting a gun. That's why I divorced him. I thought he'd change when we had children but they don't change."

Anna thought about how many times she had heard this same story and nodded sympathetically.

"I was afraid for my babies. So Lexi got me the best divorce lawyer in Queens. He cancelled all his performances for three weeks and stayed here in case George tried to do . . . anything after the papers were served."

"Did your ex-husband in fact do anything violent?" Mac asked.

"He came by here several times but we changed the locks so he couldn't get in. Lexi would go out to talk to him, there was a lot of shouting, and then George would leave. He never brought a gun or anything. He never even hit Lexi."

"Did he contest the divorce?" Anna asked.

"No, thank God!" Kathy said. "I didn't think he'd give up so easily. He was pretty possessive of me and the children. I thought it meant he loved us."

Anna and Mac looked at each other again, clearly sharing the same thought. Lexi Savenkov had probably done more than shout at George a few times.

"Is there anyone else you can think of who might not have wished your brother the best?" Mac prompted.

Kathy stared into the empty fireplace as she considered before shaking her head.

"People like Lexi. He has a spirit of mischief that makes people laugh. I always call him Puck."

Anna saw the exact moment Kathy realized Lexi wouldn't make anyone laugh ever again and it twisted her gut.

"I'm so sorry," Anna said. "Just one more question: what's your ex-husband's occupation?"

"George? He's an electrician."

As soon as she saw the dark sedan pull away from the curb, Kathy Gromyko flipped open her cell phone and hit a speed dial number.

"Nicholas? Two detectives came to tell me about Lexi. I think you should give them the piece of paper."

"Was it a young woman and a sandy-haired man?" Nicholas Vranos' baritone sounded through the phone. "Salazar and McKenzie?"

"I'm pretty sure those were their names. Wait a minute. They left a card." As Kathy scanned the room for the small white rectangle, she continued, "The woman was very striking. She had long dark red hair in a braid."

"That's Detective Salazar."

"She was very kind. I think she really cares that Lexi's dead," Kathy said, her voice breaking on the last word. She spotted the business card and checked the name on it. "The other one was Detective Lieutenant Kevin McKenzie."

"I'll give the paper to them tomorrow," the conductor said. "I need to make a copy and study it before I let go of it."

"Thank you. I know this isn't the best time for you with the concert coming up . . . ."

"For Lexi, I always have time."

"Vranos may have ignored our orders but at least we didn't have to break the bad news to her," Anna said, before she sucked the last mocha chips in the frappuccino through the straw. They were back in the car headed for the abusive ex-husband's apartment. "Not that the interview was any easier because of it."

"It's a bad sign though. He does what he wants."

"And he's used to having a lot of other people do what he wants because he's a hot shot conductor."

"Maybe we'll wrap this whole thing up tonight so we won't have to deal with Vranos anyway. Maybe Gromyko's our electrician."

"Sure, and I'm the queen of Spain."

"Lucky for us, criminals can be incredibly stupid."

"Yeah, but he doesn't look like the description of the electrician," Anna said, slotting her empty Starbucks cup in the car's console in order to pick up the photo Kathy had given them, saying she had kept it only for the children's sake.

Tilting the print to catch the glare of the neon lights on Bell Boulevard, she saw a smiling, clean-shaven man with dark eyes and dark hair holding two very young children. Kathy had described him as being of medium height and muscular build whereas the electrician at Carnegie Hall had been tall and sported a mustache. She tossed the photo on the dashboard.

"How much of Jessica Strauss' description do you think we rely on?" she asked.

"I think she knows what she saw, even if she was more worried about the audition than the victim."

"This is the address," Anna said.

They pulled up in front of a small complex of red brick apartment buildings. George Gromyko's place was on the third floor.

The man who opened the door looked like his photograph and his muscles rivaled Mac's. He was dressed in blue jeans with a crease pressed into them and a dazzling white tee shirt. The apartment he led them into was furnished in Ikea-Scandinavian style, each piece lined up perfectly with the one beside it or set at exactly a ninety degree angle. The newspaper piled on the table was centered on the blond wooden surface and a yellow coffee mug sat on a ceramic coaster.

Anna raised her eyebrows, wondering if he had been so obsessively neat when he was married. Dropping onto an oatmeal-colored chair, she pulled out her notebook and uncapped her pen.

"Did you go to work this morning?" Mac started.

"Look, I let you in. I think you should tell me why you want to know," Gromyko said, as he sat on the couch.

"There's been a murder. We're investigating it," Mac said.

"Someone I know?" Gromyko asked.

"You need to answer the question now."

"Yeah, I worked at the Hair We Are beauty shop on Bell Boulevard. The foreman can tell you that."

"What time did you leave work?"

"Three-thirty. Now I answered two of your questions so tell me who's dead," Gromyko said.

"What did you do after you left the job site?" Mac asked.

"Came home. Took a shower. Watched TV. Cooked dinner." Gromyko's look challenged Mac to complain about his short answers.

"Did you speak with anyone in the apartment complex?"

"Nah, I don't like anyone here." Suddenly Gromyko lost his sullen attitude. "My kids . . . has anything happened—?"

"No, your children are fine," Anna interrupted to reassure him.

"Thanks," he said, glaring at Mac.

"Your former brother-in-law Alexei Savenkov died this afternoon," Mac said.

"Jesus, poor Kathy!" His concern seemed genuine. Then he looked at the two police officers with sudden suspicion. "I guess Kathy told you Savenkov broke up our marriage."

"That wasn't quite how she described it," Anna said.

Angry color flooded Gromyko's cheeks.

"What'd she tell you? That it was my fault? She and the kids would still be with me if it wasn't for that scumbag brother of hers."

"So you weren't fond of your ex-brother-in-law?" Mac asked.

"Hell no, but I didn't kill him, if that's what you're trying to say," Gromyko said.

"Did he threaten you in some way at the time of your divorce?" Anna asked.

"Threaten?" His laugh was scornful. "I could have flattened him with one jab. He didn't go to the gym because he was a *musician*."

"Threats don't have to be physical," Anna said.

Gromyko wiped his hands on his neatly pressed jeans and then caved in.

"He found out something about me in the past. Nothing criminal or anything," he added, remembering they were the police. "But I didn't want Kathy or the kids to know. Savenkov made me sign away custody of my kids to keep it secret."

"You might as well tell us what it was, Mr. Gromyko," Anna said. "We'll find out eventually."

Gromyko sat silent for a moment. He got up so suddenly that both Mac and Anna started to reach for their guns, but the electrician walked across his living room to a bookcase filled with framed photos of his children. He stood with his back to them.

"When I met Kathy, I was with someone else."

Anna rolled her eyes at Mac. The guy was truly neurotic if he thought Kathy would hold that against him.

"With a man. I don't know how Savenkov found out."

That changed things.

"Have you been in contact with this guy since then?" Mac asked.

Gromyko whipped around to face them. Tears glistened on his cheeks.

"No, never. Once I met Kathy, I knew she was the person I loved. I wanted to have children with her."

"What's his name?" Anna said.

"Joe Hoffman. He was at Devine and Post, the law office. Are you going to tell Kathy?"

"Only if it's necessary for our investigation," Mac said.

Gromyko walked back to his chair and sat down before he went on the offensive.

"The guy you should talk to is Nicholas Vranos, the big music conductor. They were supposedly friends but Savenkov slept with Nicholas' wife."

"Before they were divorced?" Anna asked, remembering Vranos' reference to his ex-wife's harp.

"A year before," Gromyko said with a nasty smile. "You can't tell me that wouldn't make you want to kill someone."

"How do you know about the affair?" Anna asked.

"I caught them together at a restaurant. She had her hand in his crotch under the tablecloth so it wasn't just a friendly dinner. Savenkov didn't try to hide it. He claimed Vranos' marriage had been over for years but he hadn't bothered to get a divorce because he and his wife were too busy working. Nobody's that busy."

"That guy's a prime candidate for psychoanalysis," Anna said as Mac steered the car back toward the 59th Street Bridge. "And he's got a shaky alibi but he looks nothing like the electrician on the video tapes. I don't remember seeing anyone else who looked like Gromyko on the tapes. Do you?"

Anna waited as Mac thought. He had an almost photographic memory so she knew he was running the images they had seen earlier in the day through his mind.

"No," he said. "Nothing's clicking."

The first note of a cell phone ring sounded. When the tones arranged themselves into Billy Joel's "New York State of Mind", Mac said, "It's yours."

Anna was already pulling the phone out of her jacket pocket.

"Salazar."

"Good evening, Detective. This is Nicholas Vranos." His deep voice sent prickles down her neck. Anna tried to kill the effect by putting some space between the phone and her ear. "I have something I think you should see. Kathy Gromyko, Alexei's sister, gave it to me this evening."

"Ah, yes. You visited Ms. Gromyko before we did," Anna said. "I believe we asked you not to discuss the case with anyone except us."

"I wasn't going to let Kathy hear about Lexi's death from strangers. They are . . . were very close."

"If you'd like us to catch your friend's killer, you should follow our instructions. We have reasons for what we ask you to do."

There was a tense moment's pause, and Anna braced herself for an outburst.

"My apologies, Detective," Vranos said with tightly controlled elocution. "I'll try not to step on your toes in the future."

Ha! Anna thought. But at least he would behave himself temporarily.

"Thank you," she said. "What did Ms. Gromyko give you?"

"It's something you need to see. I'll be rehearsing at Carnegie Hall tomorrow. If you come by at about 12:30, I should be done."

"Twelve-thirty at Carnegie Hall," Anna repeated, looking at Mac to see if he was available.

He shook his head.

"Where shall I meet you?" Anna said, deciding to go it alone. His eyes wouldn't seem so mesmerizing now that she was prepared.

"In the concert hall. Isaac Stern Auditorium. Come a little early. You might be surprised at who you'll see there."

"I'll try," Anna said. "Thanks."

"So the sister gave him something she didn't mention to us," Mac said after Anna flipped her phone shut.

Anna sighed.

"Why do people make it so hard for us to do our job? We're all on the same side."

"That's where you're wrong," Mac said. "We're on neither side. We straddle them both so neither side trusts us and both sides are afraid of us. You have to get used to that."

Anna sighed again. She got out her notebook and reviewed the facts and impressions of their interview with the electrician, with Mac adding his own comments.

"So we've come full circle," she said as they finished.

"Right back where we started from," Mac agreed. "The conductor."

CHAPTER 3

The security guard at Carnegie Hall's stage door waved Anna through.

"No need to show the badge. I remember you from yesterday," he said. "Diane Engstrom, one of our artistic directors, says she needs to speak to you. She's in the House Manager's office right now."

Anna looked at her watch. She was fifteen minutes early because she'd been at Alexei Savenkov's apartment and hadn't had enough time to go back to her office to change out of her jeans and dark blue NYPD tee shirt. The apartment was so stuffed with small decorative objets d'art that it had taken longer to search it than she expected. She remembered Nicholas Vranos' comment that she'd see someone interesting if she arrived early but decided the artistic director's request took precedence.

She walked through a set of double doors and past the bulletin boards posted with rehearsal and performance schedules, usher sign-up sheets, and all the other organizational charts necessary for running a major performance venue. She noted that the sheets listing audition room reservations were publicly posted so anyone could see who would be in which room and when.

Sticking her head in the door of the office, she saw an older woman sitting at a small round table, talking on the phone. Her gray hair was pulled back in a bun with two chopsticks stuck through it and she wore scarlet lipstick. Anna pointed to the badge on her belt and the woman nodded and finished her telephone conversation promptly.

"I'm Diane Engstrom, artistic director," she said as she rose and held out her hand as though she expected Anna to kiss it. "I have something of a very confidential nature to impart to you. Let us retire to that corner behind the desk where we can't be overheard."

Anna stifled a sigh at the dramatics and followed the director to the far end of the room where they pulled up two wheeled chairs facing each other. Ms. Engstrom pulled hers forward until their knees were nearly touching and spoke in a stage whisper.

"Lexi Savenkov's death is a terrible tragedy for the music world. Just terrible. I can't believe I'll never hear him play the *Eroica* again. But it's even more dreadful for you; you'll *never* have the pleasure of hearing him." Diane Engstrom shook her head. Beneath the exaggerated manner, her sorrow seemed genuine and it took her a moment to find her voice to continue as she leaned in closer to Anna. "There's a young musician rehearsing here today who came to me with some information which is absolutely vital to the case."

Anna pulled out her notebook and pen, telling herself Diane Engstrom clearly relished drama so the "vital" information might be insignificant.

"Name?"

Diane took a card out of her skirt pocket, holding it slightly arched with the pressure of her fingertips. "This is his business card. He's very, very shy and doesn't want to be seen talking to the police so please don't approach him directly. He'd like to meet you somewhere away from here after the rehearsal."

"I completely understand, Ms. Engstrom," Anna said with her most reassuring smile. "I won't bother him here. What instrument does he play?"

"The trumpet. He's the young Chinese man in the trumpet section, very, very sweet and incredibly talented. I think he's going to develop into something special."

Diane Engstrom finally handed over the card. Anna glanced down to see "William Tsao, Trumpet, Cornet" printed on the card along with an e-mail address and various phone numbers.

"You'll find the villain who took Lexi from us and from the world, won't you?"

"Yes, ma'am," Anna said, surprising herself with the certainty of her own statement. Ms. Engstrom's hyperbole must be rubbing off on her. "Thank you for your help."

With a swirl of her skirt, the artistic director stood.

"Allow me to escort you to the rehearsal. We've got masses of security here today. It's been quite a bother."

"That's kind of you but I can just show my badge," Anna said. "Is the security here because of Mr. Savenkov's murder?"

"Lord no! I never even thought . . . it never occurred to any of us . . . ," Diane Engstrom said, her lipstick looking very bright as the blood left her face. "*Should* we have extra security?"

"It sounds like you have plenty already so I wouldn't worry," Anna said.

"Thank goodness. No, the extra guards are here because of Billy Leon."

"The lead singer of *Aluminum Zebras*?" Anna asked, following Diane Engstrom to a set of double doors manned by two security guards. She automatically flipped her jacket back to display the badge, and one of the guards nodded and opened the door. "Is *he* doing a concert at Carnegie Hall?"

The sound of violins swelled around them as they stepped through the doors.

"No, he's composed a symphony and Nicholas Vranos is conducting it. I can't imagine how Mr. Leon talked Mr. Vranos into doing that. It must be because all the proceeds are going to a charity."

They walked up a half flight of steps carpeted in deep red plush.

"Doesn't Mr. Vranos get paid to conduct?"

"Yes, dear, but he's one of the top conductors in the world. He can pick and choose his work and he doesn't generally do *gimmicky* things like conducting symphonies written by rock stars."

The red carpeting ran along a wide gently curving corridor. The outer wall sported a line of autographed photos in black frames. To their left was another set of double doors and another security guard.

"Isaac Stern Auditorium. It has the most superb acoustics in the world," Diane Engstrom said, heading for the double doors. "I'll show you where to sit to get the absolutely perfect sound."

The music poured through the door as it opened into the dim interior of the famous performance space.

They were standing near the left corner of the stage which was raised about four feet above them. The orchestra was in full voice now, all the instruments joined in a long crescendo, completely controlled by the man standing on a platform in the middle of the brilliantly lit stage, his arms raised and curved like wings. Nicholas Vranos wore pleated charcoal gray slacks and a blue button-down shirt, sleeves rolled up to his elbows. The blue fabric stretched tight across his broad back, the creases rearranging themselves as his arms rose and fell. His dark hair was disheveled, making it look longer and thicker than at the interview yesterday.

But it was his hands that held her gaze. The music seemed to spring from those long tapered fingers dancing through the air in long swooping arcs, coaxing the musicians to more, better, fuller. His hands dropped and the sound of his baton tapping the metal music stand stopped the orchestra in mid-phrase. The cessation of sound was almost shocking in its abruptness.

"We'll fix that later," he said. "Do you have a page turn at 423? All right, I'll watch your turn and then we're going. And that's an E-natural at 428, cellos."

The principal cellist said, "And that's a quarter rest at 431, maestro."

Vranos turned to the audience. The blue of his eyes was laser bright even at a distance.

"Mr. Leon, did you really *intend* to put a quarter rest there?"

Raucous guffaws came from the audience, echoed by more subdued laughter from the stage. Anna didn't get the musical joke.

Diane Engstrom touched her arm and she turned to see rows and rows of empty red velvet seats stretching away from them. Anna looked up at the horseshoe-shaped balconies, their cream plaster decorated with garlands and dentils picked out in gilt, filled with yet more red velvet chairs. It reminded her of a fancy jewelry box, the kind a ballerina sprang up and twirled in when you opened it.

Knots of people sat scattered through the orchestra seats, the largest a group of men with unkempt hair and tee shirts with bright graphics printed on them. Anna immediately recognized the bleached blond mop of hair that was Billy Leon's trademark.

She started to follow Diane Engstrom toward the back of the theater when a tall, slim man in a navy blue suit and striped tie rose from a seat near them and came over to her side.

"Hello, I'm Norman Drucker, Mr. Vranos' assistant," he whispered. "He asked me to escort you up to the stage when you arrived."

"In the middle of the rehearsal?" Anna whispered back in surprise.

Norman Drucker smiled.

"Trust me, no one will notice. They're very focused."

Ms. Engstrom waved to her and strode off to find her perfect seat. Anna shrugged and followed Drucker up the steps built into the blond wood of the stage. He led her to an empty chair placed against the left-hand stage wall, just behind the last row of violins. As Norman had promised, no one on stage paid her the slightest bit of attention.

Anna forced herself to look away from the man conducting to find the sweet, talented Chinese trumpet player. She had to shift in her chair slightly to spot him through the forest of violins. His hair was clipped short, his glasses were horn-rimmed and his baggy cargo shorts showed off muscular calves. He was leaning forward to write something on his sheet music as the basses rumbled away to his left.

The baton tapped again and the rumbling stopped abruptly. Anna looked up to see Nicholas gesture toward the trumpets.

"Now, with Mr. Leon's permission, we're going to make a little change in the last section. All trumpets, play the xeroxed sheets Norman gave you this morning. And remember, make it bright."

His arms struck their graceful upward curve. The silence was absolute. His long fingers almost imperceptibly signaled three beats and then sound seemed to spring from all around her as his arms straightened and pulsed upward.

It made a lush, cushiony cocoon with the big stringed instruments and the kettle drums thrumming low and soft. Anna thought of sinking into black velvet. The violins throbbed quietly and the clarinets threaded a minor, slightly oriental melody through the deeper notes. The music enclosed her in warm, seductive arms. Yet the acoustics were so perfect she could hear each instrument individually if she concentrated.

Suddenly, Nicholas' whole body pivoted sharply to stage left and his baton seemed to quiver with command. An explosion of trumpets pealed forth with almost overwhelming brilliance. The clarity was so extraordinary Anna gasped.

"Yes," Billy Leon shouted from the audience. "Yes, yes, yes!"

Little chills feathered up her spine, and Anna felt her eyes fill at the sheer beauty of the music. When the trumpets ceased, she wanted to jump up and scream, "No, don't stop!" Yet it was also a relief to be released from the thrall of their perfection.

She began to grasp the composer's intention; he wanted you to fall into the next section of the music with that sigh of relief. He had woven a safety net of sound for you. From that realization on, Anna was lost to her surroundings. All she was aware of was sound and Nicholas Vranos' movements because the two could not be separated.

After two different themes had been explored, the music began to weave itself into black velvet again and Anna held her breath, waiting for the exquisite blast of trumpets. But this time they began so softly she had to strain to hear their motif. As they built to their almost painfully beautiful crescendo, she casually rubbed her jacket sleeve over her cheeks to remove all traces of the tears she hadn't been able to hold back. Nicholas' arms sliced down in a swift, decisive arc and all sound ceased.

No one spoke or moved for what seemed like minutes. Then Nicholas turned and said, "I think that sounded all right."

Anna had to swallow a slightly hysterical laugh at his understatement.

The musicians rustled a bit as they waited for the composer's verdict.

"That was effing brilliant!" Billy said, standing up and clapping. "Effing brilliant!"

Nicholas swept an ironic bow and turned back to the stage. "After that evaluation, anything further would be an anticlimax. Sorry to cut short your overtime but you can all go to lunch now. Thank you, ladies and gentlemen. Excellent work!"

"Can we round to the nearest hour? Billy can afford it," a cellist joked as everyone began to straighten up their sheet music and pack up their instruments.

"How about a bonus for the trumpet section?" another voice called. "We have to carry everyone in that fourth movement."

Nicholas stepped off the podium and spoke to several of the musicians. As he turned, his eyes fell on Anna. He swept his hair back from his forehead and scrubbed his palms over his face before walking toward her. For the first time, Anna noticed dark sweat stains under his arms.

Billy Leon and his entourage surged up the stage steps and intercepted the conductor. The rock star was shorter than Anna had expected but the charisma that filled entire football stadiums crackled around him. As the two men met, Anna noticed the power of Nicholas Vranos' presence, although subtler than Billy Leon's, was in no way overwhelmed by it.

Billy reached out and pumped Nicholas' hand. "You were right, man. The second trumpet part diluted the motif. Good call."

"When I was studying the fourth movement, the extra part bothered me," Nicholas said. "I appreciate your willingness to try it my way."

One of his entourage spoke in Billy's ear. "Right," the rock star said. "I gotta run. See you here tomorrow."

"Nine o'clock," Nicholas agreed as the rock star and his posse hustled away. He turned to Anna. "My apologies for keeping you waiting so long."

"Not a problem. It was interesting to watch you work."

His blue gaze focused on her cheeks before falling to the tear stains still visible on her suede sleeve. A look of satisfaction lit his face.

"The cynical police detective is not immune to the seductions of music," he said.

"I haven't had much sleep for the past two days," Anna said to cover her embarrassment.

Vranos' voice deepened, taking on the same thrumming quality of the basses.

"Don't deny it, Lieutenant. Music brings a glimpse of heaven to earth."

CHAPTER 4

Anna had to clear her throat.

"You have something to show me," she finally managed to croak.

"Upstairs," Nicholas said. "Let me collect my music."

He strode across the stage and picked up a stack of paper and two batons from the music stand. The musicians were almost all gone, and Anna mentally castigated herself for missing William Tsao's exit. She had been too mesmerized by the conductor to do her job properly.

Nicholas waved her through the big double doors stage right. They passed through a transitional space crammed with electronic equipment, video screens showing the stages of all three performance spaces in Carnegie Hall, and yet another Steinway piano, this one a giant concert grand.

As they started up a flight of steps, Anna couldn't resist asking, "Is Billy Leon's symphony good?"

"Surprisingly so," Nicholas said, looking both pleased and startled, as though a formerly bored pupil had suddenly shown interest in her studies. "Billy's public relations machine doesn't think it's in keeping with his image to tell the public this, but he's a classically trained violinist."

"Do you often change what a composer writes?"

"No, especially if the composer is no longer living. My job is to attempt to understand what the composer was trying to accomplish and render that as faithfully as I can. However, Billy is open-minded and willing to discuss other possibilities."

They reached the top of the steps and turned left, walking toward a room labeled "Maestro's Suite".

"What exactly did you change about the trumpets today?" Anna asked. She found herself fascinated by this glimpse into the rarefied world of classical music.

Vranos' blue gaze focused on her as though he was trying to measure the genuineness of her questions.

"There was a second trumpet part that was a descant to the first," he explained. "When I looked at the piece I found it distracting, given the strength of the first trumpet motif. I felt the listener should be allowed to focus on that single beautiful line."

"It sounded pretty close to perfect to me," Anna said fervently.

"Thank you, Lieutenant. It gratifies me to know my music can move the soul of a New York City police detective," Nicholas said, bowing his head as he held the door to the suite open for her, then closed and locked it behind them. He tossed the music and batons onto the top of a baby grand piano.

"Do you mind if I take a moment to wash?" he asked.

"Go ahead. Conducting seems to be hard work," Anna said. She had heard the edge of irony in his voice as he acknowledged her compliment. He must believe she was trying to gain his confidence through flattery.

Nicholas disappeared through another door and Anna walked farther into the room to look around. It was surprisingly spare considering the great musicians who had passed through it. The black Steinway took up a third of the space and the rest contained nothing more than a dozen small wooden chairs upholstered in dark blue striped velvet and some of the standard-issue metal music stands. Deep red carpeting contrasted with the cream walls which were capped with a handsome plaster molding. Autographed black-and-white photographs of Eric Leinsdorf, Leonard Bernstein, Eugene Ormandy, and other famous conductors marched around the room at eye level. A few half-empty water bottles, a couple of rags, and some untidy piles of music further decorated the piano.

Anna peeked through the door Nicholas had vanished through. A slightly shabby sofa faced a built-in Formica vanity with a large lighted mirror and a closet. She could hear running water and assumed the closed door beside the vanity led to a bathroom. She recognized the black leather jacket slung over the back of the chair in front of the mirror. He had worn it during their first interview.

The sound of water stopped. Anna did a quick side step so she could pretend to be reading Eric Leinsdorf's inscription.

"You could get a nice rent for this place, especially with the location," Anna said when Nicholas emerged again with freshly combed hair. A few water droplets still beaded on the strong column of his neck. Anna yanked her mind away from a sudden image of licking them off his skin.

"There've been times when I've practically lived here," he said with a wry grimace.

His expression grew bleak as he flipped open a black leather briefcase and took out a plastic zip-top baggie with a sheet of paper in it.

"Kathy Gromyko found this on the floor under her front hall table yesterday after work. She thinks it dropped out of Lexi's jacket pocket when he had lunch with her just before he came here."

Anna took the bag and looked closely at its contents. The sheet of paper was white and showed three creases, two horizontal and one vertical. Several musical staves filled with notes had been handwritten on its surface. She flipped it over to find an ivory colored envelope with "Nicholas" scrawled across it included in the bag.

"Do you recognize any of the handwriting?" Anna said, studying the musical notations.

"My name on the envelope is in Lexi's handwriting. The musical doodles aren't familiar."

"Doodles?" Anna looked up at him, finding herself once again falling into those shockingly blue eyes.

She was relieved when he took the bag from her and walked over to the piano where he laid it flat on the top. Anna shook herself and followed him. She wished Mac had come;

his presence would have diluted the charged atmosphere of being alone in a small room with Nicholas Vranos.

"Whoever wrote this was playing with a transition. You see he's got the same beginning phrase each time," Nicholas underlined the repeated measures with his index finger, "then a different two measures of transition, then the same ending phrase. He was experimenting."

She discovered his hands were as fascinating as his eyes; the shift of muscle and sinew hinted at the power in those long, tapering fingers.

"Do you recognize the music?" she managed to ask.

"Yes and no," he said, frowning at the paper. "It's very much in the style of Beethoven but it's nothing he wrote."

Nicholas picked up a rag and absently wiped the handle of one of his batons before fitting it into a wooden case.

"Did you put this in the plastic bag?" Anna asked, shifting her gaze resolutely to the new evidence.

She caught his nod out of the corner of her eye.

"Thanks. How many people touched this paper that you're aware of?"

"Kathy and myself, although I tried to handle it as little as possible. I assume Lexi did since he must have put it in the envelope. And of course, the mysterious composer. Other than that . . . ." He shrugged and picked up the second baton.

"Do you believe this is what Mr. Savenkov planned to show you?"

He twisted the baton's handle inside the rag.

"If it is, there had to be something more. By itself, this sheet of paper is meaningless." He looked up suddenly and snared her in his gaze. "What did you find in Lexi's pockets, Lieutenant?"

"I'm not at liberty to discuss that with you, Mr. Vranos."

He slotted the second baton into its case.

"Why is that?"

"Standard procedure," Anna said, picking up the plastic baggie.

"It's because I'm a suspect, isn't it?" He smashed his fist down on the piano's keyboard, the ugly dissonance sounding out his anger and frustration. "Why would I kill my closest friend?"

"Maybe because he slept with your wife," Anna said, watching him closely as she deliberately made the shocking suggestion.

His response was equally shocking: his shoulders relaxed, and he laughed.

"So someone got around to telling you that little story. That was just Lexi's way of prodding me to get a divorce."

"It seems a little extreme," Anna said.

Nicholas surprised her with a rueful smile so disarming she had to steel herself not to smile back at him.

"He had to do something extreme, Lieutenant," he said and then shrugged. "I have few regrets about how I've lived my life. However, I made a monumentally stupid mistake when I married Serena. After about six months it became apparent we didn't have a marriage, we had a train wreck. So we went our separate ways. We were both traveling for work a great deal and neither one of us bothered to take the time to file for divorce. Lexi forced the issue in his own inimitable way."

"How did you find out about Mr. Savenkov and your wife?"

"Lexi told me."

"Also somewhat unusual," Anna said, although she really wondered how they could remain friends. "You said he liked to stir things up and see how people responded. How did you respond?"

"By calling him an ass and hiring a divorce lawyer."

"No jealousy, no possessiveness?"

"By that time, Serena and I had been living apart for nearly three years, and he wasn't the first person she had slept with by any means."

"So you weren't at all bothered by the fact that your best friend slept with your wife?" Anna was having a hard time believing it.

"No, I wasn't," he said, looking even more amused at her persistence. "In fact, Lexi did me a favor because Serena felt guilty enough to make an effort to sign and return the divorce papers promptly. Accomplishing anything promptly is not my ex-wife's strong suit. If it hadn't been for Lexi, my lawyer might still be chasing her around Europe."

He was doing a convincing job of sounding like a man who hadn't cared. Anna felt her grasp of a motive slipping away.

"You're wasting your time trying to turn me into a murderer, Lieutenant," he said, pushing away from the piano and taking two steps to close the distance between them. She couldn't decide if he was aware that his height made him threatening when he was that close. "You should direct your efforts in a more constructive direction."

"I wouldn't be doing your friend justice if I didn't explore every possibility thoroughly," Anna said, standing her ground.

He considered her comment as the blue beam of his eyes traveled over her face, giving her the sensation he was actually touching her.

"Point taken," he said. "What else would you like to know?"

"How did their affair end?"

"You're wondering if Serena might have killed Lexi?"

Anna gave a neutral shrug.

"Maybe she thought Lexi was in love with her and was upset when she found out he was just using her. Maybe she wanted some possessiveness from you and was unhappy about not getting it."

"I'm flattered," he said. "No, Serena might have winged a paperweight at Lexi's head but she wouldn't have shot him from behind. Besides, I'm almost positive she's been performing in Milan for the past week."

"She could have hired someone to do it for her."

"Serena isn't organized enough to hire a hit man."

Anna's cell phone vibrated and she used it as an excuse to step away from the man looming over her.

"Salazar."

"I'm in the neighborhood," Mac's voice came over the phone. "Let's have lunch at the usual place."

Anna realized she was staring at the charcoal gray wool stretched over the muscles in Nicholas Vranos' thigh and decided it was definitely time to go.

"Sure. Fifteen minutes." She'd get Mac to come with her for Tsao's interview.

She flipped her phone closed and picked up the plastic bag. "Thank you for your cooperation in turning this over to us."

"Anything to assist your investigation," he said, following her to the door which he unlocked and held open.

"I'll find Lexi Savenkov's killer," Anna repeated, choosing to look directly into his eyes. "Trust me."

"I do, Lieutenant. I'm just waiting for you to return the favor."

CHAPTER 5

"You've brought us an incredible gift, your Highness," Walter del Deo drawled in an accent that reeked of generations of New York high society. "There will be dancing in the aisles of every concert hall in the world."

The Archduke Johanne-Rudolph Habsburg-Lothringen waved a self-deprecatory hand in the direction of the slight blond man sitting across from him in a private parlor at New York City's Princeton Club. He knew del Deo was flattering him by using his title. According to an unpleasant Austrian law, the Archduke was now simply Mr. Habsburg-Lothringen but Johanne-Rudolph looked every inch the modern nobleman with his mane of white hair, his beak of a nose, and his impeccably tailored European cut blue suit. All he lacked was height.

"What else could I do, my dear Walter? As president of the International Beethoven Society, you were the natural person to receive the news of my fortunate discovery. I am very pleased to hear your experts have agreed the manuscript is authentic."

"We sent it out to the Beethoven Center in San Jose shortly after it was delivered to us," del Deo said, his mirror-polished shoes glinting in the flicker of the ornamental fire burning in the grate as he crossed his legs. "I have to admit that some of our members were skeptical at the beginning."

"How could they not be?" the Archduke said. "I myself doubted at first. After all, scholars and musicians have been searching for this for almost two centuries. Finding it was pure serendipity."

"I understand you were doing some renovation work in your home in Vienna and discovered a cache of papers?" del Deo said.

"Precisely. You know of course, my ancestor the Archduke Rudolph, whose name I also bear, was Beethoven's patron as well as his favorite pupil. In fact, he was a brilliant musician and the only pupil to whom Beethoven taught composition."

"What an extraordinary experience it must have been!" del Deo said.

Johanne-Rudolph nodded.

"Evidently, as Beethoven felt his life slipping away, he entrusted my ancestor with his unfinished composition, exhorting his pupil to decide whether he felt it could be exposed to the public without damaging the great composer's reputation. The entire package was hidden away behind a secret panel in the music room of my home and evidently forgotten. When I began a refurbishing project, the plasterers discovered the hollow behind the wall and brought me this glorious find."

The Archduke paused and stared into the flames.

"Although there is the gap in the second movement where Beethoven was obviously still refining the notes from his sketchbooks, several of which were concealed with the symphony, I felt it was too valuable an artifact to keep hidden from the world any longer."

"Have you heard it played?" del Deo asked.

"Yes, but I am not as expert a musician as my honored ancestor. What do you think of it musically?"

"Pure genius! The first movement takes everything Beethoven had done up until then and leaps beyond it. A truly mature work with an almost modern sensibility, yet unmistakably from the maestro," del Deo lauded. "One wonders why your esteemed ancestor hid it away."

The Archduke's smile was enigmatic.

"You confirm my own amateur impressions. I can only speculate that the unfinished section kept the Archduke Rudolph from rushing the symphony to the printer," he said. "Now we must discuss the sordid matter of how to handle the manuscript's disposition. Will the Beethoven Center purchase it for the sum I mentioned, as I would vastly prefer, or must I

risk having it fall into the hands of a private collector by
auctioning it to the highest bidder?"

Del Deo cleared his throat.

"We've been focused on authenticating the manuscript
and haven't yet been able to finalize the financial end of the
matter. We would, of course, need to see the remaining three
movements before we contracted for the sale."

The Archduke nodded dismissively.

"If you would give us some more time," del Deo
continued, "I am sure we can develop a mutually agreeable
arrangement."

"I flew to New York with the understanding that you were
prepared to settle the manuscript's future."

Del Deo cleared his throat again.

"The situation has changed somewhat. One of our
investors had to drop out of the consortium due to personal
reasons."

Johanne-Rudolph slammed his fist down on the arm of the
leather chair.

"You have one week to find another investor. I allow you
so much time only because I already have other appointments
here in New York."

"Thank you, your Highness. I appreciate your generosity.
We will do our best to meet your deadline," del Deo said,
standing and bowing gracefully before he left the room.

Another man, short and stocky, with a fringe of white hair
around his bald head, waited for him just outside the door. He
started to speak but del Deo shook his head and his companion
silently fell into step beside him. They took the elevator up to
another paneled room, although in this one no fire burned in
the marble fireplace.

Del Deo closed the door and turned the locking lever.

"The rotter's not going to let us buy it, Hank. Not even if
we come up with the millions he asked for. What he's got is
virtually priceless and he knows it. At an open auction, the
price will go into the stratosphere."

"I looked into Habsburg-Lothringen's financial affairs," Hank Whitehead, the vice president of the International Beethoven Society, said. "He's flat broke because he indulges himself in a very expensive lifestyle without the income to support it."

Del Deo looked as though he'd eaten something sour.

"He used us to authenticate his find so he can say it has our seal of approval."

"Then we did the right thing in photographing the manuscript," Whitehead said.

"Indubitably. Beethoven's masterpiece belongs to the world, not to some second-rate aristocrat. Now we have to get our hands on the second, third and fourth movements." He glanced at his watch. "I've got an appointment with my old pal Nicholas Vranos to persuade him to take a look at what we've got. The symphony may be written on authentic 19th century paper in authentic 19th century ink. The computer analysis may say it was composed by Beethoven, but if Nicholas disagrees I'd bet my firstborn the symphony is a fake."

"Did Jessica Strauss calm down enough to work with the artist on a sketch of the electrician?" Anna said, as she yanked the dark blue police sedan around a double-parked taxi.

"Yeah." Mac pulled out a sheet of paper, unfolded it and held it up for Anna when she stopped at the next light.

She grimaced.

"He looks like about a million other men. Any luck with Hayes Electric?"

"Nah. No record of an employee in Carnegie Hall that day. We'll pass the sketch around the company but—" Mac left the improbability of anyone recognizing him unvoiced.

"Sounds like the electrician's our man. Now we just have to find him."

"What about Nicholas Vranos?" Mac said, turning in his seat to watch his partner's reaction. "He's smart and he's cool under pressure. I can see him shooting the guy who slept with his wife and then calling 9-1-1."

She maneuvered the car into a loading zone by the Upper East Side bar William Tsao had chosen for their meeting.

"Maybe," she said, "but why would he muddy the waters with the story about Savenkov wanting to show him something? And then produce the sheet of musical doodles?"

"To muddy the waters," Mac said.

"He sure didn't seem to care about his wife and the French horn player. My gut reaction is Vranos didn't kill Savenkov," Anna said.

"Yeah, but which part of your gut is reacting?" Mac said.

"Are you implying my judgment is impaired in some way?"

Anna was genuinely hurt by Mac's suggestion. No matter how magnetic Nicholas Vranos was, she wasn't going to let him shift her own moral compass and her partner should know that.

Mac shrugged.

"Come on, Anna. He got to you. I saw it in the interview."

"I told you his eyes bothered me. They're . . . intense."

"Eyes schmeyes. You two were bothered by every square inch of each other."

"'You *two*'? I don't think so," she said. "I couldn't make a dent in his armor."

"You make a dent in every man's armor," Mac said.

He put his hand on her arm to stop her from getting out of the car.

"Remember, Vranos had motive and opportunity. Until we can prove otherwise, he's a suspect. He may be trying to muddy the waters in more ways than one."

"Have I ever let my personal feelings get in the way of an investigation?" Anna asked, looking straight at her partner.

"No," Mac said. "But you've never met someone like Nicholas Vranos before."

"I appreciate your concern, but it's not a problem."

"You've got great instincts, Anna. Don't let them get messed up by a guy who knows how to control people."

The bar was typical: dark and narrow, cringing away from the daylight that exposed its frayed upholstery and scratched floor. Anna spotted William Tsao sitting at a table about two-thirds of the way into the room and walked over.

The musician rose and shook hands politely as Anna introduced herself and her partner. He even held the chair for her.

"Diane Engstrom said you might be able to help us with information about Lexi Savenkov's death," she said.

Tsao began to fold his cocktail napkin into intricate pleats. He seemed relieved when the waitress interrupted to take orders for diet Cokes all around.

"I don't believe in spreading gossip but a man is dead," he began.

Anna gave him an appropriately somber nod of encouragement.

"And I saw and heard this myself, not secondhand."

She nodded again.

"There's another French horn player named Brian Bostridge, an excellent musician but not a genius like Alexei Savenkov. He believes Alexei has stolen jobs from him, which is not true, of course."

"Go on," Anna said as William stopped and looked at her.

"He also thinks Nicholas Vranos favors, favored, Alexei because they were friends. That is not true either."

The musician paused again and Anna gave him an encouraging smile, hoping she wouldn't have to prompt after every two sentences.

"I've heard Brian say if Alexei were out of the way, his own talent would be recognized as being the greater. I heard all this because the trumpets and French horns are near each other on the stage," Tsao said almost apologetically.

"Did he ever threaten to do Alexei Savenkov actual

physical harm?" Mac asked.

"Yes. One time he was very angry about not being chosen for a solo—French horns don't have a lot of good solos—and said he would kill Alexei. Several people heard him because he spoke quite loudly. Another time, at a party, he threw a glass of wine in Alexei's face." The young man seemed to be warming to his task at last.

"What did Alexei do?" Anna asked.

"He laughed and patted Brian on the cheek. He said something about second-rate musicians and a green-eyed monster."

"I'll bet that didn't go over well," Anna muttered, as she remembered Nicholas Vranos' comment that Lexi liked to stir things up.

"Brian tried to punch him but several people stopped him. Nicholas Vranos was one of them," their source continued. "Brian said some insulting words about Mr. Vranos as well but Mr. Vranos just shrugged and said he was drunk and should go home."

"Did Bostridge go home?" Anna asked.

"Not willingly. Three of his friends sort of surrounded him and got him out the door. I don't know where he went after that."

"Thank you, Mr. Tsao. We'll follow up on Brian Bostridge. Does he live here in New York City?"

"I don't know but the orchestra manager would. His name's Al Larrimore."

Anna made a note in her notebook.

"Thank you, Mr. Tsao. We appreciate your coming forward with this information."

The trumpeter had been sucking down Diet Coke while she wrote but he released the straw immediately.

"I know people make threats they don't mean," he said, "but people would go silent when Brian said these things, not laugh and pretend it was a joke."

Anna and Mac looked at each other as the trumpeter rose

and left after thanking them for the Coke.

"A very polite young man," Mac said.

"So you think he might believe Bostridge's public threats sounded more serious than they really were?"

"Maybe."

"He seemed pretty clear on other people reacting strongly too."

"There is that." Mac folded the bar receipt and put it in his pocket.

"Another suspect to chase down," she said. "They're coming out of the woodwork."

"Just like cockroaches," Mac agreed.

CHAPTER 6

"Walter, what a pleasure!" Nicholas said, swinging open the door to his apartment and shaking hands. He escorted his friend and fellow Beethoven enthusiast through the entrance hall and into the living room where del Deo carefully placed his cognac leather briefcase on a gleaming wood side table.

"It's good to see you, Nicholas," he said with a warmth that would have surprised those outside his innermost circle of intimates. "We should do this more often."

"We should but if you're not out of town, I am," Nicholas said, smiling. "Scotch?"

"On the rocks, thank you."

Nicholas crossed the vast Oriental rug that covered the living room floor to a brass and mahogany bar.

As his host poured two drinks, del Deo said, "You know the Chicago Symphony Orchestra is panting for you to succeed Barenboim as its music director. The board president Bill Osborn asked me to put in a good word for them. He said to name your price and he'll find the money somehow. You could cut back on travel if you took the position."

"Bill knows it has nothing to do with the money," Nicholas said, handing del Deo a cut crystal tumbler filled with single malt. "The CSO is a great institution, and I'm honored to be considered to conduct it but I can't leave New York. Now if you could persuade the Philharmonic . . . ."

"Lorin Maazel wants to confiscate my season tickets after my last review of the Philharmonic's performance so I don't think I'm the right envoy for you," del Deo said with a chuckle.

"I heard when he read your comments, he threw his baton so hard it got stuck in the wall of his office."

"Purely apocryphal, I'm sure, although they do have some cheap sheetrock walls there," del Deo said. "Why won't you leave the city? Is it because you can't run your musical empire long distance? By the way, Allegro Production's most recent recording of the 'Emperor' Concerto is brilliant."

"Thanks, we were pleased with it," Nicholas said. Lines of grief etched themselves on his face. "Thank God I persuaded Lexi to join the orchestra."

"Why's that?" Del Deo asked with a frown of concern as he noticed the shadows on Nicholas' face.

"It's the last performance he recorded."

"What the hell are you talking about?"

"I forgot. You've been in California. Lexi was murdered yesterday," Nicholas said. He looked at the glass in his hand for a moment and then finished the entire contents in one swallow.

"Oh Christ, Nicholas! I'm so terribly sorry." Del Deo reached out and gripped his friend's shoulder. "What a tragic loss to all of us in the music world but I know you will feel it the most. He was a great friend to you. My condolences."

"I appreciate it," Nicholas said, gripping del Deo's arm for a moment in acknowledgement before the two men stepped apart.

"Murdered, did you say?"

"He was shot. In a practice room in Carnegie Hall. I was meeting him there and found him."

"How perfectly horrifying! Can I do anything to help?"

Nicholas smiled without humor.

"Convince the detectives in charge I didn't shoot him."

"The police can't possibly believe you had anything to do with his death. You were the best of friends," del Deo said, looking appalled. "I've got connections in the city government. I'll request that different detectives be assigned to the case.

"Thank you for the offer but they're just being very thorough in doing their job. I can't complain about that since I want Lexi's murderer found and punished."

"But if they're wasting time trying to blame it on you, they're not exploring other avenues."

"I have every confidence in their determination to find the killer," Nicholas said with an odd glint in his blue eyes.

"Damn it, I've just thought of something," del Deo said, going pale. "Lexi was involved with the manuscript."

"What manuscript?" Nicholas said sharply.

"The one I brought for you to look at. Let me show you and then I'll explain about Lexi."

Del Deo put his glass down on the table by his briefcase. He pushed two buttons and the latches disengaged with an expensively deep click.

"I'm not going to lie to you, Nicholas. These photographs were not supposed to be taken, much less leave the Beethoven Center in San Jose. However, I feel your opinion carries more weight than a computer program as to whether this is genuine."

Del Deo slid a thick sheaf of 8 x10 photos out of a large envelope of heavy cream vellum. Nicholas frowned as he put down his own drink and took the pictures. He waved his guest to a walnut Biedermeier chair while he settled on the striped silk upholstery of a sofa in the same style.

As Nicholas scanned the first photo, del Deo heard the sharp intake of his breath. The conductor said nothing as he turned over one sheet after another, gathering speed as he read. When about twenty-five photos lay facedown beside him on the couch, he suddenly stopped, gathered them up, and almost jogged to the concert grand piano which stretched across the opposite side of the room. He arranged the photos on the music stand and flipped open the fallboard, exposing the keys.

Del Deo moved to a chair near the piano and closed his eyes in appreciation as a gentle introduction in E-flat minor rippled forth, followed by a powerful Allegro in C minor. Occasionally Nicholas faltered and cursed the illegibility of the handwritten score, but the music unfurling in the room was magnificent.

When the sound of the final descending triplets stopped vibrating, neither man spoke for a long moment.

"This can't be what I think it is," Nicholas said, as he lifted his hands from the keyboard at last. "It doesn't exist."

"Suspend your disbelief, then tell me what you think it is."

"Beethoven's Tenth Symphony."

His words hung in the air as del Deo simply looked at him.

"It's a little rough in places but it has all the elements and then some." Nicholas played a passage again. "That's pure late Beethoven." He played another. "That's what I think Beethoven would have been writing if he had written another symphony after the Ninth. But Walter, the Tenth is a myth."

"You've just played the first movement of a myth then," del Deo said. "The Archduke Johanne-Rudolph Habsburg-Lothringen found it during a renovation in his palace in Vienna."

"A descendent of Beethoven's patron?" Nicholas asked and received a nod of confirmation. "You've seen the original?"

"Yes, and it's been authenticated in every way: paper and ink analysis, handwriting analysis, musical analysis. However, as I said, your opinion trumps all of those."

"I'm flattered," Nicholas said as he stacked the photos neatly together. "Can you leave it with me for further study? I want to compare it to some of the sketchbook facsimiles I have."

"I realize now this isn't the best of times to bring you into this . . . ."

Nicholas brushed away his concern with a graceful gesture of dismissal.

"It will be a welcome distraction. And you said Lexi was involved somehow."

"Wait. I have more for you." He pulled a thinner envelope from the briefcase and brought it to the piano. "Inside this are facsimiles of two additional sketchbooks the Archduke found with the symphony. They appear to refer to the remaining three movements."

"Does the Archduke have those movements as well?" Nicholas asked as he ripped open the flap of the envelope and slid out the additional sheets. Del Deo's "yes" sent him skimming through the pages. "This will take more time.

Beethoven didn't write these to be read by anyone but himself."

"Nicholas," del Deo said, his tone suddenly harsh, "Lexi carried all of the original documents from Vienna to San Jose."

The conductor went still for a long moment.

"How the hell did Lexi get involved with the Archduke?" he finally asked.

"He was in Vienna performing and Habsburg-Lothringen hired him to act as his courier. The Archduke said he refused to entrust the symphony to someone who didn't understand its importance."

"And Lexi couldn't resist being involved in something this momentous," Nicholas said. "Did Johanne-Rudolph voice any complaints about Lexi's delivery service?"

"None at all. The documents were all locked in a metal briefcase so Lexi had no access to them on the trip. In fact, Habsburg-Lothringen was quite smug about having someone of Lexi's caliber acting as his Sherpa. Heightened the drama of the situation, I suppose."

"That explains why Lexi made the unexpected detour to California before he came back here," Nicholas muttered. "But not why someone would kill him. That paper has to be part of this."

"Paper?"

"Something Lexi's sister gave me, a sort of musical doodle sheet. Maybe it will tie into the symphony somehow."

"So you believe this manuscript led to his death?" del Deo asked.

"It seems likely. There's a great deal at stake here." Nicholas thought for a minute. "Has anyone other than Habsburg-Lothringen seen the other movements?"

"No, but he claims they're complete except for a small gap in the second movement. However, as you know, leaving transitions to be filled in later was typical of Beethoven's work habits. Habsburg-Lothringen didn't mention missing pages and that would obviously be crucial knowledge for a purchaser."

"How long can I keep these?" Nicholas asked, holding up the photographs.

"As long as you need to." Del Deo hesitated a moment. "Nicholas, you don't have to do this. You have enough on your mind with Lexi's death."

The blue blaze of Vranos' eyes was scorching.

"This is my only lead to the *alitis* who took Lexi's life," he said, "so I'll be studying it every free minute I have."

"*Alitis?*"

"Piece of scum," Vranos translated.

A clock's chime sounded from the hallway and del Deo looked at his watch. "Heavens, I have a dinner engagement. My apologies for leaving so abruptly."

"We'll coordinate our schedules better the next time," Nicholas said as they shook hands. "And Walter, watch your back."

As soon as the door closed, he strode back to the piano.

As Walter del Deo walked up the sidewalk toward a waiting limousine, an engine revved and whined into high gear. Del Deo glanced over his shoulder to see a motorbike streaking down the sidewalk straight toward him. He stepped sideways toward the building to give the obviously insane driver a clear path but the motorbike swerved to follow him.

"Watch out, you idiot!" he shouted as he tried again to dodge.

The bike grazed him, knocking him off balance. He felt his briefcase being torn out of his hand before his head slammed into the stone wall of the apartment building and he slid to the ground unconscious.

Fourteen floors above, Nicholas Vranos heard nothing but the notes of a symphony he had only dreamed about.

CHAPTER 7

"What the—"

Anna stared at the tickets she had just pulled out of the envelope she'd found lying on her desk.

Mac looked up from sorting through his own pile of papers which had accumulated during the day. Somehow—he would never explain how—Mac had wangled the luxury of an office in the Midtown North Precinct building. It was just big enough to cram two metal desks, two rolling chairs, and one visitor's chair into but the other detectives made pointed references to their preferential treatment. The snide remarks had intensified when Mac taped up a poster of a kilted highlander tossing the caber to cover the water stain on the wall beside his desk.

"Whatchya got?" he asked.

"Two tickets to the Billy Leon symphony premiere at Carnegie Hall. Plus an invitation to a party in the Rohatyn Room afterwards. Compliments of the House Manager at Carnegie Hall," Anna said, reading the card the tickets were clipped to.

"Who's that?"

"No idea," Anna said although she knew who had instigated the gift. "It's just a pre-printed card. You want to go?"

Mac snorted.

"I'd rather swim in the East River naked."

"That would be a scary sight."

Anna looked at the tickets in her hand and felt a treacherous flutter of excitement in her stomach. She would get to see Nicholas Vranos conduct a world premiere. She'd skip the party afterward, of course.

"Those tickets are worth a grand," Mac said. "You could scalp 'em."

When Anna looked up to see if he was serious, she caught him watching her closely.

"You know damn well who sent those," he said. "You're skating on thin ice, Anna. Watch yourself."

Anna's cell phone rang. She felt a cowardly wash of relief that she didn't have to respond to her partner's comments.

"Salazar," Anna said.

"This is Sergeant Terry Walsh. I've got a hit-and-run named Walter del Deo about to go to the hospital and thought you might want to come over and knock on doors . . . or at least one door."

"Why'd you think that?"

"Because Walter got knocked down by a motorbike on the sidewalk right outside the building where the famous Nicholas Vranos lives. And Walter had just paid a visit to Mr. Vranos before he got hit."

"I'm on my way," Anna said, flipping her phone closed at the same time Mac closed his. "There was a hit-and-run on the West Side. He'd been visiting Nicholas Vranos."

Mac nodded and made a grab for the car keys. Anna beat him to them.

"It's still my day to drive."

"Yeah, but you got to use the siren the last time," Mac complained.

The sidewalk was roped off with yellow tape but the drama was over: the ambulance was gone, the gawkers had dispersed, and only Sergeant Walsh, a classic Irish redhead with freckles, remained to fill them in on the details.

"The limo driver saw it happen. Said the guy on the motorbike ran down del Deo right here on the sidewalk, grabbed his briefcase and took off. When del Deo fell, he hit his head against the wall. Probably a concussion. I've talked to the guard and the doorman on duty. No help there other than to confirm del Deo was listed as visiting Vranos."

"License plate?" Mac asked.

Walsh shook his head.

"Not even a partial. Only thing we've got is that the bike had shiny chrome fenders."

"Which building is Vranos'?" Anna asked.

"This one," Walsh said, indicating an art deco skyscraper on the corner of Central Park West. "Apartment 14."

"Thanks for bringing us in," Anna said.

"It's your party," Walsh said. "Keep me in the loop."

As they approached the big bronze door, it swung inward and was held for them by a uniformed doorman with white gloves.

Mac looked at Anna.

"Swanky."

A man in a dark suit whose demeanor screamed "security" greeted them.

"Detectives McKenzie and Salazar?" he asked politely.

Anna and Mac nodded and showed their badges.

"I'm Dirk Boland, head of security for the building. I understand you'll want to talk with Mr. Vranos in 14. I'll escort you there."

He used a key to access the elevator. Anna counted at least four video cameras discreetly placed around the marble and brass encrusted lobby.

"Good security," she commented as they stepped into the elevator where another camera tracked them. She suspected there was a hidden one as well.

Boland looked pleased.

"We have several celebrities living here so we take precautions. However, we can't control what happens on the street outside."

"Of course not," Anna agreed.

The elevator was paneled in some exotic wood that looked almost tiger striped. Inlaid brass patterns further ornamented the roomy car. Anna and Mac exchanged another look.

When the doors purred open on the fourteenth floor, Boland allowed them to precede him into the hall but stepped

forward to push a button beside Nicholas Vranos' tall
mahogany door.

"It's Dirk Boland, Mr. Vranos."

"Just a minute."

It took some time before the door swung open.

"What brings you up here, Di—?" Surprise settled into
grim wariness as Nicholas contemplated Anna and Mac.
"Come in and tell me who's dead now. Christ, not Walter," he
said as realization struck.

"No, he's on his way to the hospital with a concussion,"
Anna said quickly.

Boland excused himself and left the two detectives to
enter the apartment.

The entrance hall was bigger than Anna's dining room
and was furnished with a marble-topped table supporting a
magnificent arrangement of roses, peonies, lilacs, and several
flowers Anna couldn't name. Statues were arranged in niches
around the circular walls and the floor sported an intricate inlay
of multi-colored woods.

Vranos circled around the hall table, leading them into a
living room that made 'swanky' fade into insignificance. One
side of the room offered seating for about twelve in front of a
marble fireplace. The other side easily accommodated a
concert grand piano. The wall facing them was lined with
French doors looking out across Central Park and onward to
the mansions of Fifth Avenue. Anna gave herself a mental pat
on the back when she identified the style of the furniture as
Beidermeier. It was undoubtedly not reproduction. As Anna
took in the sheer size of the space she understood why the
search team had complained bitterly about the amount of time
it had taken to check out the conductor's apartment.

With a sweeping gesture Anna recognized from his
rehearsal, Vranos offered them their pick of seats as he sank
down on a sofa, where he clasped his hands and rested his
forearms on his thighs. His hair stood out like the mane of a
lion, as though he had run his fingers through it repeatedly. He

wore a black silk shirt with the collar open and the sleeves rolled to the elbows. Dark hair, dark shirt, and dark slacks threw the blue blaze of his eyes into sharp relief. Despite the presence of two police detectives in front of him, Vranos kept glancing toward the enormous piano.

Mac outlined the accident that had befallen Vranos' recent visitor.

"How serious are Walter's injuries?" Vranos asked when Mac finished.

"The EMTs believe it's a mild concussion. Mr. del Deo was conscious and coherent when the ambulance left."

"Thank God," Vranos said. "This has become a nightmare. I'll call Walter's wife. What hospital is he in?"

"St. Luke's," Anna said. "His wife's been notified and is on her way there. We need to ask you a few questions about the incident."

Vranos nodded.

"Do you have any ideas about why someone would steal Mr. del Deo's briefcase?" Anna asked.

"Yes."

"Really?" Anna said, as Mac raised his eyebrows at the instant affirmative.

"Come with me, detectives."

Vranos stood and walked straight to the piano. Seating himself, he waited for Anna and Mac to catch up with him before bringing his hands down on the keys. A bright cascade of sound swamped Anna's senses. Her gaze was riveted by the dance of Vranos' fingers over the keyboard, the flex of tendons in the back of his hands, the shift of muscle in his bared forearms.

As the music continued without explanation, Anna could feel Mac beginning to fidget and put gentle pressure on his toe to stop him from interrupting.

Vranos raised his hands and pivoted on the piano bench.

"That is the beginning of Beethoven's Tenth Symphony."

"I don't know much about music but didn't Beethoven only write nine symphonies?" Mac asked.

"Actually, there's always been speculation that he wrote a tenth," Vranos said. "He had jotted down ideas and notes about it in what are known as his sketchbooks, hand-sewn booklets of rough paper. One of Beethoven's friends even claimed to have heard him play the first movement on the piano."

Indicating the sheets of paper propped against the piano's music stand, Vranos continued, "Walter del Deo brought me these photographs of what is purportedly the legendary Tenth. They were in Walter's briefcase until he arrived here."

Mac grabbed two velvet-upholstered gilt chairs and hauled them over to the piano. He and Anna sat.

"So you believe someone knew del Deo had these with him and was trying to steal them?" Mac asked.

"Yes." Vranos gave them a full account of del Deo's visit, including Lexi Savenkov's involvement with the manuscript's transportation.

"You think this is the genuine article?" Mac asked.

"I haven't had much time to study the music but it's brilliant and it's in the style of Beethoven. It feels right. However, there are three more movements no one but the Archduke has seen."

"What's it worth?" Anna asked.

"These are only photographs," Vranos said, "but the original would be virtually priceless."

"So in the millions?"

"Tens of millions," Vranos said.

Anna whistled. They'd found their motive and then some.

She immediately started forming and discarding scenarios in her mind.

"Where's the original of this first movement now?" Anna asked.

"As far as I know, it's still at the Center for Beethoven Studies in San Jose. They know what they have so I'm sure the security is very tight there. They've been protecting a lock of Beethoven's hair for years."

"We'll give them a courtesy call," Anna said. "They may realize how valuable the manuscript is but not how dangerous it could be." She looked at Mac. "We should send someone to talk to the Archduke as well since he's in New York. Just to make sure he's got the rest of the symphony protected." Anna turned back to the conductor. "Did you give Mr. del Deo anything in return?"

Vranos shook his head. "I had no idea why Walter was coming to see me, other than as a social call. We've become friendly through our mutual interest in Beethoven. Actually, Walter gave me something in addition to the symphony," he said, indicating another pile of papers on the piano. "They're copies of Beethoven's sketchbooks that the Archduke loaned to the Center for Beethoven Studies to help authenticate the symphony."

"Do you know if del Deo had extra copies in his briefcase?" Mac asked.

"No, I don't. Once I saw this, I wasn't particularly focused on the remainder of the contents of his briefcase."

Mac's cell phone rang. He checked the caller ID and got up. "Jessica Strauss," he said to Anna, before walking away to answer the call.

"If you talk with Habsburg-Lothringen, I wouldn't mention these copies," Vranos said. "I got the impression they weren't meant to leave San Jose."

"Would Mr. Savenkov have made copies to show to you?" Anna asked.

"No, according to Walter, they were locked in a metal briefcase for transport and Lexi didn't have access."

Anna frowned.

"Someone might have thought he had made copies. Or he might have claimed to have made copies," she said, thinking aloud.

"Or they wanted that sheet of music he was going to show me," Vranos said.

"It's being processed for fingerprints at the lab," Anna said. "Excuse me," she said as Mac beckoned her to his side where Vranos couldn't hear them.

"Jessica's remembered more about the electrician and wants to add to the sketch now, while it's clear in her mind," Mac said in a low voice. "I'm meeting her at the office."

Anna handed him the car keys.

"I'll grab a cab when I'm done here," she said. "Make sure you've got a Kleenex box handy."

"Gee, thanks for the advice. You might warn Vranos to be careful on the streets. Everyone who touches that music gets hurt."

Anna raised her eyebrows at her partner.

"That doesn't mean he couldn't have shot Savenkov," Mac said. "Maybe Vranos wanted the symphony for himself."

Anna looked around the apartment. "Seems to me he could just buy it with less trouble."

"I trust your instincts as a cop, Anna. Just don't let your other instincts get in the way."

"Maybe he appeals to my cultured artistic side," Anna said, tilting her nose in the air.

"Yeah, you spend a lot of time at the Philharmonic," Mac said. "Stay safe. This case is getting ugly."

"Same to you, partner."

Anna went back to her seat by the piano as Mac left the room.

"Mac got called back to the office. He made an excellent point though," she said. "You have possession of documents which have evidently caused one death and one assault. Your life could well be in danger."

"Does this mean I'm no longer a suspect?"

"No, but it means you could be a target."

Vranos stretched his legs out and stared at the tips of his black boots.

"What will it take to get me off the wanted list?"

"An arrest of the killer."

"This is a damned unpleasant position to be in."

"I'm sorry but it's unavoidable right now." Anna was genuinely sorry to cause him more grief. It was unfair that he'd lost his best friend and was under suspicion of killing him at the same time but until there was proof he hadn't committed the crime, that wouldn't change.

"Will you be on this case until it's solved?"

"Ye-e-es," Anna said. "Do you have a complaint about my performance?"

Vranos looked at her for a long moment before shaking his head.

"No complaints whatsoever," he said as he swung back around to the piano. "Let me play something for you, Lieutenant. Something you'll find very intriguing."

Anna glanced at her watch. She needed to start tracking down Brian Bostridge. She needed to push the fingerprint lab for the musical doodle results. She needed to . . .

"Go ahead. I'm listening," she said.

"Do you play?" he said, rearranging the music in front of him.

"I took the usual childhood lessons and rebelled after about ten years and quit."

"So you can read music. Come sit beside me. You can help," he said, sliding to the right on the bench.

Anna hesitated. Mac would be shaking his head if he were in the room. She shrugged mentally and walked behind Vranos to slip onto the seat from the left. It wasn't wide so her thigh touched his, giving her a shock of heat even through the fabric of her jeans. As he reached up to turn a page, his shoulder brushed hers and she scooted as far left as she could without falling off the slippery leather cushion.

"Here," he said. "Can you play this line?"

She looked at the mass of musical notes dancing across the page in front of her. His finger traced along one staff.

Anna forced her eyes away from the texture of the skin stretched over the back of his hand to follow the music he was indicating.

"Hmm," she said, positioning her right hand an octave below middle C before playing a few tentative notes. "Is this right?"

She turned toward him as she asked and found his face angled toward hers. His eyes were even more unsettling at close quarters; she could see striations of aquamarine, green, and sapphire. She quickly turned back to the music.

"Perfect," he said.

"Let me just play it through once," Anna said, using all her powers of concentration to dredge up her rusty musical training. It was like riding a bicycle: once she started, the buried skill resurfaced with surprising speed.

"That's an F sharp," he corrected once. As she finished, she sensed him nodding. "You're quite good at sight-reading for someone who hasn't done it in a long time. You got the rhythm right."

"It's only one hand," she said, feeling a wash of pleasure at his praise. "I couldn't do it with two."

He placed his hands on the keyboard. Something about the play of muscle and tendon in his forearms reminded her of galloping horses, tremendous power barely contained by a smooth layer of skin.

"On four," he said and counted aloud.

Anna felt him tense just before he pressed his fingers down on the keys so she knew exactly when to begin. She was tentative at first, but after two measures she recognized Billy Leon's theme and allowed herself to be swept into the sound pouring from the piano. The Steinway lived up to its reputation, her low notes sounding deep and velvety while Vranos' higher register sparkled with nearly the brilliance of the trumpets. She felt bereft when he brought his hands down in a crashing final chord and said, "Now let's play it without the second trumpet part."

Unwilling to admit she hadn't really paid attention to the presence or absence of the extra part, Anna went back to the beginning of her section.

This time Nicholas played the trumpets' melody with his right hand and used his left hand to add extra volume to Anna's motif. Anna felt the gorgeousness of the high notes deep in her chest even as she provided the foundation that supported them. She found herself inching closer to Vranos so she could pick up cues from the movement of his body. His thigh tensed and relaxed against hers as he worked the pedals to mute or sustain notes.

"Again," he commanded as they came to the end of the passage.

She returned to the beginning, and began to add her left hand to the mix, long-forgotten harmonies returning to her fingers, swelling the sound even further. Now she was touching Vranos from knee to shoulder so she could better anticipate his needs, freeing him for variations as he came to trust her to carry the underlying rhythm.

His arm brushed her breasts as he reached across her to pound out a bass chord, setting off a vibration both physical and musical that reached into her bones. The sound filled her mind, and swelled in her gut, wrapping itself around her and the man beside her, pulling them closer and closer together as they strove to create a beauty beyond the merely human.

They played the final chord as though their four hands were one. Anna closed her eyes and let her head drop back as she savored the heady illusion of being utterly attuned to another human being.

"Music is the great seducer. It has you now."

His low voice came from so close it seemed to be inside her head. She felt a whisper of warm breath on her cheek and his mouth was on hers exactly where she wanted it. She threaded her fingers into the hair curling on the back of his neck and touched the seam of his lips with her tongue. Without interrupting the kiss, he slid his hands under her elbows and slowly stood, pulling her up with him.

It was like playing the piano with him; she could still read his cues. She twisted in his grasp, offering the sensitive skin behind her ear to the heat of his mouth. He groaned and hauled her close against him, splaying his fingers over her back and waist even as he drew her earlobe into his mouth.

Anna exhaled on a long wordless sigh. She let her hands drift down onto his shoulders so she could knead the muscles under the black silk.

His hand also slid lower, cupping her behind and pressing her pelvis upward to meet his own. In her mind's eye, she could see those long fingers curled into the fabric of her jeans even as she felt his other hand exploring the curves of her back. He moved his mouth down her neck, using his tongue and the edge of his teeth to make her gasp. She arched back over his supporting arm as he tasted the skin at the hollow of her throat, the ends of his hair tickling against her skin to add an extra fillip of sensation.

He moved to balance her weight and his thigh drove between hers, sending a shock of arousal ripping through her with such intensity it jarred her out of the spell the music had woven.

She jerked in his arms and opened her eyes. He lifted his head, his hair falling in dark waves against his cheeks. He did not, however, alter either of their positions.

"Does that happen every time you play a duet?" she asked, shifting in order to put space between them without falling on her behind. Her efforts just made her more aware of his thigh between hers.

"Only on a very good day," he said. His smile let her know he recognized her dilemma.

"I could take you down but I don't want to be accused of police brutality," she said.

"I believe I'd enjoy that." He pulled them both upright and took a step away from her. "Solve this case quickly,

Lieutenant. I can think of many pleasanter things to do with you than discuss murder."

He ran his finger down the line of her neck, following the same path his lips had.

"No," she said. This time she put the bench between them.

"'No'?" He smiled as she retreated. "What exactly are you saying 'no' to?"

"I need to get back to the station," Anna said.

"Of course." He moved aside to leave a wide path to the door. His smile taunted her subtly, daring her to come closer.

As she walked past the piano, she noticed a piece of handwritten music lying flat on the black surface. She frowned as she tried to figure out why it looked familiar but couldn't make a connection in her memory. Not that her brain was functioning at its highest efficiency. She needed to get away from Nicholas Vranos so she could start thinking logically again.

His boot heels tapped softly on the wooden floor as he followed her into the entrance hall.

"Come play with me again soon," he said, as he swung open the door.

"Be careful, Mr. Vranos," Anna said.

He laughed, a deep rolling sound that enveloped her. As the door closed, his laughter metamorphosed into a melodic whistle. Billy Leon's trumpet theme followed her into the elevator.

CHAPTER 8

Anna slumped back against the polished wood of the elevator wall and started to rub the tension out of the back of her neck. The movement brought her fingers too near where Vranos had touched her and she dropped her hand as though she'd been burned.

An apt image, she thought to herself. She was playing with fire.

So was Nicholas Vranos. He had used the music to manipulate her. Of course, Mac would say it hadn't taken much manipulation.

The question she wanted to answer was *why* Vranos had done it. Her smile twisted as she debated whether her questionable charms would really drive a brilliant man who knew he was a murder suspect to ignore the fact that she was the police officer investigating the case. Was he trying to make her forget she was a police officer? Or that he was a suspect?

Or was it what Mac believed: that a man of Vranos' position and magnetism was simply accustomed to getting what he wanted when he wanted it. She'd met enough of the rich and connected to know they sometimes felt the rules didn't apply to them.

The elevator doors slid open. Anna pushed herself off the wall and strode out of the building with a nod to the guard. She shoved the incident into a compartment in the far recesses of her mind and hauled out her cell phone.

When she got to the police station, Mac was still with Jessica Strauss so Anna made a trip to the crime lab. She had picked up two chocolate-filled croissants on her way in and dropped the waxed white bag on the desk beside a black woman whose iron-gray hair hugged her elegantly sculpted skull.

"Hey, Kaya, I brought your favorite snack," Anna said, settling into an empty swivel chair next to the fingerprint technician's desk.

"You don't have to bribe me to get your paper looked at," the woman said with the music of Jamaica in her voice. "Someone's put your case on the fast track. Guess we can't have dead bodies cluttering up Carnegie Hall. Here's the report."

"Can you give me a quick summary?"

"It's got four people's prints on it. We identified Alexei Savenkov's, Nicholas Vranos', and Ekaterina Gromyko's. The other prints are unknown but judging by the position they would likely belong to the person who wrote the music." She flipped some pages to reach the illustration. "You see, it's got about half a palm print where he or she held the paper to write on it."

"Any matches?"

"Not on our database. You and Mac will have to handle an expanded search."

"Thanks, you're a peach," Anna said. "And I would never bribe a police officer."

Kaya laughed as the detective got up to head back to her office.

Anna had just hung up the phone when Mac walked in looking harassed.

"We're meeting with the orchestra manager Al Larrimore tomorrow morning for a lead on Bostridge. And I gave the Beethoven Center a warning call," Anna said. "What's up with you?"

"Nothing," Mac said. "Strauss came up with some more detail on the electrician. Here's the new sketch."

Anna took the drawing but kept her eyes on her partner.

"Is she coming to Savenkov's funeral?"

"Yeah. I promised her she'd be completely hidden at all times. We need to make that happen or she'll go to pieces on us."

"We'll keep her far from the madding crowd," Anna said. "And I know you swiped my box of tissues because she used all of yours."

Mac ignored her and started reading his email so she took a look at the new sketch. The generic face had become more individual.

"This guy looks sort of German. Or maybe he's Eastern European," Anna said. "I'm going to send this to Interpol. Maybe there's a Viennese connection."

Mac grunted.

"We've got unidentified prints on the sheet music," Anna said. "Maybe I should send those to Interpol too since Savenkov had just been in Vienna."

"Good idea," Mac said.

Anna flipped to the photo in the lab report and felt a light bulb go off like a strobe flash in her head. The sheet lying on Vranos' piano had been a copy of this music. Not a Xerox— the handwriting didn't match—but a handmade copy. That could be a good thing. After all, he was an expert; if anyone could identify the "doodles" it would be Nicholas Vranos. She'd make sure to ask him if he'd made any progress the next time she talked with him. From a distance.

"I'm going to hit the gym. I need some exercise to clear my brain." *And a few other parts of my body*, Anna added mentally. "You should go home and eat some of that healthy rabbit food Letitia fixes you. We've eaten nothing but junk for the last three days and I don't want my partner dropping dead of cholesterol poisoning."

"It's been a good run of burgers so I guess I'm due for a salad," Mac said with a sigh. "Are we meeting Larrimore at Carnegie Hall?"

"Yeah, I'll see you there since it's your day to drive." That meant Mac had to go to the station to pick up the car while Anna could go straight to Carnegie Hall.

"It would be," Mac said.

"Did you sleep last night?" Mac asked when he saw Anna in the House Manager's office at Carnegie Hall the next day.

"You look like a raccoon with those circles under your eyes."

"Thanks for making me feel so much better," Anna said. She'd deliberately worn a bright turquoise shirt to divert attention from her face. Obviously, it hadn't worked. "This case is driving me nuts. It's like a sieve. Anyone who walked into this office could have found out Savenkov reserved that practice room for the afternoon he died. We may not have even heard of the murderer yet."

She was lying about the cause of her insomnia. Her sleep had been disturbed by X-rated dreams about Nicholas Vranos with the damned Billy Leon symphony as the sound track. She wondered if you could actually do the things she'd dreamt about on top of a Steinway grand piano or if the legs would collapse under the frenzy of activity. At least it would be less public than the stage of Isaac Stern Auditorium, another setting for her subconscious fantasies. The unsatisfied arousal of the night before was already making her feel out of sorts, but the fact that Nicholas Vranos might be somewhere in this building made her downright twitchy.

"What?" she asked, realizing Mac was speaking.

"I said, where are we meeting Larrimore?"

"Oh, right here. He'll take us up to the rehearsal."

A rotund bearded man wearing a hot-pink patterned Hawaiian shirt and suede sandals walked into the office saying, "Greetings, all. I'm Al Larrimore."

His voice bounced off the walls and Anna winced before she introduced herself and Mac.

"The orchestra's about to take a break so I thought you could talk to Brian for fifteen minutes. I know he and Lexi Savenkov had their differences and Brian's a little hot-headed but I'm sure he didn't have anything to do with Lexi's murder."

He escorted them up to the big double doors opening onto the stage and left them there. Al proceeded majestically up to the platform where the conductor, a slight gray-haired man, nodded but continued to lead the orchestra. His gestures and presence seemed a pale imitation of Nicholas' dazzling performance yesterday. Even his final downbeat seemed almost indecisive to Anna.

Al announced the break and then walked back to the French horn section. He leaned down to whisper to the man sitting farthest from them, and Anna saw the musician's eyes cut instantly toward Mac and herself. Brian Bostridge laid his instrument carefully in its case before accompanying the orchestra manager across the stage.

He was a tall, slight man who walked with the stiff-shouldered swagger of the insecure. His hair was cut close to his head on the sides but rose in a thick crest of dull red and gray curls on top, creating a sort of middle-aged Mohawk. His beige short-sleeved turtleneck and brown slacks hugged a slight paunch.

"You do the interview," Mac said in a low voice. "He'll be less defensive with a woman."

"Got it," Anna said, equally quietly.

"What can I do for you, officers?" Bostridge said as he strutted up to them.

Al looked taken aback at this direct approach but he recovered.

"Why don't we go upstairs to talk?" he said, leading the way to the staircase.

They followed the orchestra manager to a private dressing room away from the lounge where the other musicians chatted and ate snacks from brown bags.

Al made sure they all had chairs and left them alone. Anna hitched her seat to a different angle so movement reflected in the large mirror wouldn't distract her, and opened the interview with standard questions about Bostridge's personal information. He gave it all willingly enough. He almost seemed to enjoy being the center of their attention.

"Do you remember where you were on Tuesday of this week?" Anna asked.

Bostridge struck a pose with one arm crossed over his

chest while he stroked his chin with the other hand.

"I believe I was in Philadephia. Yes, that's where I was. I was the soloist for a chamber ensemble there on Tuesday. We rehearsed in the morning and performed in the evening. It was very well-received by the critics."

"What time did the rehearsal end?" Anna asked.

"Around eleven."

"And the performance was at . . . ?"

"Eight."

"What did you do between those times?"

"Hmmm. Ate lunch at *Friday Saturday Sunday*. Strolled around Independence Mall. I'm a student of the American Revolution and I like to soak up the atmosphere." He glanced at Mac who was scribbling notes. "If you need anything repeated, let me know."

"Did anyone join you for lunch or your stroll?"

"No, I'm afraid my fellow musicians don't have the same interest in history as I do."

"Would anyone at the restaurant remember you?"

"The waitress might. I mentioned the concert to her."

"You and Mr. Savenkov had some professional differences," Anna said.

"Are you implying I might have murdered him? I wasn't even in the same city," Bostridge said.

"I'm interested in what your relationship was like."

Bostridge pursed his lips in thought.

"We were competitors on a sloped playing field," he said. "Savenkov knew all the right people and I had to succeed on talent alone."

"Did you ever confront him face-to-face?"

"Several times," Bostridge said with a strident laugh. "He always hid behind Nicholas Vranos. The conductor, you know. It helps to have one of the world's most influential maestros in your back pocket. I never had a chance at an orchestra that Vranos was leading."

"So Mr. Vranos deliberately excluded you from playing in

his orchestras?"

Bostridge laughed again, an even uglier sound.

"He didn't have to. Savenkov made sure no orchestra manager would hire me for a Vranos performance. It limited my opportunities here in New York severely."

A knock sounded on the door. Al Larrimore's booming voice was barely muffled by the wooden panel. "Break's over, Brian."

"One more question," Anna said. "Where were you last night between five and seven p.m.?"

"Last night? I was with a friend, a lady," he said with a smirk.

"Would you mind giving us her name?"

"Heather Tipton. She's younger than I am but has an old soul. We had drinks at the Algonquin, then dinner and after, well, I don't kiss and tell. She's here today . . . with the second violins." Bostridge stood up. "Are there any other questions I can answer quickly?"

Anna stood and offered her hand.

"No, thank you, Mr. Bostridge. You've been very helpful."

"Then I must return to rehearsal. The maestro won't take kindly to the French horn coming in late." Bostridge laughed at his own musical pun before he let go of Anna's hand and strutted out the door.

Anna flapped her right hand in the air.

"Ugh, that was like shaking a dead fish."

"His ego is the size of a whale," Mac said.

"No more puns," Anna said with a groan as she sat again. "Well, he certainly didn't hide his dislike of Savenkov."

"Not much point since he's made it so public," Mac said. "He had enough time to drive or take the train up from Philadelphia, shoot Savenkov, and get back for the performance."

"He didn't seem at all worried about providing a watertight alibi. We'll have to check the security tapes again but I suspect he won't show up on them. However, he's familiar with Carnegie Hall. He could have avoided the cameras."

"Maybe it's just his ego protecting him but he was pretty cool under questioning, not quite the harmless hothead Al Larrimore described."

"Add him to the list," Anna said as she hauled herself to her feet.

As they walked down the stairs, the orchestra began to play.

"You like this classical stuff?" Mac asked.

"It's okay. I played it on the piano when I was a kid," Anna said. "I remember liking Mozart and Debussy. I wasn't so wild about Bach."

"What about Beethoven?"

"You've already said your piece about that, Mac. I heard you the first time," Anna said, giving him a pointed look.

"I just want to know the answer to the question: do you like Beethoven?"

"He writes good symphonies. I don't remember his piano music."

"Letitia says he was a genius. She says if the Arch-high-hat Johanne-Rudolph really found the Tenth Symphony, he's got something that belongs to the whole world."

"Finders, keepers," Anna said.

"Losers, weepers," Mac responded.

"Or worse," Anna finished.

CHAPTER 9

"You've got company," the desk officer said as Anna and Mac got off the elevator at the 18th Precinct building.

"Where?" Mac asked.

"In your private suite," the man jerked his head in the direction of their glorified closet.

"Who the hell let someone in there?" Mac growled.

"Cunningham did. Says your visitor's some bigwig from the music world."

"Xavier Cunningham?" Mac said. "He's the guy who's coming to the funeral with us tomorrow, the so-called walking encyclopedia of classical music."

Anna craned her neck to look through the open door and saw two feet encased in a pair of gleaming black wingtips. The legs they were attached to were crossed at the ankles. She recognized the pose and felt a surge of what she chose to label "adrenalin" banish the exhaustion from her body.

"That's Nicholas Vranos in our office," Anna said, starting in that direction.

"She psychic?" the desk officer asked.

"Just real observant. That's why she's a good detective," Mac said, following her.

As Anna walked into the office, Vranos drew in his legs and rose in one efficient motion. He was wearing a navy blue pin-striped suit, a blue shirt, and a yellow tie with a subtle paisley pattern. The handkerchief just barely showing above his breast pocket was white. He looked like a corporate CEO rather than a musician, and his presence filled the tiny room right up to the alligatored gray paint on the ceiling.

"Detective Salazar. Detective McKenzie," he said, nodding to each one.

"Mr. Vranos," Anna nodded back.

His eyes lit with unholy glee, and she knew he was mocking the formality of their greetings after what had happened the night before. The office was stuffy so she shrugged off her linen blazer and then wished she hadn't when she remembered his remark about women wearing guns. She slung the wrinkled jacket over the back of her chair and sat down, folding her hands on the desk.

"What can we do for you, Mr. Vranos?" she asked.

Mac also sat. He leaned back in his chair wearing an expression of mild interest but Anna wasn't fooled. He was watching the exchange like a hawk.

Vranos subsided in the chair between the two desks.

"Actually, I thought I might be able to do something for you," he said. "I've been invited to lunch with the Archduke Johanne-Rudolph in about forty-five minutes. I thought you might have some questions you'd like me to ask him."

"No!" Anna spoke with more force than she intended. She moderated her voice before she continued. "We appreciate your offer but as I warned you yesterday, this case is dangerous. There's been a death and a deliberate hit-and-run, both of them apparently connected to Beethoven's Tenth Symphony. We don't want you to be the next victim."

Anna hoped the heat she'd felt when she thought about the context of yesterday's warning hadn't shown in her face. Mac would notice it in a millisecond.

"Aren't you having it both ways, Lieutenant?" the conductor said. "If I'm the murderer, it's unlikely I would be a victim too."

Anna ignored his comment and fell back into her more comfortable role as interviewer.

"Did the Archduke give a reason for his invitation?" she asked.

"He says he wants to discuss a job," Vranos said. "I'm sure it's related to the symphony."

"We'd like to know what he says on that particular topic," Anna said. "And if he has anyone with him, we'd like a description. But don't ask anything out of the ordinary. Please."

"I'll try to curb my amateur detecting zeal."

"You know Brian Bostridge?" Mac said, suddenly joining the conversation.

"The French horn player? Yes," Vranos said, shifting in his chair so he could see Mac better. "Why?"

"He didn't like Mr. Savenkov," Mac said.

Vranos' eyes narrowed and Anna suddenly found it very easy to picture him shooting someone.

"Was he in Carnegie Hall when Lexi was murdered?" he asked.

"We were hoping you might tell us if you saw him there," Mac said.

Vranos stared at the door in front of him for a long moment before shaking his head.

"No, but I wasn't there for more than twenty minutes before I found Lexi. Is Bostridge a suspect?"

Mac shrugged. "Everyone's a suspect until we find the killer."

"I see you two have rehearsed that answer."

"Do you know anything about the relationship between Mr. Savenkov and Mr. Bostridge?" Anna asked.

"Bostridge resented Lexi's talent and success, and he was vocal on the subject. Lexi didn't pay much attention to him because there was no need to. Bostridge couldn't touch Lexi's abilities. I wouldn't have him in my own orchestras because he created bad chemistry in the group."

"Didn't you once break up a fight between them?" Mac asked.

"It was hardly a fight. Bostridge was drunk and took a wild swing at Lexi. It wasn't difficult to stop him." Vranos stopped and sat forward. "Wasn't Bostridge playing a concert in Philadelphia on Tuesday? I believe Lexi mentioned he had turned down a solo there and Bostridge had probably gotten it instead."

"That's right," Mac said.

"So he has an alibi," Vranos said, sitting back again and

rubbing his eyes, the purposeful vitality drained out of him. Anna felt a surprising desire to smooth away the grim lines around the corners of his mouth.

"He's not entirely covered," Mac said.

Anna and Nicholas Vranos both looked at him, one with surprise, one with sharp attention. After a minute, Vranos shook his head again.

"I can't see Bostridge killing Lexi right before he had a solo. He's not a cold-blooded assassin, and he'd know the emotional aftereffects could ruin his performance. He's too focused on his career to run that risk. And he's a coward."

"Getting rid of Savenkov might be considered a good career move," Mac pointed out.

"If Bostridge murdered Lexi out of professional jealousy, I'll . . . on second thought, this is the wrong place to say what I'll do," Vranos said. He turned to Anna. "Will you be at Lexi's funeral tomorrow? In case the killer is stupid enough to come to gloat?"

"You may not see us but we'll be there," Anna said.

"If you're there, I'll find you," Vranos said, rising and walking to the door. He stopped and turned back into the office. "By the way, the house manager's office told me they sent you tickets to the Billy Leon performance. I hope I'll see you both there."

He nodded to them and left.

"What were you doing with the Bostridge angle?" Anna asked, as she took a deep breath. Now that Vranos was gone there seemed to be more air in the office.

"I wanted to get his reaction since he knows all the players and he understands musicians. You noticed he said Bostridge wouldn't have risked screwing up a solo performance. That's the kind of stuff I was after."

"Bostridge sounds a lot like Ms. Strauss," Anna said. "However, if I'd told Vranos that much about another suspect, you'd have bitten my head off."

"I was going with my instincts," Mac said with a shrug.

"Vranos is a smart guy. He can be useful."

"So you don't think he killed Savenkov either."

"Everyone's a suspect until we find the killer."

"Save that crap for the civilians," Anna said.

Nicholas Vranos waved away the maitre d' holding his chair. Instead he came around the linen-covered table to shake Archduke Johanne-Rudolph Habsburg-Lothringen's hand as he bowed at the same time.

"A great pleasure to see you again, Your Highness."

"I might say the same, Dr. Vranos," the older man responded, clearly pleased by the formal greeting. "Being in America is so delightful. It's very odd that your people respect titles so much more than my own country."

"Perhaps that's because we have so little direct experience with their power."

Looking not entirely sure if his nobility had been complimented or insulted, the Archduke picked up the wine list and began a monologue on whether the 2000 Chateau Margaux should be drunk so soon. Deciding that it should, he ordered it, along with their lunch.

"Since this is rather a momentous occasion," he added.

"Is it?" Vranos said.

"I'm sure you've heard the rumors—or the truth—straight from Walter del Deo's mouth since I doubt he could keep it to himself." Habsburg-Lothringen paused before he announced, "I have found Beethoven's Tenth Symphony."

Vranos lounged back in his chair.

"I heard something to that effect. I understand it's still being authenticated."

"A minor detail," the Archduke said, looking disappointed by his lack of enthusiasm. "It is authentic. I found it in the music room of my family's palace. Who else would have hidden it there but my ancestor, and Beethoven's student and patron, the Archduke Rudolph?"

"If it's genuine, you have a treasure beyond price,"

Vranos said.

The older man's eyes brightened.

"Precisely. I'm sure you'd like to see it."

"Of course," Vranos said.

"And as the world's preeminent conductor of Beethoven, you would wish to perform it. In fact, you would wish to be the first to bring it to the world."

"I would be honored to do so."

"Well, I am offering you that opportunity," the Archduke said. "You may begin to put together an orchestra worthy of the genius of the great composer."

Vranos smiled.

"When the authentication process is complete. Neither one of us wants to look foolish if the symphony is not Beethoven's."

"You need have no doubts about that. It will be proven genuine. I will have Walter send you a copy of the first movement."

"Thank you. Are all the movements complete?"

"There is one small gap in the second but I am sure you can find a clever way to smooth it over."

"Why do you think the symphony was hidden away? Was Beethoven not satisfied with it?"

"I believe the missing measures may have delayed its publication but we shall never know for certain," Habsburg-Lothringen said, shaking his head sadly. "Nothing was found with it but a few of his sketchbooks. In fact, I have brought you a small gift, knowing how you will value this."

He handed Nicholas a small flat package wrapped in cream paper so heavy it was almost like fabric. Nicholas untied the black satin ribbon and peeled back the wrapping to reveal a booklet of grayish paper.

"One of Beethoven's sketchbooks. This is far too valuable for me to accept," the conductor said, even as he turned back the first page with infinite care.

The Archduke smiled with satisfaction as he watched the

man across the table devour the musical ideas scrawled there more than two hundred years ago by one of the greatest composers of all time.

"Consider it a down payment," he said.

Vranos closed the booklet with obvious reluctance and rewrapped it.

"Even my services are not worth quite that much," he said, smiling as he held out the package to his host.

"No, no, keep it, dear boy. I insist. If anyone should have such an artifact it's you. You understand its significance, its intrinsic value, its sheer genius."

Vranos continued to hold out the sketchbook.

"Very well, I'll call it a bribe," the Archduke said. "To make sure you accept my proposition."

The conductor tucked the book into his inside breast pocket.

"I'll return it if I don't conduct the Tenth for you."

"A toast. To the genius of Beethoven!"

The two men raised glasses filled with expensive wine which glowed the color of blood.

"Holy sh—," Anna started to swear as she watched the fire hoses pour water through the windows of Lexi Savenkov's apartment on the fourth floor of an East Side brownstone. No flames were visible through the broken glass so it looked as though the firefighters had the blaze under control.

"Say it and you owe me a dollar," Mac said.

"There have to be exceptions to the cursing-for-dollars rule," she objected. "And this is clearly one of them."

"Once you start making exceptions, there's no stopping. And the next time you start I won't warn you."

Anna thought of a few curses much worse than the one she had almost spoken but she kept her mouth shut.

Mac flashed his badge at a passing fireman and asked him for details.

"Went up like a son of a bitch. Has to have been arson.

We kept it contained to the one floor but the structure may have been damaged by the heat so no one's going in until it's been inspected. Far as we can tell no one was at home but they're still checking."

"That apartment belonged to a murder victim," Anna said.

"Good thing he was already dead because he wouldn't have gotten out of there alive," the fireman said with ghoulish humor. "If you're still looking for clues, you're out of luck."

She and Mac hung around until the truck crews rolled up their hoses and got ready to depart. Anna found the commanding officer and showed him her badge.

"Clearly arson," he said. "And not an insurance job. Whoever did it just wanted the place destroyed; there's accelerant everywhere and no attempt to hide it. Looks like the guy had a really nasty enemy."

"Yeah, except the owner's already dead. Prematurely."

"No shit?" the captain said. "So why burn his place down?"

"Answer that and you've solved the case," Anna said.

A black town car pulled into the space vacated by one of the fire trucks. Nicholas Vranos got out and turned to help Kathy Gromyko out of the sedan.

"Oh my God!" she cried, taking in the destruction of her brother's former home. "Everything I had left of him is gone now."

She began to sob and Vranos immediately put his arms around her and drew her against his chest. She leaned into him, shoulders shaking.

Feeling an unwelcome twinge of envy, Anna turned her back on Vranos and the woman in his arms. "I guess there's nothing else we can do here so we might as well go back to the office."

"Your conductor friend wants to talk to you," Mac said.

Anna looked over her shoulder to see Vranos beckoning to her with one hand while he kept the other arm around Kathy Gromyko's shoulders.

"What happened?" he asked in a low voice. "The neighbors across the street called Kathy and said there was a fire in Lexi's building."

"Arson," Anna said. "Someone wanted his apartment destroyed. No one in the building was hurt but there's nothing left of his place. I'm very sorry, Ms. Gromyko."

Kathy began to sob again. Vranos turned his attention back to her, and Anna started to walk away.

"Wait, Detective. I have something to show you. Give me a minute."

Anna nodded and moved aside to let him calm his companion. He bent down to speak to her, Kathy nodded and he left her, striding toward Anna as he reached inside his suit jacket and pulled out a flat package.

"The Archduke gave me this," he said. "It's one of Beethoven's sketchbooks, discovered along with the Tenth Symphony. He's asked me to conduct the first performance."

"Did you agree to do it?"

"If the manuscript is genuine. The performance will be a significant event in musical history."

"And you want to be part of it."

"Part of it? I want it to be the definitive interpretation of Beethoven's last great work."

Anna understood then that Vranos felt about Beethoven the way she felt about her victims. They could no longer speak for themselves so someone else had to care enough to do it for them.

"What will you do with the sketchbook?"

"Study it. Compare it with the first movement of the symphony. Use it to follow the twists and turns of his thinking."

Anna nodded.

"I also want to compare it with those doodles Lexi dropped. I saw something on the first page of the sketchbook that looked vaguely familiar."

"I'll fax you a copy of the paper," Anna said.

"Thanks, but I made a handwritten copy of my own— after I put the sheet in the plastic bag, of course."

Anna breathed out a sigh of relief at his admission. She looked up at the blackened walls of Lexi Savenkov's home and remembered the gorgeous antiques and Oriental rugs in Nicholas Vranos' apartment.

"You haven't told anyone else about that sheet, have you?" she asked.

"Only Kathy," he said, catching her glance up at the smoking windows. "Do you think that's what whoever did this was trying to destroy?"

"I was in Mr. Savenkov's apartment. If you were trying to find a single sheet of paper amongst all those books and icons and paintings, you might get frustrated and just set the whole place on fire too."

"I'll take a long hard look at that paper as soon as I get back. Now I'd better take Kathy home."

Anna watched him ease the distraught woman back into the car.

Mac strolled up beside her.

"If looks could kill, I'd be arresting you."

Anna jerked her wallet out and handed him a dollar.

"What's this for?" Mac asked.

"What I'm thinking."

"Make yourself comfortable, Nicholas, if that's humanly possible in this place," Walter del Deo said, waving a welcoming hand from his hospital bed. "I hear they wouldn't let you in to see me last night because I was incoherent. I'm sorry for your trouble. Help yourself to some vintage tap water from that elegant plastic pitcher."

Vranos laughed and dropped onto the molded plastic chair. He had to adjust its position so he could stretch his legs out without hitting the bed.

"What can I get for *you*, Walter?"

"The only thing I want is a glass of good Scotch but I

suspect it wouldn't interact well with whatever drugs they've pumped into me."

"How are you feeling?"

"Fine, fine," del Deo said. "A mere bump on the head. My brain cells are all intact—or so the doctor says. My wife claims that's an immense improvement since they weren't intact before the accident."

"It's good to hear Shelley's back to her old acerbic self," Vranos said, smiling. "She was dangerously close to admitting she was worried about you when I spoke with her."

"She should have worried about the wall of your building, not my hard head."

Vranos' smile faded and he leaned toward his friend.

"Walter, who knew you had those photographs in your briefcase?"

Del Deo frowned.

"The police asked me the same thing and I swear it was only Hank Whitehead and Joseph Painter, the fellow at the Beethoven Center in San Jose who took the pictures. And Shelley, of course."

"Habsburg-Lothringen doesn't know you have them—or that I have them now?"

"I can't imagine how he would. I trust Hank implicitly and I can't see any reason Painter would spill the beans. In fact, he could conceivably get in trouble for taking the photos. Now Shelley, on the other hand . . ."

Vranos gave a short laugh as Walter grinned at him.

"If that symphony is real, it's almost priceless. People kill for a lot less than that. Be careful, Walter."

"I intend to be, I assure you." A look of delight flitted across del Deo's face. "It's an extraordinary piece of music, isn't it, Nicholas?"

Vranos' eyes lit up.

"I've spent far too little time to speak with authority but I'm impressed. There's such a perfect progression from the Ninth to this work, yet it expands on everything Beethoven had done. You can see the germs of the idea in the sketchbooks but the final work goes beyond that. It's brilliant. If it weren't for the . . . ," Vranos stopped abruptly.

Del Deo had begun to nod enthusiastically and ended with a grimace as his damaged head protested so he didn't notice the conductor's caveat.

"You should rest," Vranos said, starting to stand.

"No, no, you've just gotten my critical juices flowing and I forgot about the bump. Stay. Please."

The conductor relaxed back onto the chair.

"I hate to think this magnificent music may have caused Lexi's death," del Deo said.

"I sometimes worry whether I can judge it fairly, knowing it may be stained with his blood," Vranos said, "but I can't let go of it. The detectives on the case are pursuing the connection now."

"I don't think much of their acumen since they suspect you of murdering Lexi."

"They're just determined to do their job to the best of their ability," Vranos said. "I find myself more and more confident they'll find the murderer."

"High praise indeed. I'm surprised at your enthusiasm."

"If you'd met Detective Lieutenant Salazar, you wouldn't be."

"Really? I'd admire him?"

"Her. She's quite impressive."

"In what way?" he asked.

"Many," Vranos said, and changed the subject.

CHAPTER 10

Anna pulled the deep blue night shirt out of her drawer and slid it on over the towel that still turbaned her wet hair. Mac's wife had chosen the lace-trimmed silk for Anna as a Christmas gift, much to Mac's horror, especially when he'd found out it had a matching thong. He'd told Letitia he couldn't give his partner underwear but Letitia had told him Anna needed some feminine pampering because she wouldn't do it for herself. Anna chuckled at the memory of Mac handing her the wrapped package and then fleeing his own living room before she opened it. She rarely wore the frivolous thing but for some reason it looked appealing tonight.

Sitting down at the sinuously curving Art Deco vanity table in her bedroom, she untucked the towel, gave it a hard twist to wring out excess water, and unwrapped the terrycloth. Her hair fell in a long damp rope over her shoulder and into her lap. She began to finger comb the tangles out, her image reflected from three different angles in the triple mirror, before she noticed the "message waiting" icon on her cell phone. She checked the time: 10:18 p.m. The call had come in while she was reveling in a steaming hot shower. She folded her arms on the cool marble tabletop and put her head down for a few more seconds of peace before she picked up the phone and hit "retrieve".

"I was hoping you might still be awake, Lieutenant." Nicholas Vranos' recorded voice vibrated with rich undertones even through the tinny transmitter of the cell phone. "I've found a very interesting correlation between the sketchbook and Lexi's paper. I'll be awake for sometime longer if you care to look at it tonight."

Anna groaned and dropped her head on her arms again. Savenkov's funeral was the next day so she couldn't put Vranos off until the morning. She pushed herself upright and went back to the dresser to pull on a Columbia U. sweatshirt.

She was damned if she was going to talk to Nicholas Vranos wearing a silk nightie and nothing else.

She picked up the phone and stalked into her kitchen to grab a Diet Coke before she entered Vranos' number and hit "call".

"Mr. Vranos, this is Lieutenant Salazar returning your call," she said.

"Are you off duty?" he asked.

"Ye-e-es."

"Call me Nicholas then."

Anna pressed the cold soda can against her forehead.

"I don't think so."

She heard him sigh.

"Someone was playing with part of the Beethoven sketchbook as a transitional phrase for another piece of music."

"Could you explain that again slowly?" Anna said, taking a swig of Coke.

"It would be easier to show you. And I'd like to take you up on your offer to fax a copy of the paper to me. I want to be sure the notes are identical."

"I'd have to go to the station to get it. Maybe I could deliver it to you and see what you're talking about," Anna said, grimacing even as she made the offer. "Unless it's too late, of course."

"A perfect solution. I can't sleep so the late hour is not a problem."

His voice carried a purring quality, and she was sure he was smiling.

"I'll be there in forty minutes," Anna said and hung up.

She called herself six kinds of idiot as she yanked on a pair of black jeans, a short-sleeved black tee shirt, and a pair of black boots with a built-in ankle holster for her backup gun. She considered a moment before she buckled on her shoulder holster, covering it with a red zip-up sweatshirt. Her weapons were in place. Wincing as she jerked a brush through the tangles in her still damp hair, she braided it tightly and flung it back over her shoulder.

Thirty-five minutes later she was riding the elevator up to Vranos' apartment, holding a manila envelope containing a clear copy of the "doodles".

He opened the door before she had a chance to ring the bell. He was dressed with stark simplicity: black slacks and a white shirt, unbuttoned at the neck and rolled up to the elbows. No watch adorned his wrist, no rings decorated his long fingers.

"Good evening, Anna," he said.

"Mr. Vranos," she said, nodding as she walked past him into the foyer. The scent of lilacs hovered around the flower arrangement on the table.

He closed the door and turned around.

"I'm back on duty," she said, handing him the envelope.

"So I gather." He bowed and swept his arm out to indicate she should precede him into the living room. The gesture evoked another century, and she had a sudden vision of him in a long black cape and high leather boots with his hair tied back in a silk ribbon. She mentally added a gold earring and a black eye patch and found the image entirely satisfactory.

When she saw the piano, the imaginary pirate was banished by the memory of their last encounter there and she stopped.

If he guessed her thoughts he showed no sign of it, merely touching her elbow to indicate she should turn left instead. They walked in silence past the Biedermeier sofa and through a door which was nearly concealed in the paneling to the left of the fireplace.

Anna gasped when she stepped into the double-height room lined with books, books, and more books. Marble and bronze busts on ornate display stands punctuated the yards of shelves. In the center of the room was a massive leather-topped desk, covered with papers and illuminated by an elaborately scrolled brass chandelier hung from a chain that practically disappeared into the shadows of the ceiling.

"It's a little overdone," Vranos said, "but the previous owner was fond of this room so I haven't changed it."

"You knew him?" Anna said, as she gazed around in awe. "He must have loved to read."

"Most of this is music. He was a brilliant musical scholar and pianist."

"Who was he?"

"Paul Vogl." Vranos took a deep breath. "He was my mentor. He left this apartment to me when he died."

"I'm sorry," Anna said, uncomfortable with the emotion in the musician's voice. She turned away and noticed one display stand that supported a clear cube rather than a bust.

Vranos followed her gaze.

"That holds the baton Beethoven used to conduct his Ninth Symphony." He circled his fingers around her wrist and gave it a tug. "Come look."

Anna let him lead her across the room, the strength of his fingers reminding her of his skill on the piano. When they arrived in front of the stand, he released her.

Lying in a Lucite cradle was a simple wooden wand, rounded at the widest end, tapering to a slender point.

"He was completely deaf when he finished the Ninth," Vranos said. "But he led the orchestra for its first performance, even though he could hear nothing of the music. He was still conducting when the musicians finished the brilliant *prestissimo*. One of the singers had to turn him around to see the standing ovation his masterpiece received."

Anna heard the deep sorrow in his voice as he contemplated the fact that Beethoven had never heard one of his greatest works. She felt tears prickle in her own eyes.

"That's a terribly sad story, but at least he could see the audience loved it," she said.

"I wonder if he cared. I'm sure he would have traded all the adulation for the ability to hear his own music."

"I don't begin to understand how he could write entire symphonies within his mind, without ever being able to hear them."

"The compulsion to create cannot be stopped, no matter what obstacles you put in its way."

Anna realized he was no longer looking at the baton. His gaze had shifted to her face.

"We should take a look at the papers," Anna said, pivoting back toward the desk.

"Of course. That's why you're here."

Their footfalls were silenced by the blue and aubergine Oriental carpet that covered the oak floor almost from wall to wall, yet Anna could sense exactly how close behind her Nicholas Vranos walked. She tried to put it down to her police training but she knew she was kidding herself.

The desk was one of those massive partners' affairs that were built to accommodate two people facing each other across a vast expanse of tooled black leather. Two leather upholstered chairs on brass casters were pushed into the kneeholes on either side. Vranos ignored them and went to the side of the desk where the sketchbook and his copy of the "doodles" lay. He flipped open Anna's manila envelope and pulled out the copy, laying it beside his.

Anna waited while he compared the two. He was leaning slightly forward with his hands braced on either side of the sheets he was studying. A curve of dark hair fell forward along his temple and grazed his cheekbone. His nose was high and somewhat arched at the bridge. His frown of concentration drew a strong line down to the corner of his mouth. Even with his eyes taken out of the equation, he was still a compelling man. Anna rested her hip against the desk, folded her arms, and locked her gaze on the nearest bust, a white marble sculpture of a gentleman with wild hair and an elegant cravat.

"The copies match," Vranos said, making Anna jump. "Now let me show you how the notes compare to the sketchbook."

He shifted his handwritten copy to center position and picked up the sketchbook, holding it with his long fingers as though it were the most fragile spun glass.

"You notice that the first two and last three measures of each staff are identical all the way down the page. Those five measures do not appear anywhere in the sketchbook or in the first movement of the symphony. Now look at the three measures falling between the repeated ones. Each set of three measures is different. That's where the 'doodling' comes in."

He gave Anna a minute to find the pattern and its disruption. She nodded and he continued.

"The first two staves don't correspond to anything in the sketchbook, but look at the third, starting two measures in."

Anna counted down and across, finding herself able to read the notes without difficulty.

"Now look at this page of the sketchbook, the fourth staff," Vranos said, opening the book with just his fingertips and holding it in front of her eyes.

"Beethoven's handwriting leaves something to be desired," Anna said.

"These were his ideas, meant for no one but himself. Would I be able to read the notes you scribble down during an interview?"

"Not a chance," Anna said, concentrating on the squiggles in front of her. "Wait, I see it. These three measures match those on the paper, except for that last note."

"Whoever was experimenting with these would have had to change the last note to tie it into the following three measures," Vranos explained. "I'm further puzzled by these two odd transitions at the bottom of the sheet. You see it here: the F, G-sharp, A, D, D, E sequence."

"I see it but why is it odd?" Anna asked.

"For one thing, they repeat themselves with just minor rhythmic changes. All the other transitions are unique. The other reason is harder to explain but those measures simply aren't in the same style as the rest of the music on this page."

"So what does this mean?" Anna asked. "What's going on here?"

"The Archduke admitted there's a gap in the second movement. It looks as though someone was looking for a way to fill it in, possibly using Beethoven's own musical ideas."

"A gap? So it's an unfinished symphony. Would that reduce the value?"

"Not really, especially if the gap is as short as it appears here. Of course, it's possible the break is much longer and the 'doodler' was trying to reduce the amount of inauthentic material. There's one more point of interest. Most of the material in this sketchbook went into the first movement of the symphony. The 'doodler' was careful to choose fragments Beethoven hadn't used."

"So the 'doodler' had access to the symphony, or at least to the first movement. But if the gap wouldn't reduce the symphony's value and the Archduke admits to it anyway, why would someone murder Savenkov to get this back?" Anna was thinking out loud. "Is it possible there are more holes than the Archduke wanted the world to see? In fact, is it possible everything after the first movement is a fake, or at best, a cobbling together of those ideas out of the sketchbooks?"

"That's been done already," Vranos said. "The composer who did it never pretended it was anything other than that and it doesn't hold together in any real way."

"But he couldn't make any money doing that, could he? What if the Archduke found a cache of previously undiscovered sketchbooks rather than a completed symphony? Could he hire a composer to put the fragments of music together into coherent movements with less suspicion of fraud?"

"I suppose so," Vranos said, frowning. "It would take a great deal of skill. Then you'd have to forge Beethoven's handwriting on two-hundred-year-old paper. It would be a difficult and costly job."

"But the payoff would be enormous. I think it's time to see how the Archduke's finances stand. How sure are you the first movement is really Beethoven's work?"

Anna watched him as he considered her question, his blue eyes narrowed in concentration. She felt the air between them practically fizzing with the power of their two minds working in tandem toward the same goal. It was like playing the piano duet with him.

"It shows many characteristics of his work but seems to go beyond anything he had done before. However, that is the mark of a genius, to always push the edges of the envelope. I'd expect nothing less. If it weren't for this little page of doodles, I'd be nearly convinced it was Beethoven's work."

"What about the handwriting?"

"You know the paper and handwriting were authenticated by experts at the Center for Beethoven Studies in San Jose, but even that has a certain margin for error. Beethoven was quite ill and his handwriting changed as he deteriorated. Possibly the only thing they can say with authority is that the paper is old enough to have been used by Beethoven."

Anna was mentally sorting and listing all the information she needed to test her theory as she watched Vranos wrap up the sketchbook and lock it in a desk drawer. He slipped the key in his pocket and walked back to her, his eyes intent on her face. He reached out to pick up the end of her braid and pulled the elastic out before he began to unravel the bottom of her braid.

"Shall we play another duet?" he asked with a husky undertone in his voice.

She tried to move away but he held on, gently pulling her to a stop. She gave him a pointed look. He smiled and kept unwinding the strands of hair.

"Working with you is just as exciting as . . . playing with you," he said. He had reached the top of the braid. "There. I think that makes you off duty."

Anna usually preferred not to have anyone touch her hair but she found herself standing still as Nicholas Vranos ran his long fingers through the tangled waves. She refused to think about what Mac would say because it was no more than a faint echo of what her own conscience would shriek.

"You're still a suspect," she said in a vain attempt to raise a barrier between them.

"I know," he said, as he buried his hands in the curtain of hair and tilted her head, bringing his lips within a millimeter of hers. "That makes this all the more interesting."

His mouth came down on hers in a kiss that said he intended to have everything she would give him. He would stop only if she asked him to.

She leaned away from him to break the kiss. He started to release her even as his expression turned dark.

The tight lines of control around his mouth and the downward slant of his brows should have made her back away but the sense that together they were capable of reaching extraordinary heights was overwhelming. She slid her hands up his chest and around his neck.

He threw back his head and laughed in triumph before he engulfed her with his arms and crushed her against his body. This time he went more slowly, pressing his lips to hers gently as his hands roamed her back and shoulders and down lower to cup her behind.

Anna used her tongue to tease his bottom lip and felt his arousal against her abdomen. He shifted both hands low and lifted her so she was sitting on the desk. Driving his thigh between hers, he opened her legs so his erection pushed against the vee of her thighs. He pressed her back onto the desk, skimming his hands up under both her shirts and circling his thumbs over her lace-covered nipples as she braced her arms on the leather desk top and offered herself to his fingers and his mouth. He tried to pull her shirts farther up but encountered the shoulder holster.

"Armed and very, very dangerous," he said.

Anna started to sit up to unbuckle the harness.

"Leave it," he said, unhooking her bra and pushing it upward.

He wrapped his hands around her ribcage and brought his mouth down on one breast.

She cried out as the wet warmth and gentle friction of his tongue created a sear of deep sexual pleasure that burned straight down to where his erection touched her. She wrapped her legs around his hips and pulled him closer.

"Ah, Anna," he groaned, moving to her other breast to suckle it with more urgency.

She was pulsing against him now, her hips finding a rhythm she couldn't control.

He groaned again, the vibration exquisite against her damp skin.

She shifted to prop herself up on one arm and gently lifted his head away so she could sit up. Slowly, with her legs still locked around his hips, she unbuttoned his white shirt, enjoying the sprinkle of dark hairs over smooth skin. She played with him, kissing his bare skin lightly just above the next button to be released, flicking his flat nipples with her tongue, brushing her breasts against the soft furring, enjoying the increasingly labored rise and fall of the muscled chest she was exploring. She drew his shirt out of his waistband and undid the last button before she pushed the fabric off his shoulders and down his arms. Then she looked up.

The blue of his eyes had deepened to the point of incandescence. She felt the heat of his gaze on her lips, on her breasts, on her belly and down between her thighs. He lifted his hands to her shoulders and lowered her back onto the desk top, following her down until her breasts were crushed by his chest. He kissed her on the lips before he used the tip of his tongue to trace a line down her throat, between her breasts to her navel, only stopping when he met the top of her jeans. Her eyes had closed to savor his journey so she felt rather than saw his fingers working the button loose, yanking down the zipper and slipping both jeans and panties down her hips and thighs in one fluid motion. He left them there to slide off her boots, then finished laying her bare.

She felt his hands open her thighs and his hair brush her inner skin as his mouth touched her in an almost reverent kiss. She gasped and felt the clench of an orgasm begin. As the heat spread, she heard the whine of his zipper and a rip of foil and he was between her legs, sliding into her in one long stroke. The violence of her climax ripped a scream from her throat as he filled her, not withdrawing until the bow of her body relaxed.

As she lay shuddering on the desk, he stroked one hand lightly over the peaks of her breasts while he used the other to brace himself as he began to move inside her. She could feel him shaking as he held back his own release and stoked the after-tremors of her own toward another orgasm. The soft edges of his pants chafed gently against her thighs and the leather top of the desk dragged at her shoulder blades as Nicholas accelerated the rhythm and power of his strokes. She felt the tension coiling tighter and tighter inside her gut until she was panting his name. He slid one hand down between them, finding the spot that sent her into a cataclysm of sensation as her inner muscles contracted and eased, contracted and eased.

Her climax sent him over the edge, and his final deep thrust sent her skidding across the desk as he shouted and pulsed within her before collapsing with his head pillowed on her shoulder.

She stroked his hair, making its ends tickle the sensitized skin of her breasts.

They lay there, both still breathing hard, as his erection softened inside her. He drew in a long, shuddering breath and hauled himself upright, stripping off and disposing of his condom.

Anna knew she should move. She was still spread across his desk virtually naked with her legs draped over the edge. However, her muscles were not responding to her brain's signals. When she felt the brush of his slacks against her ankle, she opened her eyes and started to sit up.

"Don't ruin my view," Nicholas said.

He had his hip hitched onto the desk and was looking her up and down with a connoisseur's gleam in his eye. Anna used all her strength to brace herself on her elbows and cross her legs.

He ran his fingers along the line of her thigh and hip and up over one breast. She gave a little sigh of pleasure before she made her own leisurely survey of her shirtless companion. Conducting evidently developed shoulder and chest muscles because he had a lovely set, along with some handsome biceps and an abdomen like a washboard. He hadn't buttoned his pants and she could see the thicker thatch of dark hair where his penis nestled.

Anna sighed again, this time with regret, as she forced herself to sit up and jump off the desk to retrieve her jeans. Her body was humming with the satisfaction of two serious climaxes and she couldn't work up a good case of guilt yet. She shook out her jeans and leaned over to pick up the panties that fell out.

"Do you have any idea how tempting that is?" Nicholas said with a slight rasp in his voice.

Anna turned to face him before she stepped into her underwear.

"Thanks. Now I can admire your breasts since you've covered up your bottom."

Anna jerked her bra and shirts down and settled her shoulder holster more comfortably.

Nicholas slid off the desk to scoop his own shirt from the floor and shrugged into it without bothering with the buttons. As he watched her work her feet into her footgear, he said, "I notice you felt two guns were necessary when visiting my apartment. Does that tiny one in your boot really work?"

"At short range," Anna said.

"So a man has to get very close to you before you could use that on him," Nicholas said. "As close as I was."

"I told you to be careful how you approach a police officer."

He laughed and went back to the desk, sorting the papers their lovemaking had scattered and handing Anna three sheets.

"I noted the sketchbook passage on this sheet and cross-referenced it to the 'doodles'."

"Thanks." Anna reached for the papers but Nicholas did not let go immediately.

"You and I both know what happened here but no one else will," he said, his blue eyes intense.

"I was trying to put off the 'what the hell were you thinking?' self-flagellation a little longer but I appreciate your discretion."

"No regrets, Anna. Pleasure given and taken honestly is too rare to sully with guilt."

"You got me to play a duet after all," Anna said, looking away.

"The most profound kind of duet."

He reached for her, but she sidestepped him.

"I've got to get to the station early tomorrow to check on a few things and bring Mac up to speed."

He wouldn't let her walk away, catching her wrist and coming up from behind to hold her by the shoulders.

"No regrets," he whispered in her ear.

She shook her head and shrugged out of his grasp.

"Do you have a gun fetish or something?" she asked as she walked toward the door.

"A gun fetish?" He fell into step with her.

"You wouldn't let me take it off tonight."

"I didn't want to give you any time for second thoughts."

"You mentioned it at the interview too."

"Ah, that. I wanted you to see me as more than a suspect. Wait here," he said as they reached the living room. I'll call down for a cab."

"No need. I'll flag one down."

"I insist."

He picked up a sleek rosewood and brass instrument Anna wouldn't have recognized as a telephone and spoke to the doorman. He listened for several moments during which he turned a frowning gaze on Anna.

"You told Dirk Boland about the fire at Lexi's and now he's beefing up security here?"

"Absolutely. He appreciated the information, and it would have been irresponsible to withhold it."

"There's plenty of security already."

"Nicholas," she forced herself to use his first name because it verged on farce not to, "you're in danger, and I don't need another victim added to my caseload."

"Your concern is overwhelming."

Anna enjoyed the scowl that made him look like one of those minor Greek gods who was prone to the sulks. By now they had made it to the front door.

"This is the last time I'm going to do this so let's make the most of it," she said as she wrapped her arms around his neck and pulled his head down to hers.

His surprise was momentary and he put every inch of his body into fulfilling her request. By the time she dragged herself out of his arms, she was panting. They stood facing each other, and she was glad to see his breathing was ragged as well.

"An encore, Anna?" he asked.

"No, the fat lady has sung," she said, twisting the doorknob so hard it protested with a loud click as she escaped through the crack in the door.

She heard him chuckle, and once again whistling followed her down the hall. This time the melody was unfamiliar but she was pretty sure she was hearing Beethoven's Tenth Symphony.

CHAPTER 11

As she dried her hands in the police station bathroom, Anna rolled her shoulders to settle the gun harness more comfortably under her tailored black blazer. She yanked down the cuffs of her white cotton blouse and surveyed her funereal reflection in the cracked full length mirror by the door: black blazer, white shirt, black slacks and her favorite black boots with their little pistol firmly tucked inside. She had added a pair of small gold hoop earrings to appease the niggling voice saying one should dress up to go to church.

"Well, you don't *look* like an idiot," she said, noticing the circles under her eyes were even worse than the day before. "You just act like one."

The fact that her body was still humming with a deep sense of physical satisfaction didn't improve her mood since it was in direct opposition to what her brain told her she should be feeling. She hurled the crumpled paper towel at her reflection and then muttered a curse as she bent down to retrieve it from the floor and throw it away.

When she walked into her office, a slim young black man with an impressive head of dreadlocks rose from the visitor's chair and held out his hand.

"This is Sergeant Xavier Cunningham, our music expert," Mac said. "I've brought him up to date on the case, including what Vranos showed you last night."

Anna shook hands with the policeman, who was dressed much as she was although he wore only one gold earring and a paisley tie.

"A pleasure and an honor, Lieutenant," Xavier said in a soft southern drawl. "To be involved in a musical event of this magnitude is very exciting."

"We're only interested in the music as it relates to the murder," Anna said.

Mac coughed.

"Whoever shot Alexei Savenkov deserves to be shot himself," Xavier said. "The man could play the French horn like an angel. I caught his performance at Carnegie Hall last year in a Bach quartet. Brilliant!"

"So I hear," Anna said dryly. "Your role is to identify funeral attendees who might be connected with Alexei Savenkov, Nicholas Vranos, or Brian Bostridge. Are you carrying?"

Xavier nodded.

Anna eyed his flawlessly fitted suit jacket with envy. She couldn't see the bulge of a gun anywhere.

"If Johanne-Rudolph Habsburg-Lothringen is there, point him out too," Anna said. "And be very careful around our witness. She's easily upset."

"Mac warned me," Xavier said. "I've heard her perform so we can chat about that."

"She'll love it," Anna said, picking up the car keys.

Mac held out his hand. "I'm driving, Salazar. You look like you haven't slept in a week and I'm not getting killed because you fell asleep at the wheel."

It had only been two days of Nicholas Vranos-induced insomnia but Anna's guilty conscience wouldn't let her argue with her partner. She slapped the keys into his open palm and stalked out of the office, missing the look exchanged between the two men behind her.

Jessica Strauss lived in an ugly brick apartment building in a borderline neighborhood on the lower East Side.

Mac escorted the young woman to the car, holding the door so she could slide in beside Xavier in the back seat. Her long, gauzy black skirt tangled in the seatbelt and she gushed thanks at Mac for freeing it. Xavier laid the flattery on thick and soon he and the violinist were deep in conversation about various arcane musical topics. Anna made a mental note to send Sergeant Cunningham tickets to a concert of his choice as a thank you for keeping Jessica Strauss from having hysterics en route to the church.

They crossed the East River into Queens and wove through the narrow streets to arrive at the Church of St. Nicholas. The Russian Orthodox temple rose alien and exotic amidst the Korean groceries and movie rental stores, a great pile of yellow brick supporting a riot of turquoise-enameled onion domes tipped with golden crosses. Passing the multiple arches of the front entrance, Mac turned right onto a side street and drove three blocks before stopping.

It was with great reluctance that Anna interrupted the lively conversation in the back seat.

"Mac and I will walk from here so no one sees you with us. Sergeant Cunningham will take you in through the church's staff entrance and lead you to a private room from which you can watch the funeral. You'll be completely hidden at all times. We ask that you try to look at everyone who comes. Here's a pair of binoculars to help you," Anna said, handing Xavier the leather case.

Anna waited for the storm but all the violinist said was, "I'll do my best."

"Thank you," Anna said. "We'd also like you to go to the burial at the cemetery. You'll remain in the car which has tinted windows so again no one will see you. Please point out anyone who might even possibly resemble the electrician. Look especially at the shape of people's heads, ears, and hands. Those are the hardest to disguise."

At the mention of the electrician, Jessica's face lost what little color it had and her lower lip trembled. As Mac opened his door, Jessica said in a quavering voice, "Lieutenant McKenzie? You'll be in the church the whole time?"

"Yes," Mac said, "I know where you'll be and I'll stop in."

"Oh thank you. I feel safe now," Jessica said.

Mac swung out of the car to let Xavier take his place. He just shrugged when Xavier looked a question at him.

Anna waited until the sedan pulled away from the curb.

"You've got a clinger," she said, falling into step alongside her partner.

"She's fragile," Mac said.

"So you said."

"Letitia says to bring you home for dinner tonight. She says she's making haggis."

Anna laughed. Letitia always threatened Mac and Anna with boiled sheep guts when she thought they were neglecting their health. Of course, Mac's wife wouldn't touch haggis with a ten-foot pole.

"My favorite dish. I'll be there."

They walked up the steps and into the church's dimly lit vestibule.

Anna pulled a Xerox of the building's floor plan from her pocket. Consulting it, she nodded toward an ornately carved stone screen set in the wall to their left. "That's where Cunningham and Strauss should be when people are entering."

Mac narrowed his eyes and stared at the screen.

"It's good. No sign of motion or light. No one will know they're back there."

Mac pulled open one of the heavy oak doors leading inside the church. Anna stepped inside and let her gaze drift over the brilliantly colored murals of saints and angels covering every inch of the interior walls. A huge crystal chandelier hung from the vaulted ceiling, almost a twin of the doomed light fixture in the *Phantom of the Opera*. Anna checked the floor plan again.

"Through that door to the right."

They walked across the broad square paving stones, their footsteps echoing through the huge empty space. At the altar a young man dressed in black-and-white robes arranged accoutrements for the service.

As they passed through the door and began climbing the winding staircase, Anna said, "Can you believe they used to make people stand up through the whole service? And they wonder why their congregations shrank."

"It's better than kneeling," Mac said. "My knees can't hack that."

They stepped into a small gallery and looked down at the nave, checking sight lines.

"Since you're whining about your knees, you stay here," Anna said. "I'll take the gallery opposite."

"Deal. Check your earpiece."

Anna switched on the battery pack.

"Test 1,2,3," she said.

"Ditto," Mac said.

"They're fine. See you."

Anna retraced her steps and climbed up the staircase on the other side of the church. In the gallery, she positioned herself as a mirror image of Mac, two pews back and in the shadow of a column so no one below could see either detective scanning the crowd with their binoculars. Xavier checked in via his radio, saying he and Jessica Strauss were in position.

A trickle of funeral attendees soon turned into a deluge. Sunlight streamed through the stained glass windows, throwing splashes of jeweled color onto the somberly dressed crowd below. Xavier's voice came through Anna's earpiece with a running narrative of who was coming in the door next.

"The guy had a lot of friends," Anna said as she swung her binoculars to check out yet another prominent figure in the music world.

"And some enemies," Mac said as Brian Bostridge swaggered into the church.

"He probably came to make sure he's really dead," Anna said.

"Nicholas Vranos is here," Xavier said in awed tones.

Anna forced herself to swing her binoculars back to the door at a normal pace but when Nicholas stepped into view nothing could stop the jolt of awareness that ripped through her.

He wore a charcoal gray pin-striped suit and a silver and black tie against a stark white shirt. Kathy Gromyko's hand rested on his forearm and when he brought his right hand up to cover hers in a gesture of comfort, the memory of those long elegant fingers stroking her bare skin sizzled across Anna's nerve endings.

Xavier's voice faded to a meaningless drone in her ear while Anna followed Nicholas' progress up the aisle. As he moved, the colors of the stained glass windows seemed to be drawn to him, focusing first blood red, then royal blue, then blinding white on his dark figure. He handed Kathy to a seat in the front row and walked back down the aisle. Anna watched him every step of the way.

As he went back through the doors and out of sight, Anna lowered her binoculars and leaned her forehead against the cool, hard stone of the pillar.

Chanting rose from below as a group of bearded priests and acolytes processed to the front of the church, their black robes adorned with heavily embroidered stoles of white, red, and gold. Behind them, the casket swayed into view, balanced on the shoulders of eight men. Anna didn't bother to raise her binoculars because her eyes went immediately to Nicholas Vranos, positioned at the left front corner. He carried his share of the weight without apparent effort, walking with a straight measured step while some of the pallbearers staggered slightly under the massive mahogany box.

They bore their burden to the stand waiting under the huge chandelier and set it down gently. A blond man whose face identified him as the murdered man's brother, the one who had traveled from Alaska, opened the lid to reveal Alexei Savenkov's body resting on white satin cushions. Anna shuddered.

"I hate open caskets," she muttered. "The bodies look like plastic."

"Yeah, they're much more attractive in the morgue," Mac's gallows humor came back through the radio.

"At least there they look real."

Anna watched Nicholas follow Alexei's brother to the family seats and then forced herself to use her binoculars to scan the crowd. Jessica Strauss had seen no one who resembled the electrician come through the front door so Xavier was moving her to another vantage point where she could take a good look at the assembled congregation. He had pointed out the Archduke, and Anna spent some time surveying the people seated around him as the service progressed in incomprehensible Russian.

The words "Nicholas Vranos" shattered her concentration.

She swung the field glasses back toward the chancel to find Nicholas striding toward one of the lecterns. He inclined his head with respect toward the priests and took his place behind the gilded stand, bracing his hands on either side of its slanted top. Colored light splashed across the floor all around him but he stood in a pool of shadow at their center, with only the dim light of the reading lamp illuminating the stark planes of his face. He stood without speaking for a long moment, his blue gaze sweeping across the sea of faces. He was like a sorcerer, gathering the attention of every person in the church's nave into his hands so he could bend them to his will. Anna shook her head to rid herself of the thought. He was a conductor; he knew how to manage large groups.

"I am honored to have been asked by his family to speak about Alexei," he said, his deep voice penetrating to the farthest corners of the church. "You all know of his genius with music. He changed the way we think of the French horn, expanding its powers of interpretation in ways no one had ever conceived, much less matched. Those fortunate enough to hear him play jazz will never forget the extraordinary inventiveness of his mind. These things are public knowledge; everyone here has a memory of the brilliance of his musical talent."

Nicholas paused to let his audience contemplate their own recollections.

"Alexei was also a genius with friendship. He considered friendship not merely a passive connection but an active engagement. When I called to discuss some problem with an orchestra, Lexi always said, "All conductors are petty tyrants with masochistic tendencies. If you want a simple life, go back to playing the piano."

A ripple of assenting laughter greeted his words.

"Having pretended he had no sympathy for my troubles, he then listened. And when Lexi listened, he came up with ideas, extraordinary ideas, sometimes difficult ideas, but always useful ideas. He was an astute and perceptive observer of his fellow man. Innumerable times, Lexi told me I was handling a musician all wrong and suggested a different approach. If I followed his advice, I always received a fine performance from that musician.

"Lexi had a sly sense of mischief which leavened the intimidating sophistication of his mind. In rehearsals, he took pride in being able to build tension and defuse it. He valued his own talent without being impressed by it. His love of the finer things in life was exceeded only by his generosity in giving these things to others. Lexi was complex, fascinating, and inspiring.

"The person who murdered him is a thief who stole a life not just from one man but from all of us. We should all be angry at this theft."

Nicholas' voice rang out through the nave, and the crowd grew completely still. He drew in a deep breath and made a noticeable effort to speak more quietly.

"To quote one of my Russian friend's favorite proverbs, 'One does not go to Tula with one's own samovar.' Alexei loved to explain that the finest samovars are made in Tula so no true Russian would carry one there."

This time the laughter sounded relieved.

"That's a way of saying that those who are here do not need me to describe what a loss we have suffered with Alexei's death. You know already. When our grief no longer

overwhelms us, let us remember him taking our breath away
with the beauty of his music and the joy of his laughter."

He walked to the casket and reached in his pocket, pulling
out a small object that glinted briefly in the chandelier's light.
He leaned over and placed the object with infinite gentleness
on Alexei's crossed hands before returning to his place in the
front row.

Anna found herself wishing she had brought a Kleenex.

"Very moving," Xavier's voice came quietly through the
mike.

"Even murderers can make good speeches," Mac said.

"Savenkov's family doesn't think Vranos murdered him
or they wouldn't have asked him to give the eulogy," Anna
pointed out.

"They aren't NYPD," Mac said.

Anna silently cursed herself and Nicholas Vranos'
damned blue eyes. And his damned music. And his damned
long fingers. And . . . she pulled her thoughts to a stop.

"How's Strauss holding up?" she asked Xavier.

"Fine. No problem."

"But no sign of the angry electrician?"

"None."

"That would have been too easy," Mac said.

"Pros don't come to funerals," Anna observed.

"There's still the cemetery," Mac said. "He may figure he
can avoid being seen there."

"Cross your fingers," Anna said, raising her binoculars
again.

The funeral droned on. Mac left his post to reassure
Jessica when she began to press Xavier about the detective's
whereabouts.

"She wants me to escort her out of the church," Mac told
Anna a few minutes later.

"Does she know there's a risk someone will see you
together?"

Mac sighed.

"I explained that to her but she feels safer this way."

Anna started to swear but stopped herself just in time.

"Thought I was about to make a dollar," Mac said.

"I'm in total control."

"If you say so. We're going to take her out early and I'm not going outside the church. I'll meet you back at the bottom of your staircase."

"Got it. Tell me when you're going."

The priests circled around Lexi's coffin, their acolytes swinging golden censers. The clouds of scented smoke wafted upward, making Anna's nose tickle.

"We're going now," Mac's voice buzzed in her ear.

Anna straightened and began scanning the church for any movement toward the doors. The route Mac and Xavier were taking was the one used by the Sunday school children to come and go quietly during the service. It wound through classroom corridors which the church staff had assured them would be empty. Anna was far more worried about Jessica Strauss having a fit of hysterics than about anyone seeing her in the presence of police officers.

Just when she began to relax, a side door swung open and a woman dressed in black shuffled into the nave. She made her way to the end of one row and leaned down to speak with the man at the end. He stood and let the man beside him pass.

"Mac, the Archduke is moving," Anna hissed into the mike, as she yanked the church floor plan out of her pocket and shook it open. "He's got an older woman escorting him. They're going through a door that leads to the Sunday school corridors. God damn it! It intersects with your route at the second right turn."

Mac and Xavier both spoke at the same time so Anna couldn't decipher their words. She kept quiet, knowing anything she said would be a distraction.

There was another confusion of voices, then Xavier's came through clearly.

"We tried to dodge him but he walked right into us," Xavier said. "Mac's got Strauss in a classroom, trying to calm her down. He turned his mike off. I'm out in the hall but I'm going back in now."

"Keep me posted," Anna said.

The service was drawing to a close so she focused her attention back on the congregation.

Once again Nicholas lifted the corner of the casket onto his shoulder and carried it effortlessly down the long aisle. Anna could hear sobbing rising from the crowd below as Alexei Savenkov's mortal remains were borne past his friends and colleagues.

"She won't go to the cemetery and she won't let go of Mac," Xavier's voice came back on again. "Mac's called for another car to pick them up and take Strauss back to her apartment. You and I will go on to the cemetery together."

Anna kicked the stone column beside her and released her frustration with a string of curses Mac would never collect for.

CHAPTER 12

Anna and Xavier stood on a rise in the cemetery with headstones stretching out before them in rows that seemed to go on for miles. Their dark clothes and the deep shadow of an oak tree kept them virtually hidden from the funeral goers.

Xavier spotted Nicholas Vranos. Anna's gaze had been drawn to him the moment he had arrived with Kathy Gromyko, and she had carefully avoided looking at him ever since.

"He's an absolute genius with Beethoven," Xavier said. "I heard him conduct the Fifth two months ago and it was like hearing an entirely new piece of music. I noticed things I'd never heard before. Of course, he's no slouch with Mozart either."

"Hmmm," Anna said.

"He's got a whole company, you know, called Allegro Productions. There's a record label, a concert production division, and, of course, his own performing career. The man's almost as rich as he is talented. He did a brilliant television special on classical composers. I hear they tried to get him to guest star in a series because his show drew more and more female viewers every time it aired."

"Are you going to the Billy Leon symphony performance?" Anna asked to get him off the topic of Nicholas Vranos' appeal to women.

"I'd sell my soul to attend but the tickets are beyond my budget and they sold out in one hour flat."

"Want to come with me?" Anna asked, killing two birds with one stone. "Mac doesn't want to go."

Xavier's face lit up.

"Thank you from the bottom of my heart."

"I owe you for entertaining Jessica Strauss in the car." Anna made a couple of sweeps with her binoculars before saying, "You seem to admire Vranos."

"He's an incredible musician."

"So do you think he killed Savenkov?"

The light in Xavier's face went cold.

"I don't think anything until I have proof," he said. "But genius and morality have nothing to do with each other."

"So true," Anna said. She finally indulged herself by training her field glasses on Nicholas Vranos. He stood with his back ramrod straight and his head bowed. When Anna focused on his face she almost gasped. His features were drawn into harsh lines of pain as though someone had just kneed him in the gut. She turned her binoculars away to give him the privacy such emotion deserved.

"Xavier, look at the chauffeur standing by the sixth car on the right side of the road," Anna said. "Something about him reminds me of the electrician on the video."

Xavier had viewed the pertinent clips of the security tapes that morning.

"See the set of his shoulders and the shape of his ear?" Anna asked, her excitement growing.

"It could be," Xavier agreed. "Want to go have a talk with him?"

"Let's wait and see who gets in the car he's driving. I've got the license plate."

Anna was still watching the chauffeur when a flash of light caught her eye. She dropped the binoculars and scanned the area behind the car.

"I'm going to get a different angle," she said to Xavier, switching on her earpiece.

She strolled casually until she was behind a mausoleum, then ducked and sprinted from gravestone to gravestone until she had a better view. She crouched in a shadow and waited. The flash came again and she swung up her binoculars to focus on its location.

"Holy sh—," she breathed, spotting the back wheel of a motorcycle. The fender was polished chrome, just like the bike that had run down Walter del Deo.

"What have you got?" Xavier asked.

"A very shiny motorcycle. I'm going to get closer."

Anna moved again, walking slowly when she was in the open, dodging swiftly when she had cover.

"Gotcha," she whispered as she peered through a viburnum bush and saw a figure hunkered down behind the white marble gravestone where the bike was parked. The man wore a gray and red helmet and was dressed in jeans and a black leather jacket. He seemed to be intent upon the crowd of mourners gathered around the grave.

"Xavier, I've got a concealed biker behind the white double headstone two rows south of the road. Can you get three cruisers to close off the entrances? Remind them about the service entrance on the northwest side. No sirens, no lights. I don't want to spook him."

"I'm on it," Xavier said. "I'll work down to the west side of the gravestone as soon as the cruisers are en route."

Anna slid her gun out of its holster and started moving again, working her way around behind the biker. She winced and froze as a police siren blared. The biker tensed and twisted around toward the sound. Anna followed suit, spotting a police car racing along the street just outside the cemetery's spiked black fence. If it was one of the cruisers Xavier had called for, she'd have the driver's head on a silver platter. It wasn't: the flashing lights kept going well past the wrought iron gates. The siren had made the biker nervous though; he fidgeted and looked around repeatedly.

"Xavier, be very careful when you move," Anna murmured.

"Will do."

He was careful but it didn't matter. One of the limousine drivers got bored with waiting and started wandering down the row of headstones, his cigarette glowing as he idly read the incised names.

The biker became increasingly agitated, finally straightening and grabbing the motorcycle. He wrenched it around so it was facing toward Anna's hiding place and threw his leg over the seat.

"He's moving," Anna whispered.

"The cruisers are at the entrances. He can't get out," Xavier murmured back.

Anna started to relax until she realized the cyclist wasn't aiming toward the roadway. She glanced around and saw a gravel path leading to a small pedestrian gate that was marked as locked and out-of-use on the cemetery map. Now it stood wide open.

She swore under her breath.

"He's headed out a small gate to the east. He must have opened it somehow. I'm going to try to beat him there."

"I'm right behind you," Xavier said.

Anna didn't bother to hide as she sprinted for the gate. She heard gravel spray as the cycle's motor revved and whined into high gear.

"He spotted you," Xavier said, his voice jarred by the pounding of his own running. "He's going to beat you to the gate."

"Not if I knock him off the bike," Anna said. She veered right, setting her right foot on a low headstone, then leaping onto a higher one before she launched herself at the biker as he came even with her. She aimed for his body, hoping to make him jerk the handlebars so he'd skid in the gravel. She felt her shoulder slam into his and his helmet cracked her on the side of the head. Then she was flying through the air unencumbered. She tucked her head and rolled as she hit grass. For a few seconds, she lay on her back staring at empty blue sky, sucking air into her flattened lungs. Then she sat up and propelled herself to her feet, gun still in hand.

The cycle lay on its side, the engine idling. Its driver had been flung completely off and was curled into a ball on the gravel path. Anna approached cautiously, her gun pointed directly at the prone figure.

"I'm a police officer and I will shoot if you try to escape," she said. "Do you understand?"

The driver moaned, an odd high-pitched sound.

Xavier raced up and trained his gun on the cyclist as he killed the motorcycle's engine. He nodded and Anna holstered her weapon in order to reach down and ease the biker's helmet off.

"It's a woman!" Xavier said as long blond hair spilled out over the gravel.

"I . . . can't . . . breathe," the woman gasped out, holding her ribs.

"Try to relax and take your hands away from your sides," Anna said. "You got the wind knocked out of you so your diaphragm's in spasm."

Anna hoped it was nothing worse.

Xavier kept his gun steady as the woman slowly relaxed and uncurled herself so she was lying on her side and breathing more normally.

Anna looked up to see if the burial service had been interrupted but the gathering of dark suits was still focused inward. However, a few of the limo drivers had wandered over to see what was going on. None of them was the one Anna had been observing.

"Police," Anna said, holding up her badge. "Everything's under control. Please go back to your cars."

Muttering and glancing back over their shoulders, the onlookers dispersed.

Anna bent down to the woman.

"May I check you for broken bones? I'm a certified emergency medical technician."

The women gasped out a "yes" so Anna did a quick examination and decided the cyclist was bruised but unbroken. She helped the biker to a sitting position and then said, "What's your name?"

The woman pushed her hair back from her face and looked away. She was a large woman with broad shoulders which explained why Anna and Xavier had mistaken her for a man. Although Anna guessed she was in her late thirties, the pouches under her pale blue eyes and the lines bracketing her mouth made her look older.

"Please answer my question, ma'am," Anna insisted.

"I am Karin Gadde," the woman said with a marked accent.

"Where are you from?"

"*Wien*," she said, using the Austrian name for Vienna.

"Why are you here?"

"I was watching the burial."

"Why?"

Karin Gadde looked away again.

"I wished to speak with Herr Habsburg-Lothringen."

Anna and Xavier exchanged a glance.

"Xavier, would you mind bringing the car down here?" Anna said. "Ma'am, we'd like to talk with you further and you'll be more comfortable in the car than on the ground."

The woman nodded, her shoulders still heaving as she breathed laboriously. Xavier righted the motorcycle and took the key out of the ignition before jogging to the dark sedan. Anna led the cyclist out to the road as Xavier pulled up and helped her climb stiffly into the back of the car.

It required some prodding but Karin Gadde finally told them her story.

"I have—had—a younger brother named Franz. He was a musical genius, a prodigy from childhood. My parents died when I was twenty but he was only nine so I raised him. I tried to give him all the musical training his brilliance deserved, but the money," she shrugged, "well, it was always difficult to find. So when Herr Habsburg-Lothringen offered to hire him, to become his patron, it seemed like a gift. Franz would have enough money to finish his advanced degree in composition."

Tears coursed silently down Karin Gadde's cheeks.

"Franz was content but he joked about how strange Habsburg-Lothringen was. He demanded great secrecy. Franz couldn't talk about what he was working on and he couldn't carry paper into or out of his patron's palace; at the beginning,

Herr Habsburg-Lothringen's assistant Karl searched him every time he left. Franz had an excellent memory though and occasionally he would play for me something he had written for his patron, beautiful music. And I have none of it."

Karin Gadde's mouth thinned to an angry line.

"Five months ago my brother was killed by an automobile whose driver did not stop to help the man he ran down. The police say it was an accident but I don't believe this. He would not have ridden into the street recklessly as the police claim."

"Perhaps he was distracted by something, by thinking about the music he was working on," Anna said.

"No!" Karin said with a sharp shake of her head. "Franz was riding his new bicycle—he had bought it with the money from his job—and he was very, very careful with it. It was his treasure, the first new bicycle he had ever owned. But that is not what convinced me he was deliberately killed."

"What convinced you?" Anna asked.

"Two days after he died, his apartment burned. Nothing was left of it." Karin's voice broke on a sob. "I have nothing left of him. It was not an accident."

Anna felt the skin on the back of her neck prickle as the flames of Savenkov's apartment blazed to life in her memory. Karin Gadde was probably right. Xavier pulled a packet of Kleenex from his pocket and passed it back to Anna, meeting her eyes in the rearview mirror. He knew about Alexei Savenkov's apartment fire.

"Why did you steal Walter del Deo's briefcase?" Anna asked as Karin wiped her eyes.

"I didn't know whose briefcase it was," Karin said. "I just knew he had met with Habsburg-Lothringen so I followed him. I thought he might have something of Franz's, some of his music, in his briefcase and I wanted it."

"So you admit to knocking him down with your motorcycle and robbing him?"

"Yes, I did it," Karin said, leaning her head against the seat back and closing her eyes. "So you will arrest me now."

"I'm afraid I have to," Anna said although she felt a certain sympathy for the woman.

"I am so tired," Karin said. "I have been following Herr Habsburg-Lothringen for so long now, all the way to New York City. He wouldn't see me at his hotel so I was forced to chase him to a burial. And still I have nothing of Franz."

"Sergeant Cunningham and I are going to leave you in the car for a moment but we'll be right outside. Please don't try to leave."

Karin Gadde nodded without opening her eyes.

"You're good," Xavier said as they stood three paces from the car, watching the still figure inside.

Anna shook her head.

"I almost let her get away."

"I didn't mean your Superman routine although it was impressive. I meant the way you handled Gadde. You got her talking about her brother and then hit her with the assault and robbery. She confessed without a blink. Nice work."

"Thanks," Anna said. "Mac taught me the oblique approach."

"Really? I would have guessed he went straight for the jugular every time."

"Mac's a lot more subtle than people think," Anna said. "We need to get Karin Gadde back to the station. Can you take her? I want to stay and get a better look at that chauffeur. The burial ceremony has to be over soon."

"Russian Orthodox services can be quite long," Xavier said, looking at his watch. "I'd say you have at least another fifteen minutes. I'll call for a truck to pick up the motorcycle and another car for you."

"That was good back up, Sergeant," Anna said, shaking his hand. "I'd be happy to work with you again even if Beethoven's not involved."

Xavier looked pleased as he slid into the driver's seat.

Anna found a vantage point behind an overgrown hemlock. She could see both the chauffeur and the funeral crowd easily although her main focus was the uniformed man. He appeared to lounge casually against his car but there was nothing casual about his gaze; he was surveying the cemetery as intently as she was. She couldn't actually see the color of his eyes but she guessed they were light: blue or gray. He was clean shaven and had blond hair but Anna dismissed the easily changed details of facial hair and coloring. If the man was a pro—and Anna was increasingly convinced he was—he knew all those tricks. She systematically memorized his face so she could get a sketch worked up to show Jessica Strauss.

The service ended and the crowd began to disperse toward the waiting limousines and cars, forming long dark tentacles that threaded through the headstones. The Archduke waylaid Nicholas Vranos as he escorted Kathy to her car. Kathy continued on with her brother while the two men stopped to talk. The Archduke made an angry gesture and stalked off toward the road. Anna stood very still as she watched the blond chauffeur open the door for the Viennese nobleman.

"Bingo!" she breathed before adding, "Shit!" as the chauffeur looked directly at her and gave a mocking salute before he disappeared into the driver's seat.

"Is it standard police procedure to launch yourself at a moving motorcycle?" asked a low baritone voice beside her left ear. "You could have broken your neck."

"The only reason you're not flat on your back with a gun pointed at your head is because I knew it was you," Anna said.

Strong hands wrapped around her upper arms and she felt the heat of Nicholas Vranos' body behind her.

"How did you know?" he asked, his breath against her cheek making goose bumps rise on her arms.

Anna realized she had walked into a trap of her own making. *She had known because she couldn't stop herself from knowing.*

"Years of training," she lied. She kept the binoculars up but all her attention was focused on the man behind her.

"Will you have dinner with me tonight? Not as a detective but as my guest."

"Not a good idea."

"I buried my closest friend today. I'd like company."

Anna remembered the expression on the conductor's face as he stared down into the grave where Alexei Savenkov now lay.

He released his grip on her right arm and feathered his fingertips up the side of her neck.

"Please, Anna." His low voice seemed to penetrate to her very bones.

Letting the binoculars fall to the end of their strap, she twisted out of his grasp to face him. Her refusal died in her throat.

The lines of pain were still etched there but entwined with them was a simmer of desire, the classic denial of death with its opposite.

He sensed her surprise and the advantage it gave him.

"At my apartment at eight," he said. "I'll play the Beethoven for you."

Pivoting on his heel, he strode back toward the road. Anna stood frozen as he ducked into the open door of the family's limousine.

She began to raise the binoculars but stopped when they were halfway to her eyes. Swearing under her breath, she lowered the field glasses and stomped over to the green police sedan which had glided into the cemetery five minutes before.

"Problems?" the plainclothes driver asked.

"Yeah, and I made them all for myself," Anna said.

The driver laughed.

"Back to the precinct?" he asked.

"Anywhere but here," Anna said, propping her chin on her hand and staring out the window. "And thanks for the ride."

By the time they pulled into the precinct parking lot, Anna had convinced herself she was going to call Nicholas Vranos to tell him she wasn't coming. Later. Right now she needed to talk to Mac.

He wasn't in their office but two reports lay on her desk. One was a fax from Philadelphia where an officer had tracked down the waitress Brian Bostridge claimed would remember him. She did but for reasons he would not have found flattering. However, she confirmed his alibi and eliminated him from the list of suspects. Anna heaved a sigh of relief at having cleared some mud from the murky waters of the case.

The second report was an e-mail from Interpol. Her breathing quickened as she read it: the fingerprints on the musical "doodle" sheet belonged to a hit-and-run victim named Franz Gadde.

"Holy shi—"

"You owe me a dollar," Mac said from the doorway.

"Damn it, Mac—"

"Two."

Anna waved the printout at him.

"Give me a break. Those are Franz Gadde's fingerprints on the doodle sheet," she said.

"Who's he?" her partner said, slumping into his chair like a man exhausted.

"Xavier didn't tell you?"

"I've been with Jessica Strauss ever since we left the church. Running into the Archduke really spooked her. Turns out she's convinced someone's been following her. I just got her calmed down and sent her home with 24-hour surveillance."

"Rough day," Anna said. "Sorry she's glommed onto you."

He shrugged.

"I think she's looking for a father figure," he said. "When she's not hysterical, she keeps asking me for advice."

"About?"

"Financial stuff. Where she should live. What jobs she should take. Nothing I know anything about."

"Weird," Anna said, but it did happen. Most people were wary of cops if they didn't hate them outright. However, some found the badge comforting, a beacon of safety and security.

"By the way, she hates your boyfriend the conductor. Says he plays favorites in his orchestras."

Anna ignored the "boyfriend" crack.

"She and Bostridge," she said.

"We've heard it from two people. Maybe he does play favorites."

"According to Diane Engstrom, Al Larrimore makes all the hiring decisions for Vranos' New York performances. I don't know about the overseas ones. Even if he does play favorites, what does that have to do with Savenkov's murder?"

"Just wondering how much we don't know about Vranos," Mac said with a shrug. "So who's Franz Gadde?"

Anna grabbed the subject change with alacrity and filled him in on her busy afternoon at the cemetery and showed him the reports.

"Figures I miss all the fun," Mac groused. "So we got Bostridge out of the way. We've maybe found the electrician. The Arch-Hoo-Haw is in this up to his neck. And now we've got to be really careful because the murderer is going to get nervous."

"Um-hmm," Anna said, staring down at the Interpol report. Her eyes kept coming back to Franz Gadde's name. For a few seconds, she let her mind cast around for whatever connection it was trying to make but when nothing clicked, she looked up at Mac.

"At least Karin Gadde will finally have something that belonged to her brother," she said.

CHAPTER 13

Anna stood on the eastern sidewalk of Central Park West with her head tipped back and her hands shoved in the pockets of her brown suede slacks. She shifted her shoulders and grimaced when the bruises from her landing on the cemetery's hard earth protested.

Her gaze was focused on the 14th floor. An ornate Art Deco railing ran across the entire front of the building, outlining a terrace illuminated by the light spilling from the tall French doors of Nicholas Vranos' living room. It was ten minutes past eight o'clock.

The hum of traffic, punctuated by an occasional siren or taxi horn, was nothing but background noise for the debate raging in Anna's mind. Reaching a conclusion, she shook her head decisively and turned on her heel, walking into the park and away from the building. Then a mournful arpeggio of piano notes cascaded down from the open doors above and a shudder ran through her.

"How does he know?" she whispered, stopping in her tracks. She pivoted and paced slowly across the street, almost like a sleep walker, coming to a halt in front of the big bronze doors of the apartment building. One side swung open silently and she blinked in the blaze of light that spilled over her and onto the sidewalk.

"Lieutenant Salazar. "Mr. Vranos is expecting you," a disembodied voice said.

Anna shook herself as her eyes adjusted to the brightness and she saw the doorman waiting patiently for her to enter. Nicholas Vranos was a man, not a magician. She had to keep reminding herself of that. It was hard to believe sometimes when he seemed able to draw her to him in spite of every warning her brain screamed at her.

"Thanks," she said, striding into the lobby.

On the ride up in the elevator, she fidgeted with the sleek leather handbag she had slung over her shoulder; her Glock was nestled inside it in a built-in holster. She felt naked without her shoulder holster but she had decided guests didn't wear their weapons. *Not even in their boots*, she thought, glancing down at the soft brown leather civilian boots she wore and missing the weight of the Smith and Wesson subcompact against her ankle.

She knew she was splitting hairs: taking her guns off didn't make her any less of a detective on Alexei Savenkov's case or Nicholas Vranos any less of a suspect. No matter what she felt or Mac thought or the dead man's family believed, Nicholas had not been cleared of his friend's murder and she should not be here.

The elevator doors opened and Nicholas Vranos stood in the hallway waiting for her. He was dressed in charcoal slacks and a silvery gray shirt. A smile smoothed some of the lines from his face.

"You came," he said, holding out his hand as though to pull her from the elevator.

She stepped through the doors and put her hand in his. His long fingers closed around hers in a grip both dominating and protective.

"Against my better judgment," she said.

"Judgment should always be tempered by compassion."

She wasn't sure compassion was what had led her there.

"Come in. Would you like some wine or something stronger?" he asked, drawing her through the open door of his apartment.

"Wine would be good, thank you. Red, if you have it."

He tucked her hand underneath his elbow as he escorted her across the vast living room to the brass and wood bar. Decanters of all shapes and sizes were arrayed on its shelves while two dozen bottles of wine were racked in a glass-fronted cellar below.

"I have a 1994 *Opus One* already breathing but if you'd prefer something else, take your pick."

"Is it well focused but bigboned with a slight underlayer of smelly gym socks?" Anna asked.

He threw back his head and laughed.

"Puncturing my pretensions?" he said, picking up a carafe of deep red wine and pouring from it into two crystal balloon glasses.

"I took a wine-tasting course a couple of years ago," she said, putting her bag down on the bar and carefully accepting the fragile glass. "When you mentioned 'breathing' it reminded me of the strange descriptions the professor used."

She took a sip and closed her eyes for a moment of pure sensory appreciation. There was no way to describe the flavor of this wine in words. Even "superb" seemed weak.

"Definitely not smelly gym socks," she said after she let the wine slide down her throat. "This is a lot better than the stuff they gave us at the class."

"I hope so," he said, taking a drink himself. "It's a personal favorite but hard to get because the production is limited."

Anna swirled the wine in her glass, admiring the richness of the color and the weight of the liquid. It was an excellent way to avoid looking at her host.

"It's from California, isn't it?" she asked, taking another sip.

"Yes. It's a joint venture between the Mondavi family and the Comte de Rothschild."

There was an undercurrent of amusement in his voice now. He knew she was deliberately keeping the conversation impersonal.

"I should go," Anna said, putting the glass down harder than she meant to.

"No," he said sharply, catching her wrist in an unyielding grip. "Let me play for you."

He left his own wine on the bar and led her across the room to the sleek black monster of a piano.

"Tonight, ambiguity is banished," he said, his voice taking on a low hypnotic cadence. "Tonight you are simply a fascinating and very beautiful woman." He used just the tips of his fingers to brush up along her jaw line and around the curve of her ear. "Tonight, I am simply a man who wants you here."

Anna swallowed hard and his fingertips followed the movement of her throat. For a long moment, they simply watched each other.

"And for tonight, this," he said, gesturing to the sheets of music spread across the piano's stand, "is the authentic first movement of Beethoven's Tenth Symphony."

He sat on the leather topped bench and tugged gently at her wrist.

"Sit with me."

"I can't play this," Anna said after one glance at the handwritten notes in the photographs.

"Not to play. Just to feel it."

She remembered the day they had played together, the sense that their bodies had fused into one.

She slid onto the bench beside him.

He raised his hands to the keyboard. She felt him gather himself on a deep breath and then his fingers curved into the keys and music poured from the instrument in front of them.

It swirled like the wine, full and rich and infinitely sensuous. It filled her mind until all she could contain there was the sound and the feel of the man beside her, his thigh warm and hard against hers, his shoulder flexing as his hands flew across the keys, and his face utterly intent on the notes in front of him. She lost all sense of time passing.

A series of heartbreakingly beautiful chords rose and fell and suddenly there was silence.

Anna stared at Nicholas' hands still poised on the keyboard as though willing them to bring forth more glorious sound.

"Is that all?" she asked.

"Yes. Frustrating, isn't it?" he said, reaching up to flip over the final page so the right side of the music stand stood bare. "He leaves you on the edge of your seat and the resolution of the next movement is denied us."

"It's . . . it's like the wine: you can't describe it," Anna said.

"When I play it, I believe it's real," he said, his gaze still on the sheets of music. She could see the intensity of his longing for this to be the final explosion of Beethoven's genius. "When I look at Franz Gadde's paper, I doubt it. The Tenth is like the unicorn, a glorious myth."

"No ambiguities," Anna reminded him. "Everything is just what it appears to be on the surface."

He turned from the music and smiled, something still so rare in her experience with him that it had the same effect on her as her leap over the motorcycle. She had to tell herself to breathe.

"Thank you for reminding me of my own rules," he said. "Would you like dinner now? There is nothing less ambiguous than good food."

Anna had forgotten a meal was included in the invitation but she discovered she was ravenous. She nodded.

Nicholas left her at the piano to retrieve the bottle of *Opus One* from the bar. Anna stayed on the bench, examining the facsimiles of Beethoven's composition. How Nicholas could translate those tiny black squiggles into such magnificent sound was beyond her comprehension. Of course, Beethoven's creation of those squiggles without hearing them was even more incomprehensible.

"Dinner?" Nicholas asked, breaking into her reverie. He helped her up from the bench and led her to a set of closed double doors near the foyer. As he pulled open the oak panel, air scented with garlic wafted around her and her stomach growled.

"I think I forgot to eat lunch," she said as Nicholas raised an eyebrow. "What a beautiful room!"

Her host left her to absorb the details as he lit the two candelabra sitting on the table and dimmed the lights.

Anna admired the birds-eye maple paneling covering the lower half of the walls and what looked like pale blue watered silk above it. A carved molding defined the edge of the domed ceiling where a delicate crystal chandelier hung from a plaster rosette. The long polished table was made of several woods of differing shades and grains, inlaid in geometric patterns. Two places were set across from each other at one end. Although the china and crystal were obviously expensive, Anna was relieved to see that the array of silverware was relatively simple, no weirdly shaped knives she couldn't figure out what to do with.

Nicholas pulled out a chair and Anna practically jogged across the cream and blue Oriental rug.

He seated himself across from her and then lifted the lid of a serving bowl sitting on a silver stand.

"Would you like some *kavouri?*" he asked, uncovering a serving dish filled with miniature crab cakes.

"Yes, please," Anna said. "Did you make them?"

"No, my culinary skills are very limited. Christos made dinner."

"Christos?" Anna asked.

"From *Vranos Estiatorio* in Brooklyn."

"Any relation?"

"No and yes. I'll tell you the story later. For now, as Christos would say, *kali oreksi!* Eat heartily!"

After the first taste, Anna had to force herself not to just pick up the crab cakes with her fingers and swallow them whole. As she chewed the last forkful, she debated whether it would be gauche to ask for seconds. She looked up to find Nicholas watching her across the table with a slight smile playing around his lips.

"More?" he asked.

"How did you guess?"

He refilled her empty plate.

"You ate *prestissimo*."

"Is that a polite way of saying I inhaled them?"

"Now that the edge of your hunger has been blunted you can savor this serving. Pleasure should not be rushed."

Anna flushed as she remembered the speed with which she had climaxed the other night.

"Although the greatest pleasure can't be controlled," he continued, once again seeming to look inside her mind. "It insists on its own tempo."

"Hmmm," Anna agreed, keeping her eyes on her plate. "So how long have you lived in this amazing apartment?"

He was silent for so long that Anna looked up. Her host was twirling the stem of his wine glass between his long fingers. She watched his shoulders rise and fall on a long, deep breath.

"The answer is complicated," he said.

Anna put down her fork.

"Tell me. I want to know."

His eyes met hers.

"Who will I be telling? The lieutenant or Anna?"

"Both. I can't separate the two, no matter how much I'd like to pretend otherwise. I'm a lieutenant because I'm Anna."

"How do you stay so uncorrupted by the ugliness you see every day?" he asked, leaning forward. "How do you keep that pristine integrity from getting smudged?"

"I have a good partner," Anna said.

"Lieutenant McKenzie?"

"Mac believes in the same things I do. We keep each other strong when we need to."

A shadow crossed Nicholas' face.

"Did Alexei do that for you?" Anna asked.

"Perhaps." He stood up and swept the two appetizer plates from the table. "Let me get our main course."

Anna started to rise to help him but he waved her back to her chair. He left the empty dishes on the sideboard and took a filled plate from a silver warming box. Anna took a long sip of wine as she watched him stride around the table. As he leaned down to set the plate in front of her, she felt the slightest brush of his chest against her back. She sucked in a breath as she fought the temptation to lean back into him. Instead she stared down at the plate in front of her.

"Lamb chops, *horta*, and Greek potatoes," Nicholas said as he strolled back around the table to collect his own plate and a basket of artisan bread.

As she leaned forward to breathe in the fragrant steam rising from the dish, Anna noticed the black band around the rim of the plate was decorated in gold with musical notes.

"Are these notes a real piece of music or are they just decorations?"

Nicholas ran his finger partway around the rim of his plate.

"This is a theme from Mozart's *Magic Flute*," he said. "I'm not sure which piece yours is. Paul had this china made; these are his personal favorites from the classics."

"Your mentor?" Anna asked.

He nodded.

"He's part of the complicated answer about your relatives," Anna said, picking up her knife and fork and digging in. She was deliberately focusing her attention somewhere other than Nicholas, a technique she used in interviews to make the other person feel less pressured.

"Paul made me," Nicholas said.

Anna flicked a quick glance at him. He sat back in his chair with one arm draped over the back. The other hand lay on the table, fingers drumming quietly. He seemed intent on a painted landscape hanging to Anna's left but clearly he was seeing a completely different scene.

"I was dropped on the steps of a convent in Louisiana when I was an infant. The sisters weren't in the business of raising children so I went into the state child welfare system and was adopted. Despite hiring a private investigator when I was financially able to, my biological parents are still unknown and probably dead by now."

He said it dispassionately but Anna made a mental note to try official channels; she would have fuller access to otherwise sealed records.

"My adoptive parents were fundamentalist Christians who felt it was their duty to help a poor bastard child."

Anna winced. She could almost hear the self-righteous voices driving that dagger into a lonely child's heart.

"They weren't physically neglectful. I was fed and clothed and educated to a certain point. However, their particular set of beliefs included the sinfulness of all forms of music. Except hymns, of course. I was allowed, required, in fact, to play those on the church piano but if I strayed into anything else . . . well, I was punished."

He turned his blue gaze directly on her.

"Some people believe that kind of upbringing makes one capable of killing without a qualm."

"It can," Anna said. "But sociopaths come from all backgrounds. There's a profile but no standard blueprint."

He picked up his wine glass and swallowed the remainder of its contents. He added some wine to Anna's glass and refilled his own.

"Of course, I had the usual fantasies about who my real parents were. My favorite was having a world-famous opera singer for a mother and a concert pianist for a father. However, my adoptive parents assured me that my biological parents were hardened sinners who would burn in hell.

"When I was fourteen, I stole one Sunday's collection money from the church, my small act of revenge, and got myself to New York City. I had heard of the Juilliard School and decided I wanted to go there."

He laughed at his younger self's ignorance with a low, raw sound.

"They weren't receptive to a scruffy fourteen-year-old who could play fifty-nine variations of 'Nearer My God to Thee'."

"Their loss," Anna said.

He laughed again, with real amusement this time.

"Not all New Yorkers were unkind," he continued. "I wandered into a Greek restaurant in Brooklyn where the owner, Christos Vranos, took pity on me, paid me in cash for doing odd jobs, and let me sleep on the office couch."

"Of course. *Vranos'* is famous for being a musician's hangout. I guess that's no coincidence."

Nicholas nodded and continued, his words coming faster and more fluently.

"When Christos wasn't lecturing me on the proper way to cook lamb, I haunted music stores and traded any work they wanted me to do for sheet music, books on music, and playing whatever instruments they were selling. That's where Paul found me, massacring a Mozart concerto on an old Steinway in a used piano store. What he heard in my untrained performance I'll never know but he offered to pay for lessons and let me use the piano here in his apartment to practice on."

Anna imagined a younger Nicholas with shaggy hair and faded jeans, hunched in the corner of a dark, dusty store crammed with battered pianos, coaxing a glorious sound from the once-proud instrument. His youth, his extraordinary eyes, and his raw talent must have burned like a flame in the dismal surroundings.

"Paul had good instincts," she said. "Who was he?"

"Paul Vogl was a musician and gentleman scholar from an immensely wealthy Viennese family, who intended to make a brief visit to New York to hear real jazz. Once here, he and his wife Maria never left. When he found me, he was in his early fifties and had been here for twenty years. Unfortunately, Maria had died of emphysema two years before so I never knew her."

"And they had no children?" Anna asked.

"Much to their regret, no," Nicholas said. "So Paul devoted all his time to the study of music . . . and to educating an ignorant boy from Louisiana."

"I'd never have guessed you were from the South and I pride myself on my ear for accents."

"I eradicated all traces of my childhood from my life," he said, his voice implacable.

"Including your original surname."

"The day we met, I told Paul my name was Nicholas Vranos. When Paul adopted me, I wanted to take his name. He was such an unassuming man though, he wouldn't let me. Vogl, however, is my middle name."

Anna knew that and had noted the odd concatenation of ethnicities, but New York City was a "great melting pot" and such combinations occurred frequently.

"So you lived here from age fourteen on?"

"Not quite. I knew something about the dangers of being picked up by strangers. Paul won my trust though and I moved in here within a year of our first meeting."

"And he gave you all this," Anna said, sweeping her hand around.

"He gave me music," Nicholas said, completely dismissing their opulent surroundings. "He gave me all the knowledge I was capable of absorbing although I could never learn everything he knew."

"He was the father from your dreams," Anna said. "How old were you when he died?"

"Old enough to understand what I'd lost," Nicholas said. "He died four years ago."

"I'm so sorry."

She wanted to reach across the table and lay her hand on his but the expanse of polished wood stretched too far between them. A thought struck her and she spoke without thinking first.

"That's when you married Serena, wasn't it?" she asked.

"Yes, Detective, that undoubtedly explains the timing of my ill-fated foray into matrimony."

The heavy irony in his voice made Anna frown. She wanted to meet the woman who consistently evoked such overt bitterness from this supremely controlled man. At the same time, he still hauled his ex-wife's harp around Carnegie Hall. The dynamics of failed marriages were endlessly bizarre.

"Eat your dinner, Anna," he said as he picked up his own fork. "Christos will be insulted if you don't."

Anna recognized the "No Trespassing" sign he'd just posted. She regretted interrupting the narrative of his life—she would have liked to hear the story of his career—but she couldn't help questioning his motives for sharing it with her.

"Your ability to listen must be very useful in your profession," Nicholas commented after they had eaten in silence for a few minutes. "I haven't told anyone that story in years."

"Do many people know it?"

Nicholas shrugged.

"Some version of it, but my p.r. department romanticizes it as much as they can. Lexi knew all the ugly details." He gave a harsh laugh. "Speaking of ugly, I was notified today that Brian Bostridge has filed a complaint against me with the musicians' union. Evidently I have maliciously and deliberately blocked the advancement of his career."

"What does that mean for you?"

He shrugged.

"A few hearings. A new Jaguar for my lawyer. It's a minor annoyance."

A series of melodious but insistent electronic tones provoked a growl of irritation from her host. He rose and walked over to a small brass panel by the door.

"What is it, Stan?" he asked.

"I'm sorry to disturb you but Miss Reyes is asking to come up."

Nicholas muttered a curse.

"Thank you. Send her up." He turned to Anna. "Speaking of the devil . . . my apologies but I know from experience Serena won't leave until I see her. However, I'll make sure her visit is short. Perhaps you should retire to the library temporarily."

For a long moment their eyes locked as the memory of what had happened there not so many hours ago seared the air between them. Anna looked away as she pushed her chair back from the table.

"I think I can find it."

CHAPTER 14

"Serena, the next time do me the courtesy of calling before you arrive on my doorstep," Anna heard Nicholas say as she stood listening at the library door. He hadn't closed the door completely which Anna accepted as tacit permission to eavesdrop, something the detective in her intended to do anyway.

"Darling, I just got back from Tokyo so I missed Lexi's funeral," came the response in a throaty voice with the slightest of Spanish accents. "I came straight here to express my sympathy."

"Thank you." Nicholas' voice held a heavy dose of irony.

Anna shifted so she could catch a sliver of a view through the crack. Serena Reyes, Nicholas' ex-wife, was tall and thin with red hair cut almost brutally short around her face. Her enormous brown eyes and strong bone structure were accentuated by the extreme hair style. She wore a dark blue jumpsuit with a collection of gold chains slung around her hips, and she balanced confidently on spike-heeled black boots with more chains draped around the ankles.

"And I had to find out what happened. He was murdered?" Serena continued.

"Yes," her ex-husband said.

"In Carnegie Hall?"

"Yes."

"For God's sake, Nicholas, talk to me. Don't make me pull it out of you like teeth." Multiple rings flashed on her fingers as she gestured in exasperation.

Nicholas gave her a brief and unembellished summary of the facts of his friend's death.

"You found him? My poor darling."

Serena flung open her arms and moved out of Anna's line of sight. A moment later, she stepped back into view with a sad smile on her face.

"I forget. My arms are no longer a comfort to you," she said. "Lexi was closer to you than even I was. You must mourn his loss."

"In my own way, Serena. Not yours."

"That was always the problem, wasn't it? Our ways are so different." Serena looked away for a silent moment. "Why have the police not caught his killer? Are they incompetent or just lazy?"

"Neither. It's a complex case." Anna could swear she heard the tiniest hint of amusement in his voice. He knew she was listening. "I'm on the list of suspects as well."

"You?" his ex-wife said. "Why would you shoot your best friend?"

"Over you, my dear. The fury of a cuckolded husband."

Serena laughed and then looked sad again.

"Some fury would have been welcome," she said. "You didn't give a damn who I slept with by then."

"Fortunately for both of us. However, love and money are the most predictable of motives so the police feel I have a good one."

"Money," she repeated, looking thoughtful. "I saw Lexi in Vienna and he was being his usual cryptic self but he mentioned money. He'd found something in a palace. I assumed it was one of his usual artifacts and—"

"What palace?" Nicholas' tone was sharp.

"Oh God, I can't remember," Serena said, putting her hand to her forehead. "Lexi always dropped so many names. It was something very fancy, like a prince."

Anna held her breath.

"An archduke," Serena said. "That was it. An archduke with a long name."

"Johanne-Rudolph Habsburg-Lothringen."

"That sounds familiar."

"What did he find there?"

Serena thought again.

"Music? Or a drawing? I think he said something about a sketchbook."

"Serena, try to remember exactly what he said about what he'd found."

Anna watched in fascination as Serena's face went utterly still. She was clearly listening to something in her mind and Anna had a sense of how she would look in a performance.

"He said there was more than money at stake and he needed your opinion on something he'd gotten at the Archduke's palace. I made a snide comment about your opinion." She grimaced at her ex-husband in a comically affectionate way that made Anna want to smack her. "Then he mentioned music and a sketchbook."

"'Music and a sketchbook'," Nicholas repeated slowly.

"Not 'and', 'in'," Serena corrected. "Music *in* a sketchbook."

Anna had to stifle a gasp. If Savenkov had found the sheet of doodles *in* the sketchbook, it would indicate the Archduke was at least considering forgery.

"Did he say anything about Beethoven?" Nicholas asked.

Serena shook her head but she was a musician and made the connection herself.

"You think he found one of Beethoven's sketchbooks? But he wouldn't have simply walked out with it. Lexi was never dishonest, just a bit . . . manipulative."

"The Archduke may have given it to him. He finds them handy as bribes."

"I should have known Beethoven was involved if Lexi wanted your opinion. What's going on, Nicholas?" his ex-wife asked.

"Something someone will kill for. Don't discuss what you've told me with anyone except the police," he said. "You should talk to them first thing tomorrow morning. I'll get you the detective's card and your coat."

Serena moved out of Anna's view again.

"Darling, let me stay tonight," she heard her purr. "You shouldn't be alone."

"Your solicitude overwhelms me." Nicholas' voice could have cut glass.

"Are you still holding it against me that I went on tour after Paul died?"

"If we don't learn from our mistakes, we're condemned to repeat them," Nicholas said.

His ex-wife sauntered back where Anna could see her. Her hands were planted on her hips and she worried her lower lip with her teeth as she waited for him to return.

The irritation on her face vanished as Nicholas came up behind her holding a long mink coat. She slid her arms into the fur and turned.

"If I'm in danger, darling, shouldn't I stay here with all your security systems?"

"You're only in danger if you talk about it. Try to use some discretion for a change."

"You wouldn't be at all upset if they found me shot, would you?"

"On the contrary, I would mourn the loss of a great musical talent," he said.

Serena snarled and drew back her hand. Anna waited for the sound of palm against cheek but Nicholas caught his ex-wife's wrist and forced her arm down to her side. Some men found that sort of physical violence from a woman exciting; Anna was relieved to see Nicholas' face showed nothing but a faint contempt. Serena rubbed her wrist as she stalked around him without a word.

He followed her and Anna lost sight of both of them, hearing only Nicholas' deep baritone saying, "Call Lieutenant Salazar tomorrow, Serena."

Anna thought she heard the door close but waited a minute for safety's sake. When the silence stretched and Nicholas did not open the library door, she pushed it open and scanned the room. At first she thought it was empty but then she saw him standing in front of the piano, staring at the symphony on the music stand. She walked across the vast expanse of carpet and came up to the piano.

"It's a fake," he said without looking at her. "It's brilliant but it's a fake."

His lips twisted as he picked up the pile of papers and dropped them on the floor.

"Lexi knew and he was going to tell me." His voice was harsh with anger as he pivoted towards her. "The Archduke killed him to silence him."

"Possibly," Anna said, keeping her voice low and calm. "But we have to prove that."

He wrapped his fingers around her upper arms and pulled her closer.

"Prove it, Anna," he ground out, "or I'll kill the Archduke myself."

"If you do that, you're just as guilty as he is. Trust me to do my job."

She met his searing blue gaze without flinching as he stared down at her. The snarl left his lips and his grip on her arms loosened from bruising to firm. He scanned the close-fitting V-necked sweater she wore.

"Have I earned your trust then?" he asked. "There's obviously no gun under that sweater. Is there one in your shoe?"

Anna shook her head.

"Guests don't wear guns."

He lowered his head very, very slowly and touched her lips with his. His hands slid over the soft peach-colored wool of her sweater, warming her back with his palms.

There were questions she needed to ask him about Serena's visit but his own question overrode hers. It was a question he was asking with his body, as much as his words, a question of denying death its power over the living.

But had he earned her trust?

She stood still under the careful brush of his mouth on hers, trying to decide if trust had anything to do with the dark fascination she felt for this man. Then she threaded her fingers through his gleaming hair and tilted his head so their lips met fully. That was the only answer she had.

CHAPTER 15

As his arms tightened around her, Anna arched into him, wrapping her own arms around his neck and teasing his tongue with hers. He groaned and ran his hands down her back to cup her behind and pull her harder against him, his fingers kneading the soft suede of her slacks. Her breasts were crushed against the solid wall of his chest so his slightest movement sent streaks of exquisite heat into the growing ache at her core. She skimmed the inside of her knee upward and locked her leg around his hip so she could feel him pushing between her thighs.

"Oh God, Anna," he breathed into her mouth before gripping her other leg and lifting it around his hip so she was stretched open and pressed tight against his erection. His long fingers were like steel bands around her thighs, both supporting her and pulling her against him. Anna gasped and let her head fall back and her eyes close as the pressure sent ripples of delicious tension through her. She felt his teeth graze her neck, and then he pulled back and eased her down so her feet touched the floor.

She opened her eyes to find out what had gone wrong.

"This time we're going to be comfortable," he said, taking her hand. He pulled her after him, his long strides making her almost jog to keep up.

"The couch would be fine with me," Anna said as they passed it. "I always wanted to make love on an antique."

His laugh was only slightly strained.

"My bed is even older so you'll get your wish."

They crossed the foyer and entered a long hallway strewn with Oriental runners and lit by bronze sconces in the shape of human hands holding torches.

Nicholas saw her eyeing them and said, "Paul's little joke. You know, I never realized before how long this hall is."

He stooped and put his arm behind her knees, sweeping her up in his arms before he continued down the corridor at a faster pace.

She started to squirm in protest but he bent his head to kiss her and she subsided.

"You seem to be walking *prestissimo*," she teased him with his own word when he released her lips. "What happened to savoring the pleasure?"

"Oh, I plan to savor you for a very long time but strolling down a hall is not my idea of foreplay."

Anna laughed and reached down to stroke the bulge in his slacks. He hissed in a sharp breath and rolled her toward him so she could no longer reach his erection.

"*Andante*," he said through gritted teeth. "We don't want to reach the climax in the first movement."

"I thought each movement had a climax," Anna said as he swung her sideways through a door. She had a kaleidoscopic impression of paneled walls, a burgundy Oriental rug, and long blue and gold drapes before she was tossed into the depths of the gold velvet quilt covering his bed. Nicholas followed her down, stretching himself out halfway on top of her and sliding his hand between her thighs to stroke her as she had stroked him.

"Ohhhh!" Anna gasped as electricity seemed to shoot through her and she jerked under his questing fingers.

He withdrew his hand and rolled off the bed and onto his feet so he was standing over her. His smile was a tantalizing mixture of lust and mischief.

"Tonight I don't want to think of anything but you," he said, sliding his hands up under her sweater and dragging it upward as she lifted her arms. He balled it up and hurled it across the room before working his hands under her back and unhooking her black lace bra. It followed the sweater before he stood and simply looked down at her.

With her breasts exposed to his intense gaze, Anna felt vulnerable and started to cross her arms over her chest but he caught her wrists. Gently forcing her to bend her elbows, he raised her arms over her head and clipped them together in one of his hands. With his other hand, he pulled her long braid out from under her and wrapped it around her wrists, anchoring it with his hand.

If his eyes had seemed intense before, they positively scorched her skin now. Then she forgot his eyes completely as he drew his free hand down the valley between her breasts and around to cup one while his mouth came down on the other.

He tongued her nipple to an excruciatingly sensitive hardness before shifting to her other breast. She planted both boots on the bed and bowed upward, wanting him to take more of her into the wet and warmth of his mouth. Having her hands trapped above her head so her breasts seemed to offer themselves to him was arousing in a way she hadn't expected.

Yet she wanted to touch him too. She started to tug her hands apart, thinking it would be easy to free herself but she discovered her hair made a more effective rope than she thought.

He felt her efforts and lifted his head briefly.

"Ah, you see, you're completely at my mercy. My only regret is that I didn't take off all of your clothes first. But perhaps I can get around that problem."

He kept her hair tightly around her wrists with one hand while he used the other to unfasten the waistband of her slacks and pull down her zipper. With impressive dexterity, he worked her slacks down to the top of her thighs, revealing the black satin and lace panties she wore. They were no barrier to his strong fingers as he pushed aside the smooth fabric and slid into the even smoother folds between her legs.

He controlled her completely, pinning her above with one hand and below with the other by thrusting into her with those long, powerful fingers. She opened her eyes to see him watching his fingers stroking into her. It was too much.

"If you do that one more time, I'm going to come without you," she managed to gasp out.

He stilled with his fingers inside her then brought his head down for a long, searching kiss. He carefully slipped his hand out of her and let go of her hair.

"Don't move," he said, using both hands to remove her boots and pull her slacks and panties down and off. He started toward the night table beside the bed but stopped before he reached it.

"Do we trust each other enough to not use a condom?" he asked.

Anna looked at him.

"I can vouch for myself, Pill and all," she said. "And you?"

"Clean as a whistle."

"Apt for a musician. You can leave off the protection."

She watched his gaze devour her as he unbuckled his belt and unzipped his slacks. It was like having a laser beam on her bare skin; she thought she would go up in flames.

Then he was on top of her, still fully clothed, pressing her into the soft quilt as his knees drove between hers. The silk of his shirt and the wool of his slacks abraded her sensitized skin and she swallowed a moan when he pushed into her fully. He let her feel helpless beneath his weight for a moment before he braced himself on his elbows and began a slow rhythm of thrust and withdrawal.

Something in the back of her mind was shocked at her pleasure in his domination. This man was playing her the way he played the Steinway: with total control. She didn't give a damn. Every nerve ending in her body craved more of him and she moved the only parts of her body free of his command, her legs. Once again, she wrapped them around his hips, making him drive deeper inside her until the tension wound one more turn and exploded, making her shout and arch so hard she pushed even his weight upward. She thrashed mindlessly beneath him in the throes of her orgasm while he stayed motionless, riding it out so her pleasure took center stage.

When she relaxed back onto the bed, he lifted himself up onto his palms to thrust harder and deeper than before, the muscles in his neck and arms straining with the effort. He called out her name as she felt him pump his own climax into her, sending an echo of orgasm through her own still trembling muscles.

Then he sank down to cover her with his body, his head buried in her shoulder. She whimpered her loss as his erection subsided and he slid out of her.

"Am I crushing you?" he asked, lifting his head and shifting sideways.

"Yes but that wasn't why I complained," she said. "I was regretting your absence inside me."

He made a sound somewhere between a laugh and a moan.

"Believe me, I regret it too."

He saw her trying to work her wrists loose and reached up to unknot her braid.

"Do you know how erotic it is to use your own hair to tie you up?"

"Yes," she said, grinning as she felt a small sense of superiority when she remembered Serena's very short hair.

He smiled back at her, a smile that banished all the lines and shadows from his face. Then he rolled onto his back, spreading his arms wide and closing his eyes with a lesser version of the smile still lingering on his lips.

Anna curled her legs under her and sat up beside him, feeling very naked beside a man who still wore even his shoes. She crossed her arms over her chest and looked around for some article of clothing. She located a couple of heaps in opposite corners of the room and started to get up. His arm curled around her waist like a whip and he hauled her down on top of him.

"You're not putting anything back on that body," he said, running his palm from her shoulder down to the curve of her behind. "Every inch of your skin is now my playground."

"You have to give to get," Anna said as she started to unbutton his shirt.

"Focus is very important to a musician. I wanted to focus entirely on you."

She undid the last of his shirt buttons and shoved the silk away from his chest. She skimmed her palm over the muscles of his abdomen, enjoying their contraction. He made no move to stop her as she moved upward, drawing her fingers up the column of his neck so she could trace the strong bones of his jaw and cheek. His eyes were closed as she smoothed his dark eyebrows with her fingertip and explored the whorls of his ear before following the sharp line of his nose down to the curves of his mouth. As she trailed her finger along the cleft in his chin, he opened his eyes. Their extraordinary blue still stunned her.

"You're pure fire, Anna. You cleanse my soul."

"Frankly, I haven't been thinking much about your soul in the last half an hour or so," Anna said.

He laughed and thrust his fingers into her hair, pulling her down for a kiss that curled her toes before it led to other things.

They made love twice more before they slid under the velvet quilt and into the sleep of satisfied exhaustion. As she curled up against the big, warm body beside her, the sense she had missed something which had been chewing at the edges of her mind fell into a clear pattern and she sighed with relief. Tomorrow . . .

"Tish, I'm worried about Anna," Mac said, after he chewed and swallowed the last bite of the huge chef's salad his wife had served him for dinner. His partner had called earlier and apologized for having to miss dinner but she had given no real explanation for her absence.

"Ach, it's no wonder what with the nasty folks you two run into," Letitia said. She'd left Scotland twenty-three years before but her voice retained her homeland's burr.

Mac hesitated.

"She's not gotten herself shot again, has she?" Letitia asked, putting her mug of tea down with a thump.

Mac shook his head and looked uncomfortable.

"Well, what is it then, Kevin? We've been married twenty-two years and I've heard it all. Out with it, man."

"Anna's involved with a suspect."

"'Involved'? What does that signify exactly?"

"You know, physically."

"As in sex?"

Mac flushed and nodded.

"She'd never do such a thing," Letitia said.

"It's Nicholas Vranos, the conductor."

"Ahhhh," Letitia said. "That explains a great deal. He's a bonnie man besides being talented and famous. I saw him on the telly and if I weren't happily married to you, I would have been getting his autograph myself. You told me you don't believe he shot the French horn player."

"It doesn't matter if he did or not. Right now, he's a suspect and it looks bad for Anna."

Letitia picked up her tea and took a sip.

"It's tearing her apart, Tish," Mac continued. "She looks guilty every time his name comes up."

"Our Anna would never let her feelings get in the way of her duty," Letitia said.

"Even if Vranos is cleared, I'm worried."

"Because?"

"He's a high and mighty international conductor who hobnobs with presidents and kings. Anna's just, well, she's just a cop. I think he's playing her for the information he can get. He's not going to hang around once this case is closed."

"You're underestimating the lass," Letitia said. "Vranos would be lucky to have *her* decide to stick with *him*."

"I know that," Mac said testily. "But she's a good cop and I don't want to see her hurt."

"You're a good cop too," Letitia said, covering her husband's hand with her own. "You can find the killer before

Anna gets into trouble. But you can't stop her from being hurt. No one can do that."

CHAPTER 16

Anna's internal alarm snapped her eyelids open at 5:00 A.M. She muffled a groan at the brevity of her sleep before she tried to slip out of Nicholas' bed without disturbing him. As she shifted, she realized he had entwined himself with her. He was spooned up against her back, his head anchoring her long, unbound hair to the pillow, his left arm snaked around her waist. He had driven his thigh between hers and torqued his ankle up and around her calf to lock her leg against him.

As she tried to disentangle her legs, she felt his breathing change as his grip turned to iron.

"I have to get up," she whispered, thinking he was reacting in his sleep.

"Why?" his voice rumbled in her ear.

"I've got work to do. There are some questions I need to ask you and something I've got to double check before I leave."

She could feel his erection growing against her buttocks. He rolled her onto her back and was inside her before she guessed his intent. Then he began his foreplay, stroking her breasts, nipping little kisses down her neck, and whispering flattering adjectives as he explored every part of her body. The contrast of his light touch above with the hardening of his arousal inside her drove all thought of escape from her mind.

As her hips began to pulse against him, he pushed up onto his elbows and looked down at her in the dimness of the room.

"Ask me your questions," he said. "I can't lie to you now."

She searched his face, trying to understand what he was thinking but it was too dark to read his expression. She shook her head.

"This is when men tell the biggest lies," she said, panting.

"You're wrong," he said, bending to kiss her eyelids. "They tell the biggest lies to get here."

Then he began to thrust into her, making her forget any questions. When it came, her climax ripped through her with brutal abruptness and power. Nicholas, too, seemed to almost wrench his pleasure from their joining. They lay side by side shuddering when it was done. When her legs felt strong enough to support her, Anna scooted to the edge of the bed.

She thought she heard him breathe her name but he let her go.

She found the marble-lined bathroom and showered in a huge glass enclosure, reveling in the multiple jets spouting from several levels of the high tech brass fixture. She could definitely get used to that. She borrowed her host's comb to unsnarl the tangles in her hair and braided it wet. Before venturing back into the bedroom, she wrapped herself snugly in one of the enormous bath towels hanging over brass rods.

The lamp on the bedside table threw a pool of light over Nicholas as he lay wrapped in the sheets, watching her. His dark hair fell around his face in tousled waves while his bare chest and shoulders glowed olive against the white sheets. One leg was bent at the knee and the sheet had slipped sideways to expose the strong arch of his bare foot.

"You look like one of those sulky Greek gods," she said, recalling an earlier thought she'd had.

"'Sulky'?" he said, raising his eyebrow. "Spent, not sulky."

"You seem to have a grudge against my clothes," she said as she began to retrieve them from the recesses of his room.

"Always. As a god, I invoke the privilege of having you naked at all times." He threw off the sheets and got up.

The sight was spectacular.

"If I can invoke the same privilege, that's fine," she said, forcing herself to drag her gaze upward to meet his eyes.

He started toward her and she held her clothes-laden hands out in front of her to ward him off.

"No, I really have to get dressed," she said as he prowled closer.

"That may constitute blasphemy," he said but veered toward the bathroom.

Anna threw on her clothes. When she turned around he was leaning against the bathroom door jamb, wearing nothing but a pair of black silk pajama pants.

"What do you need to check?" he asked.

"The musical doodle sheet," Anna said, trying very hard to ignore the ripple of his shoulder muscles when he pushed off the doorframe.

"It's in the library," he said, taking her hand as he drew even with her and interlocking his fingers with hers. "We'll use the back entrance."

As they walked down the hall, Anna kept her gaze resolutely straightforward in the hope that all she would be distracted by was the heat of his palm against hers. Unfortunately, she kept catching glimpses of his bare arm and chest out of the corner of her eye.

"Don't you own a robe?" she asked irritably.

"A couple," he said.

"Don't smirk. It's annoying."

He raised an eyebrow as his lips curved out of a smirk and into a genuine smile.

"Someone got up on the wrong side of the bed."

"Someone got up from the wrong bed," Anna muttered as he held open a door for her.

They had entered the library from a different side this time. When Nicholas swung the door closed, she realized it was actually a hinged section of the bookshelves.

"Very Gothic," she said.

He sauntered over to the desk. Anna gave up and simply drank in the sight of his body, half-covered with nothing more than thin, clinging silk. He twisted a section of decorative molding on the desk's edge and a small drawer sprang open.

His blue gaze dared her to comment again as he pulled two sheets of paper out of the compartment and laid them on the desktop. One was the photocopy of the doodle sheet and one was his own handmade copy.

She walked over to the desk and scanned down the photocopy until she found what she wanted.

"These notes," she said, pointing to one of the inserted measures. "They're F, G-sharp, A, D, D, E, aren't they?

"That's right."

"And these are the same?" she said, moving down to the next staff.

"Yes."

He was frowning down at the paper, trying to find the significance in the sequence of notes.

"He was signing his work," she said, tracing along the measure with her finger.

"Who was signing his work?"

"Franz Gadde."

CHAPTER 17

"Who the hell is Franz Gadde?" Nicholas asked.

"The brother of the motorcyclist I tackled in the cemetery," Anna said. "He was studying for his Ph.D. in composition and working in secrecy for the Archduke when he was killed in a hit-and-run. His handprint is on the original doodle sheet."

"The bastard," Nicholas said.

"Who? The Archduke?"

"No, Gadde. To try to pass off his own work as Beethoven's."

"He may not have known that was the Archduke's intention," Anna said. "Karin Gadde is convinced his death wasn't an accident. If Franz was in on the plan, why kill him?"

"One less person to worry about keeping silent?" Nicholas' eyes were blazing when he lifted them to Anna's face. "If you don't put Habsburg-Lothringen in jail, I will put him in hell."

"That won't help," she said, laying her palm against his chest. A muscle twitched beneath her touch and she dropped her hand. "Are you sure the symphony is a fake?"

He gave a short, dark laugh.

"How ironic to ask me that instead of the opposite." He crossed his arms and leaned his hip against the desk. "Given what you've told me, I think it's more likely it's a fraud than that it's genuine. But it's a brilliant fraud. If I could see the remaining three movements I could be more certain."

"Maybe I can arrange that," Anna said.

"No, I can arrange it," Nicholas said, straightening. "The Archduke wants my seal of approval. I can't give it until I look at the rest of the symphony."

"Too dangerous," Anna said, shaking her head. "Let me—"

"No, Lieutenant. I have access and he needs me."

So they were back to cop and suspect now.

"You could create more problems than you solve," she said. "If Habsburg-Lothringen gets wind of your suspicions, he's likely to go after you."

"The Archduke will know only that I'm ecstatic over the first movement but want to see the other three before I endorse his find."

"Can I stop you?" she asked.

"No."

"Let me know when you're meeting him and what happens," she said, turning toward the door into the living room.

"What about the questions you wanted to ask me?" he said.

She pivoted slowly back.

"All right. If your ex-wife was in Vienna and Tokyo until last night why were you carrying her harp around Carnegie Hall the afternoon Lexi was killed?"

"Your attention to detail is admirable. The harp was a wedding gift from me to Serena, a rather valuable gift which she had left here. It was the subject of some . . . discussion in the divorce settlement. We had just resolved its fate, and I was in the process of delivering it to its new owner."

"Who would that be?"

He rattled off a woman's name.

"I never went back to get it out of the storage closet in the Maestro's Suite so she still doesn't have it. However, she will confirm it was promised to her."

"Why was the harp a problem in the divorce?" Anna asked.

"It was given with a certain commitment. Since that commitment no longer existed, I felt it should be passed on to someone else."

Serena Reyes had done some damage to her ex-husband.

"Thanks," Anna said. "I've got to get to work. Call me when you're going to meet with the Archduke and call me again when you're done. Please."

She started toward the door again.

He padded along beside her, waiting as she retrieved her handbag from the bar.

When they reached the front door, she stopped and laid her hand against his cheek.

"Remember what you told Serena: someone's willing to kill for this. Be careful."

He turned his head to kiss her palm but the lines of pain were back around his mouth.

"I'm sorry the symphony isn't real," she said.

"Thank you," he said. "Thank you for coming here."

He leaned down to kiss her forehead before he swung open the door.

As Anna walked down the hall toward the elevator, no tendrils of sound came curling behind her to tease her mind. Her angel of music was silent.

CHAPTER 18

"That's right, the Pierre. You've got the photo of Vranos. If he goes in, make sure he comes out. When he comes out, follow him. Thanks," Anna said, hanging up her office phone.

Her line buzzed again. It was the desk officer saying a Serena Reyes wanted to talk to her.

Mac walked in right on cue.

"We've got an interview," Anna said. "Vranos' ex."

"How'd she find us?" Mac asked, as he shrugged back into the jacket he had started to take off.

"Let's go talk to her."

A night's contemplation had added nothing new to Serena Reyes' story of her meeting with Lexi. Mac took the lead and asked some follow-up questions but he elicited no more useful information.

After the harpist had left, Mac said, "Now there's someone with an agenda and her name is at the top of it. Makes you wonder about your boyfriend's taste in women."

"Yeah, it does," she said.

"You didn't seem real surprised by anything she said," Mac said as they walked back into their office.

"I made a connection last night that has me pretty convinced the manuscript is a forgery." She pulled a copy of the doodle sheet out of her file and handed it to her partner. "Check out the fourth and fifth staves. The middle two measures have the notes F, G-sharp, A, D, D, E. Guess what that spells?"

"F. Gadde," Mac said with a whistle. "He wanted to put his stamp on it. But he could have just been filling the gap in the second movement the Archduke admitted was there."

"Yeah, well, there's what Reyes told us," Anna pointed out before she took a deep breath. "And Vranos thinks it's a fake. Brilliant, he says, but a fake."

Mac gave her a sharp glance.

"You been hanging out with the conductor and not telling me?"

Anna nodded and took the paper out of his hand, putting it back in the file folder so she could avoid his eyes.

"Anna," he said softly. "You're making a big problem for yourself."

"You know he didn't murder Savenkov," she said, glancing up briefly before looking away again.

"It doesn't matter. We can't prove it. Vranos has got motive, opportunity, and worse than no alibi."

"I know, I know," Anna muttered.

"Ask yourself why he's messing with you in the middle of a murder case where he's a suspect," Mac said. "He's a smart guy; he's got to realize what the complications are."

"He's alone," Anna said. "He's got no one close now that Savenkov's gone."

"Oh Christ!" Mac said. "This is worse than I thought. Don't you realize you have to be like Caesar's wife, above suspicion?"

"Now you're quoting Plutarch to me?"

"If that's what it takes. How many times have you complained that you have to be twice as good as any of the men around here just to stay even? Well, this is the same thing. In fact, it's even more so."

"No one needs to know," Anna said, finally looking him in the eye.

Mac sighed.

"They always find out," he said. "But it won't be from me."

"Thanks, partner. For the warning too."

Mac shrugged off her gratitude and went back to his desk.

"I got no help from the limo company," he said. "Everything was done in the Archduke's name. They never saw the driver."

"Figures."

Anna was trying to concentrate on Karin Gadde's paperwork when her cell phone rang.

"I'm meeting Habsburg-Lothringen in an hour at the Princeton Club," Nicholas said when she answered.

Anna swallowed a curse.

"Why there?" she asked.

"It was his choice."

"Call me when it's over."

"I have a rehearsal this afternoon at Carnegie Hall."

"I'll find you," Anna said.

"My day is looking up."

Anna's wasn't. She rerouted her surveillance cop from the Pierre to the Princeton Club. She considered going herself but was afraid the chauffeur might spot her. She pulled out the file on another unsolved homicide, hoping it would distract her from the dangers of the upcoming meeting.

"Your Excellency," Nicholas said, lowering his head in what might be taken as a bow as he shook the Archduke's hand. "Thank you for meeting with me on such short notice."

"Don't mention it. After all, we have the same goal. To set the master's glorious music in front of the world."

The Archduke sat and gestured toward the leather chair opposite him.

"I've studied the first movement and it's brilliant, truly extraordinary," Nicholas said, sitting down and leaning forward. "However, I have some reservations about a few of the motifs. I'd like to see if they appear in the later movements and how they're handled."

"'Reservations'?"

"Perhaps 'questions' would be a better description," Nicholas said. "I want to see how they're developed. And frankly, now that I've seen the first movement, I'm itching to see the rest."

"Ah, that I can understand. Perhaps we can arrange it, although you'd have to examine them where they're being stored. I can't allow such delicate documents to be hauled around like a daily newspaper."

"I'm at your disposal."

"Now, sir?" The Archduke was taken aback but after a moment's thought he allowed himself a small smile. "Why not? It will move us more swiftly toward our goal."

"Excellent." Nicholas gave the nobleman an answering smile.

"We'll have to summon a taxi," the older man said, rising. "It's in a bank vault a few blocks from here."

"I have a car waiting outside," Nicholas said, holding the private parlor's door open.

"Good man."

Twenty minutes later, the Archduke and Nicholas were ushered into a vault buried deep in the bowels of a well-known international bank. The vault door's thickness measured in feet while a sophisticated climate-control system put forth a soft, on-going hum that tormented Nicholas' highly tuned hearing. The Archduke and the bank officer pressed the tips of their thumbs against the scanners built into the safe deposit box before its door swung open with a quiet click. The Archduke slid the metal container out of its compartment and followed the bank officer into a small brightly-lit room. A glass-topped table and two utilitarian chrome-and-leather chairs stood on a white tile floor.

The bank officer noticed Nicholas' raised eyebrow.

"It's deliberately stark," the woman said. "The designer was instructed to leave as little potential for concealment of an object as possible. You wouldn't believe the scams that involve safe deposit boxes, especially at this very high end of the spectrum. The room has a security camera as well."

"I'd like to have at least an hour to study the manuscript," Nicholas said as the Archduke took a smaller gray metal box out of the bank's container.

"The room is yours as long as you need it," the banker said.

The Archduke opened the gray box and reverently lifted out a thick brown leather portfolio. Placing it on the table, he loosened the ties holding the portfolio closed and gently flipped the top back.

A pile of thick yellowed paper with discolored edges and slashes of musical staves in brownish ink stood revealed.

The Archduke waved his hand in a dramatic flourish.

"Beethoven's Tenth Symphony, written in his own hand."

CHAPTER 19

"You'll see the places where he made changes even as he wrote out the final version" the Archduke said. "He was probably going to send this to a professional copyist but he ran out of time."

"One wonders why the Archduke Rudolph had it in his possession and why he hid it," Nicholas said, his eyes riveted on the papers.

"It's one of those mysteries we can only speculate upon," the Archduke said. "Perhaps my forefather was paying for the printing and so took on the task of transporting the manuscript."

He reached into the recesses of the bank box and pulled out a pair of white cotton gloves.

"Please wear these. The oils in your fingers can damage the documents," he said, offering the gloves to the conductor.

"Of course," Nicholas said, pulling the gloves over his long fingers and flexing his hands in them.

"I believe I'll accompany this lovely lady to the officers' lounge," the Archduke said.

"Push this button when you're ready to leave," the banker said to Nicholas, indicating a stainless steel box mounted on the wall near the door. "Someone will come within a couple of minutes to unlock the door and let you out."

"Thank you," he said before turning to the Archduke. "I'll try to read quickly."

"Take your time, dear man," the nobleman said. "They have an excellent selection of reading materials in the lounge. I won't be bored."

From the bank's security control center, a guard watching the array of video screens saw the tall, dark-haired man in the high-security vault take a small pad of paper and a pen from his pocket. He laid them on the table beside a pile of what looked like old papers and began turning the pages over.

Suddenly, he stopped and leaned down to study the top of the stack. He scanned through several more pages before picking up his pen and jotting down a note on his notepad. He bent over to look more closely, fiddling absentmindedly with his pen.

The blond man sitting beside the guard uttered an exclamation which the bank employee, whose grandmother had grown up in Berlin, recognized as being in German. The blond fellow, Mr. Schmidt, had been ushered in and seated with a brief introduction by one of the bank's senior vice presidents who had said to extend their guest every courtesy. Schmidt had sat silently until now, his eyes on the scene in the vault. The guard peered at the screen to see what had upset his companion but the tall man was handling the papers with great care. He seemed completely focused on them and oblivious to his surroundings.

The guard scanned the other monitors and came back to the vault screen, finding nothing changing in the view. After half an hour, Schmidt began swearing with a fluency and viciousness that stretched the guard's comprehension of the German language to its limits.

"Problem?" the guard asked, again examining the screen in front of him.

"Nothing I can't deal with later," the German said. He got up and stalked out of the room, leaving the guard eyeing his screens with more attention than usual. A few minutes later, a monitor showed Mr. Schmidt walking straight across the bank lobby and out the front doors.

The guard kept a close watch on the vault camera but nothing changed for the next forty minutes. Then the room's occupant strode to the door and rang the call bell. While waiting, he stowed his pad and pen in his suit jacket pocket and meticulously restacked the papers although he left the portfolio open.

The senior vice president entered with the older man who had opened the portfolio. The tall man made a gesture toward the papers. The older man shook his head, and everything was packed up and returned to its home in the vault. The guard let out a sigh of relief as the door closed behind them. They were no longer his problem.

"Hiya, Frank," Anna said, nodding to the Carnegie Hall security guard as she walked through the stage door.

"Good to see you, Lieutenant. Go right on in."

She strode past the office, up the stairs and into the corridor outside Isaac Stern Hall. Music rolled through the entrance door as she pulled it open and stepped into the concert space.

There were many more people scattered through the seats than at the last rehearsal. The retinue around Billy Leon's blond mop had swelled by at least fifteen. Anna smiled at Nicholas' assistant, Norman Drucker, but waved him back to his seat as he started to rise. She scanned the entire auditorium, checking for anyone who looked as though they might plan to shoot Nicholas Vranos before she got to do it herself.

He had called to tell her he had photographs of the Beethoven manuscript, taken right under the lenses of who knew how many security cameras, watched by who knew how many suspicious sets of eyes. Before she had a chance to tell him what a dangerous idiot he was, he had ordered her to meet him at Carnegie Hall and hung up.

Anna crossed her arms and leaned against the wall of the auditorium, waiting for the music to end. Nicholas was wearing another of his blue dress shirts, and she couldn't help watching the play of the fabric across his shoulders as his arms curved and swooped like a falcon's wings. That led to all too vivid memories of how those shoulders looked without a shirt, and Anna shifted her gaze to the violin section.

The trumpets began to play their heartbreakingly brilliant motif. Anna listened for a few seconds before bolting for the door and slipping out into the corridor where the music was blessedly muted. She walked over to one of the photographs hanging on the wall and pretended to study it.

"Get a grip, Salazar," she muttered. "You're letting a pair of pretty blue eyes and some nice muscle definition distract you from your job."

Of course, that was a lie. Nicholas Vranos fascinated her in ways she couldn't explain even to herself. He created beauty, commanded others, and yet seemed utterly solitary. He was brilliant, famous, talented, wealthy, and completely beyond her reach. Yet she kept reaching for him. Stranger still, he kept reaching for her.

Which came back to the question she saw in Mac's eyes every time she mentioned Nicholas' name: was he just using her?

"Anna. Why did you leave the rehearsal?"

She turned to find him striding toward her.

"How did you know I was there? You were in the middle of conducting."

"I can feel it the moment you walk in a room," he said, an odd smile playing around the corners of his mouth. "I was waiting for you to arrive before I called a break. There's an office with a computer we can use. I haven't had a chance to look at the photos myself."

He put his hand on the small of her back to steer her down the hall toward the steps back to the administrative area. His touch was light but she felt the heat of his palm radiating deep inside her.

"Lead the way," she said, stepping away from him.

He raised an eyebrow at her but dropped his hand.

After a few turns, Nicholas held open a door leading to a small interior office. Anna waited for him to close the door behind him before saying in a low, furious voice, "You realize that by taking photographs of the manuscript you have endangered yourself and warned the Archduke you are suspicious of the authenticity of his find. You may have made it that much more difficult to solve this case because now he'll be on his guard. Don't ever do anything like that again without discussing it with me first," she said. "I don't need any more complications to this case than I already have."

She stopped because her companion had pulled a cable and a small cylindrical object out of his pocket and was attaching it to the computer. She realized the camera was shaped like a pen and felt some hope that perhaps he hadn't aroused the Archduke's suspicions.

"I'm listening, Lieutenant," he said, without taking his eyes off the computer screen.

"Nicholas, look at me," she said, wrapping her hand around his upper arm and pulling him around.

He let her turn him away from the computer but he crossed his arms and frowned down at her, his blue eyes intent but cold.

Anna decided to try a different approach. She reached up and laid her palm against his cheek.

"I don't want you to end up dead," she said.

He covered her hand with his own, threading his fingers through hers.

"Are you worried about my life or the case?" he asked, turning his head to kiss the inside of her wrist.

"Both. They go together."

"How can I be a suspect and be in danger of being murdered?"

As he spoke, he held her hand against his mouth so she felt the brush of his lips and the heat and moisture of his breath. A shiver shook her.

"You're not a suspect," she said as she tried to disentangle her fingers from his.

He allowed her to lower her hand but kept their fingers entwined.

"I'm not?"

"You know damned well I wouldn't be . . . wouldn't have . . ." she couldn't come up with an acceptable phrase so she left it blank, "if I thought you'd killed Lexi or anyone else."

"Thank you," he said, his blue gaze now scorching. "I hoped you'd say that."

"I shouldn't have because officially you're not cleared. It changes nothing in the investigation."

"It changes a great deal for me," he said, bringing her hand to his lips again before he released it and turned back to the computer. "I wish I had more time but I need to show you this."

Anna watched his long fingers manipulate the mouse and wondered how much trouble she'd gotten herself into now.

"Yes," he murmured triumphantly as an image of the music came up on the screen. He clicked through several photographs before he stopped. "You see, this is the gap in the second movement. I think they put it in as an explanation of why Beethoven wouldn't have simply handed this over to the printer."

"'They'?"

He turned and the sharp planes of his face were suddenly very pronounced.

"It's definitely a forgery. Franz Gadde's signature is in the fourth movement. Fortunately, the son of a bitch who did the copying wasn't enough of a musician to catch it." He clicked through several more images before he stopped and pointed. "You see. A theme and variations on F, G, A, D, D, E. That's the most glaring clue but I found other places where the transitions are clearly modern. Whatever sketchbooks Gadde was working from must have had some major gaps he chose to fill in with his own ideas."

"I'm sorry," Anna said.

"So am I," he said, bracing himself on his hands as he dropped his head for a moment. "It's a brilliant construction but it isn't Beethoven's."

He straightened and looked at his watch.

"I have to get back to the rehearsal. You can take the camera and the cable with you."

She put her hand on his forearm.

"At least two people have died because the Archduke needs the world to believe this is real," she said. "He knows you have doubts, at the very least. Be very, very careful."

"Luckily, I have you to watch my back."

CHAPTER 20

As soon as the door closed behind Nicholas, Anna turned back to the computer screen and noted the file number of the relevant photograph. She disconnected the pen-camera and stowed it in her jacket pocket before pulling out her cell phone. The signal was weak but it worked.

"Mac, Vranos has proof the Beethoven is a forgery. He saw the rest of the manuscript and found the Franz Gadde signature incorporated into the fourth movement."

"How the hell'd he do that?"

"Don't ask. I told him he's a dangerous idiot but I don't believe he paid any attention to my opinion. We need to put a tail on Vranos for his own protection."

"So he did something to make His High-Hatness suspicious?"

Anna sighed.

"He might have. It's hard to tell. I just have a bad feeling about this. I'm coming back to the office now."

"No, you're not because I'm on my way out and you're meeting me. We've got a dead body with a knife sticking out of it in a stockroom at Bloomingdale's."

"You've got to be kidding me!"

"Wish I was. See you there."

Anna had just finished with the last witness at Bloomie's when her cell phone vibrated in her hip pocket.

"Anna, it's Nicholas."

"You sound exhausted."

"It was a long rehearsal. The concert's tomorrow and Billy's nervous so I had to do some handholding."

"I see," Anna said. "Where are you?"

"At home."

"Good. I can stop worrying about you for a while. By the way, I have an officer following you 24/7 for your own safety." Anna braced herself for the explosion.

"You're wasting the taxpayers' money," was all he said. "Will you have dinner with me tonight?"

"I can't. I've got another case I have to work."

"Come later then."

His voice had deepened and she knew where his mind was. Every molecule in her body yearned to say *yes* but she needed to think and he would distract her in all sorts of ways she was trying not to imagine.

"No, it's better if I don't," she said. "But I want to."

"Then that will have to be enough for tonight," he said, his voice dropping even lower. "I'll use the time to plan what I'll do with our next night together."

"What happened to spontaneity?"

"Preparation is the key to a superlative performance."

Anna groaned. She could feel heat pooling low in her gut as she imagined Nicholas Vranos deciding how to kiss her, where to touch her, where she would touch him . . . .

"I've got to go," she said. "I'll see you tomorrow."

"Good night, Lieutenant," he said.

She could hear him laughing as she flipped her phone closed.

Mac had ducked under the yellow plastic police tape and joined her outside the crime scene as she ended the call.

"Why can't kids join the marching band instead of a gang?" Mac said with a heavy sigh.

"I can't picture LaShawn playing the flute," Anna said, watching as the young man's body was wheeled away on a gurney.

"What about the tuba? That's big and macho. I hate it when the kids die."

"Me too. Especially when other kids kill them."

"Well, at least this case was open-and-shut," Mac said. "Two rival gang members, three witnesses, and we're done."

"We need to talk about the Savenkov case," Anna said. "You won't like this but I want to stir things up. I think we need to have a chat with Walter del Deo at the Beethoven Society."

"Why?"

Anna pulled him into the buyer's office they'd been using for interviews.

"I want del Deo to approach Habsburg-Lothringen with an offer to buy the Beethoven manuscript for some outrageous sum of money, funded by a group of private investors or something. But say that he's concerned because Vranos has reservations about the authenticity of the symphony."

"Christ, Anna, you'll put Vranos' head right in the Archduke's crosshairs!"

"It's already there." Anna fished the pen-camera out of her pocket and held it up. "He took photographs of the manuscript in the bank vault this morning with this. Those places have security cameras everywhere and you know someone was watching him very closely."

Mac took the camera and examined it from all angles.

"Neat little gizmo. Vranos is pretty good with his hands. Maybe no one realized he was taking photos."

"Maybe. But it's more likely they did."

"And maybe they think he just wanted to look at some of the pages again."

"Mac, the Archduke can't afford to have any doubt thrown on the symphony. He needs the money soon or he won't be able to hold onto his palace or his fancy cars or his yacht in Monte Carlo. Vranos is already at risk and we can't keep a twenty-four-hour tail on him forever."

"So you get del Deo to do this and then what happens?"

"We watch Vranos like a hawk and wait for the Archduke to panic. You always tell me people do stupid things when they panic."

"Stupid, *dangerous* things," Mac corrected. "And Vranos is willing to go along with this?"

"He will be," Anna said.

Mac looked at her.

"He wants Savenkov's murderer found, and he's royally pissed off that Habsburg-Lothringen is trying to sully Beethoven's name with a fake symphony. It's weird but he cares a lot about that." Anna gave Mac a pleading look. "I wanted to run the plan by you before I mentioned it to anyone else."

"So if I say no, you'll give it up?"

Anna half-shrugged.

"Yeah, that's what I thought," Mac said. "Call your boyfriend but I'll deny everything if this goes south."

"More likely you'll say it was all your idea," Anna said, giving his shoulder a quick squeeze. She would have hugged him but that would have embarrassed him.

She flipped her phone open again and hit redial.

Nicholas answered immediately.

"Changed your mind, Lieutenant?"

"Yes and no," she said, drawing the moment out just a bit to bother him. "We'd like to prod the Archduke into taking action but it might be dangerous to you."

"You mean you're asking for my help?"

He sounded far too gratified about it.

"We just want to use your name," Anna said before she explained the plan. As she finished, she warned, "This is like waving a red flag in front of an angry bull so I want you to think carefully before you agree."

"Do it," he said without hesitation. "Tell me when you're meeting with Walter and I'll be there."

"That's not—," Anna began.

"I'll be there," he said in a tone which brooked no argument.

"Fine. I'll get back to you.

She disconnected and turned to Mac.

"Vranos is on board. Now I've got to track down del Deo."

Mac just shook his head.

"Nicholas, this is very dangerous for you," Walter del Deo said, looking worried. "If you really believe the Archduke was involved with Lexi's death, this will very likely make you his next target."

"That's exactly what the police and I hope will happen," Nicholas said, his posture completely relaxed.

"We'll be protecting him around the clock," Anna said. "We believe Mr. Vranos is already in danger and we want to make sure we're alert and prepared when the Archduke makes his move. This way we'll have a pretty good idea when it's coming."

Del Deo stood up and paced across his study. It was early evening and a small fire was framed by a black marble mantel. Anna, Mac, and Nicholas sat in large green leather chairs grouped around a low mahogany table. Book cases surrounded them on three sides and the flames picked out glints of gold on the leather-bound volumes' spines.

Del Deo turned and glanced back and forth between Anna and Mac.

"Are you confident you can protect Nicholas?"

Anna let Mac answer. She suspected del Deo would trust another man's word more than hers.

"Yes, sir. Mr. Vranos has excellent security in his building and we will be working closely with their people. In addition to plainclothes police officers, Lieutenant Salazar or myself will be with him at all times."

Nicholas caught Anna's eye as the slightest of wicked smiles tilted the corners of his mouth.

Del Deo took a deep breath and nodded to Nicholas.

"All right, I'll do as you ask. But we need to get the details exactly right."

Nicholas and del Deo filled in names and financial information as Anna and Mac outlined how much pressure they wanted to put on the Archduke. Anna suggested one person for the list of investors which made both Nicholas and del Deo stare at her in surprise but she just said, "He'll do it."

After an hour or so, they were all satisfied they had a plausible story fleshed out.

"I'll set up a meeting tomorrow morning," del Deo said.

They all stood and shook hands. Del Deo opened the study door but gestured for Anna to stay behind after the two other men filed out. She could hear them still talking as she faced their host and co-conspirator.

"Lieutenant Salazar, I'm still very reluctant to put Nicholas in harm's way. You have to understand something about him: he's absolutely brilliant. One might even call him a genius when it comes to his ability to interpret Beethoven. It would be a great loss to the world of music if he were to be, well," del Deo seemed to have a hard time saying the words, "if he were killed as Mr. Savenkov was."

"We won't let that happen," Anna said.

"Beyond that, I consider him a good friend. We are perhaps not as close as he and Mr. Savenkov were but, nonetheless, any injury to him would cause personal grief to me. If I felt my actions were responsible for this, I would be most distressed."

"I understand. I can assure you that, if necessary, I will put my own life on the line to protect him," Anna said.

He searched her face for a long minute.

"You've convinced me, young lady. You'll hear from me as soon as I make contact."

Anna wondered why del Deo had chosen her to have that conversation with. Had Nicholas said something about her or was it written on her face for anyone to see?

Nicholas and Mac were standing by the brown police sedan.

"I understand Mac's taking the first shift tomorrow because you have an appointment in the morning," Nicholas said, his eyes glinting with suppressed laughter.

Anna rolled her eyes. Her appointment was with Kelly Sinclair, assistant to Rafael Castaños, one of haute couture's hottest designers. She and Mac had rescued his daughter from the basement of a serial killer in their first case working together. Anna still had nightmares about what they had seen in that basement but the designer's daughter was alive and relatively unscathed.

While working on the case, Anna had grown to respect Kelly's loyalty to her boss and the two women struck up a friendship, which grew after the grateful Castaños had offered to dress Anna and Letitia for the rest of their lives. Of course, they couldn't accept any of his outrageously expensive clothing but Anna would call Kelly for a loaner when she needed a dressy outfit for police work, something that happened far more often than she liked.

"Yeah, I have to borrow something to wear for the concert since it's formal."

"And you view this with the same enthusiasm you would a trip to the bowels of Hell, according to Lieutenant McKenzie."

She shrugged and sent an annoyed glance toward her partner. Mac had one of those "we're superior males" expressions on his face.

"Watch it or I'll tell the story about the last time you wore a tux," she said. "Had some problems with it, didn't you?"

Mac's neck burned red but he appeared unmoved by her threat.

"Anna will be back in action by noon and we'll have plenty of help," Mac said.

"I'm not concerned," Nicholas said, his lips curling into a feral smile. "Let him come."

CHAPTER 21

"I'm sorry I'm so grouchy," Anna said to Kelly as the designer's assistant carefully draped a chiffon scarf around Anna's neck. "There's a meeting going down in half an hour and I can't believe I'm trying on clothes instead of staking it out."

Kelly laughed and stepped back to assess the effect of her work. She'd been through this with Anna before.

"You're a lot pleasanter than some of our customers," she said.

"Yeah, but they're paying," Anna pointed out.

"Not necessarily." Kelly shook her head at the dress. "This one's no good."

Anna sighed as Kelly efficiently stripped off the gown, leaving Anna bare except for the thong panties Kelly had insisted she wear. Anna was glad there were no other customers around at the moment because Rafael's showroom walls were all frosted pink glass. She always felt exposed, even though she knew you couldn't see more than flickers of movement through the thick glass.

"Can't you just give me a pair of black satin slacks and a sparkly shirt?" she pleaded.

Kelly looked appalled.

"This is the Billy Leon premiere! Rafael has his reputation to consider."

"No one's going to notice a police detective lurking in the shadows," Anna said.

"With your looks and our dress, you will definitely get noticed."

"But—"

Kelly dropped another dress over Anna's head, cutting off whatever objection she'd been about to make. The azure silk chiffon pooled around Anna's waist since there were no straps to hold it up. Kelly pulled the bodice up into place and slid the zipper up under Anna's armpit.

"This is promising," Kelly said, looking at the reflection in the mirror.

Anna took a look. The vivid blue chiffon cupped her breasts, giving them a sexy push upward. The dress clung to her torso and hips before falling straight to the floor in back. In front, the fabric was drawn up from one side and tucked into her cleavage, showing an under-layer of sky blue chiffon and a flash of calf and ankle. Kelly had already forced her to don a pair of silver sandals whose tiny straps wound over her arches and around her ankles.

"Walk," Kelly commanded.

Anna was amazed to discover she could move quite freely in what looked like a formfitting gown. That was one of the requirements she had for anything Kelly wanted her to wear.

Now the assistant sighed.

"I wish you'd let me give you three inch heels. Those are too low to give your walk the right sway."

"Are you kidding? These are bad enough," Anna said, twisting her foot so she could peer down at the kitten heels on her sandals.

"We-e-ell," the assistant said, folding her arms and contemplating Anna.

"I like this one," Anna said before Kelly decided it didn't work and made her try on something else. She threw back her shoulders, thrust her hips forward and tried her best to pose like a model. "It looks great."

"It'll do."

Anna's posture sagged in relief.

"Now for a bag and a wrap."

Kelly disappeared into a back room, and Anna looked at her cell phone lying frustratingly silent on a leather and Lucite chair in the cavernous fitting room. Was del Deo still talking to the Archduke?

"Here we go. One *large* clutch purse and a stole," Kelly said, her emphasis referring to another requirement Anna had made clear. The purse had to hold her radio receiver, her cell phone, her badge and her Smith and Wesson subcompact. She handed Anna a blue silk bag, shot with silver threads, fastened with a deep blue sapphire which Anna hoped was a fake. The stole she draped around her shoulders was made of the same sky blue chiffon as the under dress.

"Why bother with this?" Anna asked, rubbing the translucent material between her fingers. "It certainly won't keep me warm."

"It finishes the outfit," Kelly said. "Details are everything so I also brought you earrings."

"I've got perfectly good diamond studs."

"Shut up and let me put these on you." Kelly deftly removed Anna's small gold hoops and fastened the new earrings in place. "And your hair," she said, taking Anna's braid and winding it up around her head. "Very regal but not quite right."

Anna sighed again but stood still as Kelly took the elastic off the end of the braid and unraveled it, spreading the long, dark fall around her shoulders before she stepped back to view the effect.

"Oh, yes," she breathed. "Sex in silver sandals."

Then she moved aside so Anna could see the mirror.

"Who *is* that?" Anna said, staring at her reflection. Drops of aquamarines strung on tiny glistening silver chains cascaded from her earlobes. Her hair created a dark frame for her bare shoulders and the brilliant blue of the dress which called attention to every curve in her body. The slightest movement of air stirred the chiffon of the stole or the under dress or her loose hair so the effect was of constant flowing motion.

"I can't wear this. It's too . . . conspicuous."

"That's what you and Mac said you wanted," Kelly pointed out. "So the bad guys would know where you were all the time and not be nervous, wasn't it?"

That had been their strategy since the chauffeur had clearly recognized Anna as a cop. They had decided she should look like she was at the Billy Leon concert purely as a spectator.

"Yeah, but this is . . ."

"Perfect," Kelly said, starting to undo the ensemble. "And easy. All you need to add on your own is some subtle makeup. Why are you smiling like that?"

Anna was visualizing what Nicholas Vranos' reaction to the outfit would be.

"Okay, out with it," Kelly said. "Who's going to be blown away when he sees you in this dress?"

"You wouldn't believe me if I told you," Anna said.

"Try me."

"I can't. It's related to a case."

Kelly was smoothing and hanging all of Anna's party attire.

"This case?" she asked.

Anna picked up her jeans and yanked them on.

"Yeah, that's how I met him."

"And just how blown away is he going to be?"

"What do you mean?"

Kelly sat down on one of the Lucite chairs and crossed her long legs.

"I mean, is he going to be taking the dress off of you later on tonight?"

"No. I'm working."

"And if you weren't?"

Anna made a minute adjustment to her shoulder holster.

"Then it might be a possibility," she said.

"Okay, if you won't tell me who it is, at least tell me how serious it is."

"Serious? I haven't known him long enough to answer that."

"You told me a murder case is like an accident: it strips away all the surface deceptions so you can see the person underneath," Kelly pointed out.

"I said that? That must have been when I was new to the force."

"All right, *could* it be serious?"

Anna looked at the toe of her boot, then at the dress hanging by the mirror, and finally at her friend.

"It could be for me," she said.

"But not for him?"

Anna shrugged.

"I don't know. He lives in a different world but he seems to want me around."

"All right, I'll let it go because I know you're itching to be out of here," Kelly said, "but we're going to finish this conversation when the case is over. And I'm going to want details then."

Anna laughed.

"You should be doing my interviews. You make me look like a softy when it comes to getting answers."

Her friend stood up and wrapped her arms around Anna in a real hug.

"You *are* a softy. You still believe in truth, justice and the American way. That's why I love you."

Anna was laying the dress bag across the back seat of the brown sedan when her cell phone finally rang.

"Lieutenant Salazar," Walter del Deo's cultured tones came clearly through the receiver. "My meeting with the Archduke seems to have been quite successful. I believe you would say he took the bait."

"How do you know?" Anna asked.

"Because he's already contacted Nicholas Vranos about setting up a meeting."

"What did Mr. Vranos say?"

"That it will have to wait until tomorrow as he has an important performance tonight."

Anna had to bite her tongue not to spit out a four-letter word. Undoubtedly it was a bad time to have a meeting;

Nicholas needed to focus on the concert. However, she knew he was also playing the Archduke, trying to increase the time pressure which meant increasing the danger to himself as well.

"Thank you very much, sir. We appreciate your cooperation."

"Not at all. I found it quite exhilarating."

Anna sighed as she punched the disconnect button. Civilians thought police work was exciting until they were faced with the bloody consequences. Now all she had to do was make sure that in this case there were none.

CHAPTER 22

Anna sat beside Xavier Cunningham squarely in the midst of Billy Leon's entourage, the members of which were all dressed in creative variations on the theme of the tuxedo. Somehow the anonymous Carnegie Hall House Manager had given her tickets in the best box in the concert hall. Xavier was ecstatic and Anna was on edge.

Billy had already turned and introduced himself to both of them, clearly wondering why they were seated in the box of honor. Amazingly, the rock star seemed nervous, and Anna found herself telling him how brilliant she had found his composition during rehearsals. His answering smile was blinding, and she suddenly understood why he had legions of fans.

She knew Nicholas had arrived safely at the concert hall. Now all she had to worry about was whether the Archduke was desperate enough to shoot the conductor in public. Despite all the metal detectors at the entrances and the plainclothes policemen posted around the auditorium, they probably couldn't stop a determined assassin from putting a bullet through the back of Nicholas' head as he stood completely exposed on the stage.

She fidgeted with her purse, feeling the reassuring outline of her gun. Of course, the subcompact pistol was too small to be useful at anything other than close range but it comforted her to know it was there.

"No one will shoot him in the middle of a concert," Xavier murmured in her ear. "It would point too obviously to the Archduke."

"I know," Anna muttered. "I'm just antsy."

"No kidding."

The orchestra, which had been warming up with random musical phrases, fell silent as the first violinist stood and played a single note. The other instrumentalists joined in, creating a new cacophony before the lights dimmed and the musicians lowered their instruments in expectant silence. The door opened stage right and Nicholas Vranos strode onstage, looking magnificent in his white tie and tails as applause swelled into a near roar.

Anna drew in a quick breath as he stepped onto the podium and seemed to gather the attention of the entire audience with his gaze before he bowed and turned to the orchestra. The applause ended instantly.

He picked up his baton, stood for a moment with his head bowed and then raised his arms in that bird-of-prey curve. The musicians sat poised in utter stillness and the audience seemed to hold its breath. His arms came down in a slashing cue and sound poured forth from the stage, swelling into the grand space with an almost physical force.

Anna stole a glance at the spectators sitting around her and found their eyes locked on the stage. Xavier looked almost hypnotized and Billy Leon sat like a statue. She kept scanning the auditorium while pretending to keep her eyes on the stage since she was supposed to be there as a civilian.

Three of the symphony's movements were finished and Anna took a deep breath in the stillness before the fourth movement began. Nicholas briefly blotted his forehead with a white handkerchief before he once again swept the musicians and the audience into a maelstrom of sound.

Anna recognized the introduction to the trumpet motif and found herself being pulled inexorably into the beauty of the music. She fought the seduction but the rumbling of the kettle drums seemed to vibrate in her very bones and she couldn't stop the tears welling in her eyes as the trumpets burst forth in the theme she now knew so well. As the brilliant notes soared and fell, a rapturous gasp rose from the audience. Billy Leon's face lit up with a grin like the Cheshire Cat's. Whatever the audience had felt about the first three movements, the young composer had clearly grabbed them with this one.

Anna let her gaze rest on the man who commanded the entire hall. The white cuffs at his wrists seemed to sketch glowing hieroglyphs in the air as his arms soared and fell, coaxing, ordering, soothing, and demanding ever more from his orchestra. She followed him, immersing herself in the music of the night.

The conductor made a sweeping downward slash and the final note ended. For a long moment, no one moved and nothing broke the silence as the memory of the music seemed to linger in the great hall.

Then Nicholas turned to face the audience and inclined his head to acknowledge their presence and free them from the spell of the symphony. Anna's throat tightened with a strange possessive burst of pride as she joined the spectators surging to their feet, clapping and shouting, "Bravo! Bravo!" A contingent of security guards arrived at the box and hustled Billy Leon down to the stage where he joined Nicholas in an extended curtain call. Shouts of "Yeah, Billy!" mingled with the more traditional Italian praise. Nicholas waved the musicians to their feet repeatedly as the applause continued unabated.

"I guess it was a success," Anna said to Xavier as they stood clapping.

"Surprisingly good for a debut composer," he murmured back. "Leon's second movement was a bit derivative of the third movement of Mozart's Symphony No. 40 but the other three were quite original. I predict his fourth movement will become a popular classic."

"When an audience gasps, it's a pretty good indication people like it so I think you're safe on that one."

"Of course, having Nicholas Vranos interpret the music brings out depths Leon probably didn't even know it had."

"Is that true?" Anna asked. "Does the conductor make that much of a difference?"

"He can, especially with a new piece like this one. I hope they recorded this performance so I can listen to it again and compare it with future interpretations."

"I'm pretty sure I heard Vranos mention that Leon had paid a pile of money to get it recorded in Carnegie Hall."

"Fantastic!" her companion enthused. "You've more than paid me back for dealing with Ms. Strauss."

Nicholas and Billy Leon bowed once more and then Nicholas gestured for the composer to precede him toward the stage exit. The applause rose to a crescendo before it fizzled out as the doors swung closed behind the two men. The spectators began streaming out of the concert hall, raising a buzz of excited conversation.

One of Leon's entourage, a young man dressed in a scarlet tuxedo with matching hair, held the door of the box open for Anna. He gave her a comprehensive head-to-toe inspection before leering at her appreciatively. She chuckled and the young man started to follow her until Xavier stepped into his path, blocking it subtly but effectively before he turned to accompany Anna downstairs.

An usher rushed up to them.

"Lieutenant Salazar? Mr. Vranos asked me to escort you backstage."

"I'll see you at the party," Xavier said, relinquishing her arm.

Anna followed the usher through the labyrinth of backstage Carnegie Hall. As they approached the Maestro's Suite, a jangle of voices surged down the hallway. The usher gestured her toward the door and she stepped in and stopped, halted by the crowd and the racket.

Billy Leon and his posse held court around the piano, surrounded by men in traditional renditions of black tie and a sprinkling of women, mostly in black as well.

A waiter pressed a flute of champagne into Anna's hand. She started to hand it back but noticed everyone in the room was holding a glass. So she kept it as a prop and tucked herself into a corner to watch Nicholas Vranos. He stood in the back of the small room, receiving the homage of his guests with the grace of an emperor. His damp hair showed comb marks but the energy of the performance still rolled off him in waves.

He pivoted and caught sight of Anna. The blue of his eyes seemed to burn with extra intensity as she raised her glass to him in a silent toast. He turned to say something to the couple beside him before advancing through the crowd toward her corner retreat. People moved aside as he walked.

The congratulatory words died on her lips when she received no greeting or welcoming smile. He took her glass from her, seized her wrist and said, "Come with me," pulling her along behind him through the door into the maestro's private dressing room.

He closed the door and locked it before he used his grip on her wrist to pull her in front of the lighted mirror while he stood behind her.

The azure of her dress, the red glints in her hair, and, most strikingly, the cream of her skin were heightened by the black frame of his formal dress. When Anna swallowed, she could both feel it and see it, an oddly reverberant experience. She tried again to compliment his musical performance but the words fled as he cupped his hands around her shoulders. Once again, she could feel the warmth of his palms against her bare skin even as she watched those long fingers stroke across her collarbone.

She raised her eyes long enough to look into the reflection of his and wished she hadn't. His eyes were hooded and intent, allowing her no doubt of his focus. He slid his hands down her arms, feathering his fingertips over the thin skin inside her elbows and evoking a tiny shiver. When he reached her hands, he flattened his palms and thrust his fingers between hers, trapping them against her thighs.

For a moment, they stood that way, the only movement the arrhythmic rise and fall of Anna's breasts as her breathing accelerated out of her control. Her face in the mirror seemed a stranger's, soft, almost dazed, her eyelids heavy and languorous.

Suddenly, he pulled their joined hands upward so their arms crossed over her waist, the black of his sleeves slashing across the brilliant blue of her dress as he forced her back against the wall of his chest and thighs. She felt the caress of fine wool against her bare back and the hard pressure of one of his diamond and onyx studs. Anna had the briefly lucid thought that he had effectively immobilized her, a police officer, before he lowered his head and brushed his lips against the side of her neck. She moaned and let her eyes close and her head fall back against his shoulder.

A whiff of warm breath wafted across her skin as he gave a quietly triumphant laugh. He released her hands, freeing his own to cup her breasts as his mouth skimmed down her neck and he nipped at her shoulder.

"We can't do this here," she whispered, reaching back to steady herself by grabbing whatever she could reach. Her hands massaged dark wool over muscled thighs and she felt a shudder pass through the big body pressed against hers.

"We already are," he rasped.

She swallowed all protests as he shifted one of his hands lower, over her hipbone, down her abdomen until he reached the beginning of the dress's deep slit. She felt his fingertips slide under the fabric and over the bare skin of her inner thigh. He encountered the satin of her panties and pushed it aside. Anna whimpered when his progress halted.

"Open your eyes," he said.

With her head tilted back against his shoulder, Anna lifted her eyelids the smallest amount, afraid the image in the mirror would shock her into sanity. His left arm drew a dark diagonal up to her right breast where his thumb circled the nipple clearly visible against the soft gathers of chiffon. His right arm angled down toward her bare thigh. The white cuff with its glinting black cufflink drew her eye to his hand as he held aside the fabric of the dress and panties with his thumb.

As Anna watched, he plunged two fingers down along her already damp folds and inside her. She arched into his hand, driving it even deeper, and bit back a cry. His left arm tightened around her so she could feel his erection pressing against her as he began to slide his fingers in and out. She watched, fascinated and shocked at what was happening one thin door's width away from a room full of strangers.

"Come for me," he whispered in her ear. "Let me feel you around my fingers."

Anna closed her eyes and let go of all thought. Two more strokes of his clever fingers and an orgasm ripped through her. Her body bowed against his hands, releasing all the pent-up tension of the day so hard and fast that the pleasure tipped almost into pain in its intensity. The scream trapped in her throat came out as a ragged moan of his name.

He was turning her and pulling her leg up against his hip when a knock sounded on the door.

"Yes," Nicholas barked.

"Mr. Vranos, the party is beginning," a voice said.

He swore while Anna threw back her head and laughed. When he let go of her thigh, she kept her leg locked around his hip.

"You can't go out in public like this," she said, rolling her pelvis against the solid bulge in his elegant evening trousers. She enjoyed the tremor that shook him.

He growled and seized her face between his hands, slanting his lips across hers with the thirst of a man dying in the desert. He raised his head and his voice to speak almost normally. "Thanks, I'll be there shortly."

Anna found his zipper as he ran his hands up her thighs to stretch her open wider. She freed his erection and guided him between her legs. She felt his knees bend and then he buried himself deep inside her with a low groan of satisfaction. The little ripples of her fading orgasm surged again as he stroked up into her, lifting her onto her toes at the apex of each thrust. The tiny teeth of his open zipper bit softly against the sensitive folds between her legs. She locked her arms around his neck, threading her fingers into the dark curls at his nape and reveling in the muscles working under her hands.

He threw back his head with a strangled cry of release and she felt the pulse of his climax inside her. She buried her face against his chest to muffle her own howl of pleasure as a second orgasm exploded through her, leaving her muscles quivering with exhaustion.

For a long moment, they held the position. When Anna's thigh muscles twitched against his fingers, Nicholas slid out of her and carefully lowered her so she could stand without his support. As soon as both her feet were on the ground, he dropped his head onto her shoulder, his arms wrapped tightly around her.

"I heard cymbals and trumpets but possibly it was only in my imagination," he murmured, his deep voice vibrating against her collarbone.

"For me, it was the 'Hallelujah Chorus'," Anna said, running her hands over the breadth of his back.

His shoulders shook.

"A religious experience?" he said, raising his head so she could see the laughter lighting his face.

His performance in front of the mirror had been an exercise in deliberate seduction, his lovemaking had been powerful, but the pure amusement in his smile took her breath away.

She smiled back and felt the thread of more than a physical connection twisting tight between them.

He released her, grasping her shoulders to steady her as she swayed slightly. Kissing her gently on the forehead, he stepped back and pulled a handkerchief from his pocket, offering it to her. Anna looked at it in surprise.

"To clean up," he said.

Anna felt a blush creep up her neck as she realized what he meant her to do with it.

"Most men are not so thoughtful," she said.

He turned away to give her some privacy and she used his small gift before walking to the mirror to see how much damage had been done to her borrowed finery. Amazingly, the dress showed only one faint crease slanting across the front which could easily be attributed to sitting through the symphony. Her hair required some smoothing, and she realized she had no idea where her purse was.

Nicholas came up behind her and held out the glittery clutch and the chiffon stole which he had retrieved from the floor.

"They seem to have survived unscathed," he said, taking the handkerchief and tossing it in a trash can.

As she accepted her things, she met his eyes in the mirror. Without breaking the contact of their gazes, he gathered her hair in his hands, holding it away from her neck as he pressed his lips to the same spot he had claimed earlier.

"Don't leave the party without me," he said.

The planes of his face were once again drawn into their mask of control, and a pang of disappointment lanced through Anna. She suspected Nicholas was so implacable in his pursuit of Lexi's murderer because his friend was one of the few people who had gotten behind the mask.

"Maestro!" Anna recognized Billy Leon's voice as a series of thuds sounded on the door. "Time to party."

Nicholas lowered her hair and adjusted his white tie in the mirror as Anna jerked open her bag and seized a tiny brush. A few quick strokes gave the illusion of propriety before she shoved the brush back into the frivolous purse.

Nicholas offered the crook of his arm to her, saying, "Shall we, Lieutenant?"

She took a deep breath and slid her hand onto his forearm. "We can't disappoint your fans," she said.

He unlocked the door and swung it open.

"I just remembered: you're the lady cop," Billy said, waving an open bottle of champagne in Anna's direction. "Let the man have a night off from death once in a while, why don't you?"

"The lieutenant is my guest tonight," Nicholas said.

"Hey, man, sorry. No need to get pissy about it," Billy said, backing away when he saw the expression on the conductor's face. "Let's hit the chow."

Nicholas let Billy and his band members leave first before he led Anna down the hall.

"There is no way I'm walking into the party beside you," Anna said when he showed no sign of relinquishing her hand as they walked down the steps.

"Why not?"

"Because I don't want to draw attention to myself."

Nicholas laughed.

"Anna, my love, you're not dressed to avoid attention. In fact, I think Billy's drummer, the fellow in that very subtle red tuxedo, has designs on your virtue. Consider me your protection."

Anna made a sound somewhere between a snort and a laugh.

"Are you choking?" Nicholas asked with exaggerated concern.

"No, but you should be."

"I simply want to make my entrance with the most beautiful woman in the building on my arm. It's my reward for a hard day's work."

"Nice try. In fact, it was a very nice try but I'm not doing it. And you've already gotten your reward, buster."

"Oh, no. That was just the beginning of my reward," he murmured as he raised her palm to his lips before he released her from his grasp. "I'll see you after the party, Lieutenant."

CHAPTER 23

Anna dropped out of the procession as Nicholas strode forward to join the waiting Billy Leon. She was sure the afterglow of sex was obvious to anyone who looked at her, and she wanted to give her inner muscles time to stop quivering. It was distracting.

She could hear the applause as the two men entered the Felix Rohatyn Room side by side. This was where the big donors got to schmooze with the conductor and the composer face-to-face. After an hour and a half there, they were going on to another party at a nearby restaurant where Nicholas and Billy would each make a speech for those who were listed below the "Platinum" level on the list of benefactors in the program. Anna had heard someone say that having your name in the upper echelons meant a donation of over one hundred thousand dollars, a number that boggled her mind.

She decided to check in with Mac on the transportation arrangements and slipped her radio earpiece over her ear.

"Mac? You out there?"

"This is Xavier. Mac's in the auditorium where the radios don't work. I'll get him."

That afternoon they had discovered their communications were cut off inside the concert hall. Nothing worked: radios, cell phones, and walkie-talkies all went to static. When Mac complained, Nicholas had laughed and said he was sure the hall had been deliberately designed that way although no one would admit it.

"Hey, Salazar. How's the champagne?" Mac said.

"Bubbly. What's the latest?"

"We've got the limos ready with our drivers. We'll have uniforms on the street here and at Cipriani's. There's been no sign of a shooter so I'm pulling the plainclothes out of here. You've got the five cops in the party itself who'll be watching Vranos all the way. Leon's got his own professional security guards who've been brought into the loop. And I'll be at the stage door coordinating. At least my radio works down there."

"Want to trade places?"

"Not a chance," Mac said. "It's bad enough I had to put on a monkey suit. You couldn't force me to stand around talking to a bunch of billionaires."

"What if I told you they're serving single malt Scotch?"

"That would only make me hesitate before saying no."

Anna laughed.

"Anything else up?" she asked, trying to delay her appearance at the party.

"Well, Jessica Strauss called and went on about how Lexi Savenkov would have been playing in this concert if he'd still been alive and how he'd been replaced by, uh, George Ponzio, I think it was, who's not good enough to play Carnegie Hall, and more in the same vein."

"The way she fixates on Savenkov, you'd think there'd been something between them."

"Yeah, but we came up with nothing on that front."

"I know. If that's it, I'll see you at 11:30," she said before she removed the earpiece and tucked it back in her purse. She made sure her subcompact was still easily accessible before snapping the sapphire catch closed again.

The hum of conversation swelled to a dull roar as she approached the doors to the party. She squared her shoulders and did her best to slip unobtrusively through the door and along the wall toward the room's corner.

"Hey, I'm Frankie Crum. You know, the Aluminum Zebras' drummer," the young man in the red tux said, grabbing her hand and shaking it before she got halfway to her goal. "What's your name, gorgeous?"

"Anna Salazar," she said, withdrawing her hand from the vigorous pumping.

"Tell me you're not with the conductor. You don't look like the stuffy classical type."

"We're working together," she said, taking a step away.

His face brightened.

"Oh, is that all? Great. Let's get you a drink." He raised his arm over his head and snapped his fingers. "Hey, waitress, over here. We need a drink."

A young woman holding a round silver tray loaded with a selection of beverages changed course. As she walked up to them, Frankie grinned hugely and said, "Hey, sorry to shout at you like that but it's too crowded to move in here. It's amazing how you get around without spilling a drop."

The waitress, who had been looking a bit peeved, melted beneath his barrage and told him if there was anything he wanted that wasn't on the tray, she'd go get it for him.

"No, no, this is fine. It's the good stuff," he said, picking off two flutes of champagne and handing one to Anna. He clinked his glass against hers. "Here's to rock and roll and beautiful women, not necessarily in that order."

Anna found his exuberance as hard to resist as the waitress had and she caught herself smiling at him before she pretended to take a sip of champagne.

The air around her changed. That was the only way to describe what happened just before she felt a touch at the small of her back and a voice beside her ear.

"Ah, Anna, I've been waiting for you," Nicholas said. "I see Frankie has found you already. He has an unerring eye for female beauty."

"Thanks, man," the drummer said. "Good show tonight, even though it's not my thing. Billy's lit about it."

"Thank you. If you'll excuse us, there's someone I'd like Anna to meet," Nicholas said to Frankie.

"Sure, man. Anna, we're partying back at the hotel after Cipriani's. You can ride in the limo with us," Frankie said.

Anna felt the conductor stiffen even as she opened her mouth to refuse.

"I think not," Nicholas said.

"I'm working tonight so I can't," Anna hurried to say. "Thanks for the invitation though."

Frankie looked from the conductor to Anna and raised his eyebrows. "Whatever you say. See you later, gorgeous."

Nicholas' hand in the small of her back pushed Anna inexorably toward the corner she'd been headed for earlier. She watched him flash a brilliant smile and speak a brief word of acknowledgement to the people they passed without allowing any of them to waylay him. It was an impressive performance.

"Where've you been?" he said when they reached the bit of empty space.

"Checking in with Mac," Anna said. "I'm on duty tonight, remember?"

She considered giving him some grief about his abruptness with Frankie Crum but decided she'd enjoyed the flare of possessiveness.

"So you are," he said, a wicked glint sparking in his eyes.

"Do you really want me to meet someone or was that just an excuse to drag me over here?"

"Both. I'm heartily sick of making small talk and I want you to meet a music professor. From Austria."

"Sounds like I want to meet him too." Anna started to move away.

"In a minute."

He lifted his hand to her shoulder and feathered his fingers down the length of her arm until he reached her wrist. Turning it slightly upward, he lightly brushed his thumb back and forth across the sensitive skin, setting up a series of tingling waves that raced up her arm, rippled across her scalp and plunged down over her breasts and lower.

"How do you do that?" Anna whispered, her gaze riveted on the elegant sweep of his thumb as it moved back and forth across the veins of her wrist.

"Do what?" he asked.

Anna looked up to find him staring down at her, with a smile curling his lips and that same glint in his eye.

She pulled her wrist away.

"Stop playing with me."

"The thought of playing with you is the only thing getting me through this party," he said, before looking at his watch. "I'm going to give you fifteen minutes with the professor and then we're taking a break from work."

"I'm on duty. No breaks."

"I misspoke; the break is mine. You'll still be guarding me very closely, I assure you."

"There are five other cops here watching you too," Anna pointed out.

He steered her into the crowd.

"Professor Koubek, I'd like you to meet Lieutenant Salazar," Nicholas said as they stopped in front of a short, slender man with a brown Vandyke beard. "She'd like to hear what you told me about your student."

"A pleasure, Lieutenant," the man said, shaking Anna's hand.

Nicholas' attention was claimed by a redhead with a French accent, and he left Anna alone with the professor.

"Dr. Vranos tells me you are interested in Franz Gadde," Koubek said. "His death was a great tragedy. He was one of the most talented students I've ever had. No, *the* most talented. Head and shoulders above any others, really. How he could have ridden his bicycle in front of a car . . . well, he was such a precise, careful young man. I can't imagine it."

"When did he study with you?"

"He was studying with me when he died. I was his adviser, I believe you call it in this country. We were beginning the work of his doctoral thesis. He told me he was finishing up a project he thought would be a perfect thesis but he had to get permission to use it since it had been commissioned by a private patron. We met the week before Franz died and he was quite excited, for Franz who as I said, was usually very controlled. He planned to write a commentary to accompany it, explaining why he had made the musical choices he had. He felt I would be extremely pleased and interested in the project."

"Did, er, *Dr.* Vranos tell you we think Mr. Gadde may have been murdered because of this project?"

"Oh dear me, no! Murdered because of a composition? Why?"

"It's part of an ongoing investigation so I'd rather not go into detail. I simply want you to be careful who you mention this to."

"Murdered! I'll be very careful if you'll tell me the story when you're able," the professor said.

"That's a deal. May I ask you another question?"

Koubek nodded.

"You called him *Dr.* Vranos."

"I forgot that in the United States, you don't use academic titles outside of universities. The maestro holds Ph.D.s in at least two musical disciplines I know of. I met Dr. Vranos when I attended one of his master classes. I believe I learned more about Beethoven in those six hours than in all my years of study."

"Thanks for clearing that up," Anna said before the professor turned to another guest.

"Anna! How wonderful to see you!" A small, slim woman with her auburn hair piled on top of her head and a warm smile lighting her face wrapped her arms around Anna and hugged her.

"Kate!" Anna said. "I didn't notice your name on the guest list."

"Well, I'm not, strictly speaking, a guest. Mr. Leon is donating all the funds raised by this event to the National Literacy Foundation, and I'm a member of the board of trustees. I think I was listed under 'Staff' as 'Kate Johnson and guest' which of course did severe damage to Randall's ego."

A tall man with black hair and eyes and slashing cheekbones strolled up behind Kate and slung one arm around her waist as he leaned forward to kiss Anna on the cheek.

"Anna Salazar, good to see you here even though I suspect you're working. You owe us a visit."

"Soon, Randall, I promise. It's just that New Jersey is so far away," Anna said, smiling. "I didn't think you were much of a classical music lover."

"I'm just Kate's arm candy at this shindig," he said, his Texas twang thickening for effect. "Billy Leon's mother didn't learn to read until she was thirty-four and it was a National Literacy volunteer who taught her. So Leon's giving the money from tonight to Kate's favorite charity."

"Thanks again for letting us put your name down as an investor for the Beethoven manuscript. It lends a lot of credibility," Anna said in a low voice.

Randall nodded.

"How are Clay and Patrick?" Anna asked at normal volume.

"Clay's over there soaking up the rock star atmosphere," Kate said, waving toward a handsome blond teenager hovering on the outskirts of Billy's entourage. "He's going to Princeton in the fall, something I'm trying not to think about. Patrick stayed home to work on a science project which involves landing a video camera on an asteroid. He wasn't excited about either the classical music or wearing a tuxedo."

"If Patrick's involved in it, I fully expect to see videos from that asteroid in the next six months," Anna said.

"I think he's already written a funding proposal for NASA," Randall said, pride underlying his dry tone. Although Clay and Patrick were Kate's sons, Randall had adopted them when he married her.

Once again Anna knew the moment Nicholas got within five feet of her so she wasn't surprised when he came up beside her and held out his hand to Kate, saying, "I'm Nicholas Vranos."

"I know," Kate said, grinning at the absurdity of his introduction as she shook his hand. "I'm Kate Johnson and this is my husband Randall. What a magnificent performance! We were enthralled."

Nicholas dipped his head slightly and gave her his most charming smile. "Thank you. It was a pleasure to conduct music written by such a talented composer."

Anna gave him full marks for knowing about the Johnson's connection with the rock star.

Nicholas turned to Randall. The two tall dark-haired men in their black formalwear made a striking tableau as they gripped each other's hands in greeting. The financier and the conductor both exuded a subtle sense of power and authority which were surprisingly similar. They almost seemed to recognize kindred spirits in each other.

"Thank you, sir, for letting us use your name," Nicholas said.

"I'm always happy to help the good guys," Randall said.

"I'm curious as to how you and Lieutenant Salazar know each other so well."

"My headquarters are here in New York," Randall said. "A few years ago, one of my managers at RJ Enterprises got mixed up in an ugly situation. The lieutenant pretty much solved the problem single-handedly."

"Thanks, but I had the resources of the entire NYPD to draw on, not to mention your own impressive security organization, so it was hardly single-handed," Anna protested. "All I really did was to speed up the process a bit."

"Don't let her fool you," Randall said to Nicholas. "She's one smart lady and a damn good cop."

"I know. I've seen her in action," the conductor said, brushing the palm of his hand very deliberately across her behind. She resisted the urge to jam her kitten heel down on his instep.

"You've built yourself a nice business with Allegro Productions," Randall said, changing the subject for Anna's sake. "I'm always looking for a good investment so if you ever have a need for some extra capital, get in touch with me."

"Much obliged," Nicholas said. "I may take you up on your offer. I'm starting a series of music festivals in Eastern Europe. The project is still in the planning stages but you might be interested in participating farther down the road."

Kate rolled her eyes in laughing exasperation. "This is the one place I thought we were safe from business conversations."

"Darlin', this is the best place to do business," Randall said. "Wouldn't you enjoy being a patron of the arts?"

"If you're involved, our patronage will undoubtedly turn a profit," Kate snorted, even as she smiled up at her husband.

"Nicholas here has no problem with that philosophy; he does a fine job of it himself. Here's my cell phone number," Randall said, slipping a business card out of his breast pocket and handing it to Nicholas with a wink. "I'll expect your call."

"Thanks," Nicholas said, pocketing the card. "Now the lieutenant and I have to discuss some police business. If you'll excuse us."

Without waiting for Anna to say her good-byes, he locked his arm around her waist and propelled her through the crowd toward the door. She twisted around to give a farewell wave to the Johnsons over her shoulder.

"Well, that was abrupt," she said, leaning back against his arm to slow their progress slightly.

"Your fifteen minutes was up," he said, tightening his grip to keep her moving.

Anna longingly eyed a tray of endive slathered with crème fraîche and caviar as they sped past the waiter offering it.

"That was caviar you dragged me away from," she complained.

"I'll make it worth your while," Nicholas said, his voice dropping to a seductive growl.

Anna forgot the fish eggs as he swept her out the door and into the empty curving gallery lined with doors leading into the First Tier boxes. Nicholas led her around the gallery to a box well away from the party's hubbub.

He drew a key out of his formal vest's watch pocket and opened the door, pulling her into the tiny dark vestibule where the box holders could hang their coats before proceeding to their seats. He yanked the door shut and pinned her against the wall with the length of his body.

"Ahhhh," he said on a long breath of satisfaction. "Now I can really play with you."

He plunged his hands into her hair and tilted her face to his before lowering his lips to hers for a serious kiss.

Anna felt her good intentions go swirling down the drain as he seemed to engulf her body with soft, smooth wool stretched over the heat and play of muscle and sinew, creating an erotic counterpoint to the hard, cold plaster wall she was crushed against. Yet instead of feeling suffocated, she wanted to be even closer. She seized his lapels and pulled him in a fraction of a millimeter more to deepen the kiss.

She felt the vibration of his groan all the way down to her toes before he lifted his head to say, "I have an idea."

CHAPTER 24

Anna nearly slid down the wall into a heap when he let go of her. He took a step into the box and seized one of the high wooden chairs from the back row.

At that moment she heard a distinctive sound, one she hated. She hurled herself at Nicholas, ramming her knee into the back of his to make sure he went down fast. He fell hard on the carpeting, cursing furiously, as Anna dropped on top of him and stayed there.

"Someone's shooting at you with a silenced gun," she whispered. "Be quiet."

"Evidently, they hit me," he muttered back. "My left arm hurts like hell."

Now Anna took over the swearing. She lifted her head to see if she could find the shooter but only empty red velvet seats filled her view. She craned her neck to check the wall behind them, feeling some relief when she located a small round hole which meant the bullet wasn't lodged in Nicholas' arm. She just hoped it hadn't torn anything critical in its passage through. Her biggest concern was whether the shooter was above them and could shoot down into the box. Since no further shots had been fired, she was fervently hoping that was not the case.

"We need to move back into the vestibule," she said. "We're too exposed here. Can you crawl?"

"In a three-legged way," he said. "But probably not with you on top of me, as much as I'm enjoying it."

"You can't be hurt too badly if you can still think about sex," Anna said, her anxiety for him easing slightly. "Stay low and move to the wall away from the doorknob. He may decide to shoot through the door or shoot out the lock."

She carefully shifted off to Nicholas' right, scanning the concert hall for any sign of movement as he backed into the shadows of the coatroom. As soon as she knew he was in, she skittered backward herself. He sat propped against the wall, peering down at his upper left arm. She knelt beside him and took a look.

Blood glistened darkly on the black wool of his tailcoat while it painted the shredded edges of the shirt underneath scarlet. She carefully pulled the sodden fabric away from the wound and breathed out a sigh.

"It's a graze, a deep one, but you'll be fine," she said, looking up at him with an encouraging smile. "It's going to burn like the dickens so it's a good thing your conducting is over for the day."

She picked up the blue chiffon stole which had fallen from her elbows to the floor.

"Rafael will have my head for this," she said, as she folded it three times and tied it over the bloody wound.

Nicholas winced as she tightened the knot.

"Tell him I'll happily pay him for it," he said.

"He'll probably get you to autograph it and display it in his showroom."

Nicholas chuckled and she gave him full marks for staying cool under pressure.

Anna retrieved her clutch, pulled out the subcompact pistol, flipped off the safety catch, slipped a spare magazine into the bodice of her dress, and hooked her radio earpiece firmly in place, with the hope they'd reach a spot where she could transmit.

She unwound the silver straps of her sandals while mentally reviewing the layout of the gallery as she remembered it. There was no cover there, just a long smooth stretch of burgundy carpeting and locked doors. If the gunman was the pro she suspected, he'd have moved already, possibly to a place where he could take them out as they came through the door. She looked down at the tiny gun in her hand; it was useless at any real distance. She made a mental note to increase her size requirement for evening bags so she could carry her beloved Glock in the future.

"I wondered where you were hiding your gun, because it certainly wasn't under your dress" Nicholas murmured. "That doesn't look big enough to kill a mouse."

"Oh, it's quite lethal at close range," Anna said.

"Are we going to sit tight until the cavalry arrives?"

"I'd like to but I'm not sure we have that luxury."

"Then perhaps we could work our way over to the end balcony and jump onto the stage."

She leaned out of the shadows and surveyed his proposed route with narrowed eyes. They'd have to get over the dividers between four more boxes before they reached the last one but she could make herself and her gun conspicuous to cover Nicholas and possibly draw the shooter's fire. The jump to the stage was hefty but doable now that she was barefoot. Unfortunately, she knew the doors stage left led to nothing more than a storage area where they would be trapped again. They'd have to get all the way across the expanse of blond wood to stage right to escape. However, there was a grand piano, a cluster of kettle drums, and the conductor's podium to give them a modicum of cover. If they moved fast enough, they could make it.

She also remembered a security camera was permanently focused on the stage. Mac would have someone watching those monitors closely so he'd send in the troops pronto, not to mention locking down the building to trap the shooter. She was hoping the video camera might even cover some of the boxes they had to climb through. Mac would send in the cavalry even sooner and they might not have to cross the open stage. As her partner often lamented, Anna preferred action to immobility so she nodded.

"You're going to go first all the way," Anna said. "If you hear a sort of spitting sound, get back into the nearest coatroom. Wait for me when you get to the last box and we'll decide on a route across the stage. How's your arm feeling?"

"Fine," he said, pulling himself into a crouching position.

"Liar. I've been shot myself and it gets worse before it gets better." She copied his pose. "Okay, go."

Nicholas seemed to explode past her as he hurled himself over the railing between the boxes. Anna spun out of the vestibule, her arms extended so the gun was in plain sight as she followed him into the next box. There was no movement anywhere she could see and no shots were fired.

However, as Nicholas leapt over the next divider, a flurry of shots hissed and thudded around him, sending chips of plaster flying.

Anna squeezed off two shots from her pistol in the direction she thought the bullets had come from before she catapulted herself over the railing and crawled back toward the little coatroom. This box was smaller so it wasn't a separate room but rather an alcove.

"Nicholas, are you all right?" she whispered frantically as she slithered up beside his prone body.

"Fortunately, his marksmanship isn't up to par," he said, lifting his head and coming to his knees. The dark fabric of his tailcoat was sprinkled with plaster dust so the shots had come closer than Anna wanted to think about.

"This time I'm going to go first," Anna said. "It will confuse him."

"You mean you're hoping he'll shoot at you and not me. I don't think so," Nicholas said, taking off before Anna could do anything to stop him. Anna cursed and leapt to her feet to draw the shooter's attention, firing two more shots in the same direction she had before. It didn't deter the other gunman though and she heard the spit of two more silenced rounds, although this time the plaster rained around her. She dove for the railing.

"Don't do that again, Anna," Nicholas growled from the shadows of the alcove as she scooted toward him.

"I was covering you. Standard procedure," she said, pulling her extra magazine out of the bodice of her dress and slotting it into the pistol.

He circled her left wrist with his fingers and applied pressure.

"Don't do that again," he repeated with more emphasis. "You will not make yourself a target to protect me."

She looked pointedly down at her captured wrist. His grip loosened infinitesimally.

"Anna?"

"All right, I won't stand up again but I'm still going to cover you."

He released her.

"I'm going," he said.

This time no bullets spit across the concert hall.

"Well, either he's figured out he'll have a shot at us as we cross the stage or he's moving for a better angle," Anna said as they crouched in the third box.

"Last one," Nicholas said and rocketed into the next box as Anna fired two of her remaining four rounds to keep the gunman off balance.

"I've got two shots left," she told Nicholas when they reached the protection of the box which projected just slightly over the very front edge of the stage. "I'll use them while you're making the jump because I'm not going to be able to take the gun with me. I'll need both hands to grip the balcony railing."

He was frowning.

"Then you'll have no protection. I'll try to draw attention to the stage as you're jumping. Just give me a few seconds after I get down there."

"What are you—" she asked thin air as the conductor went for the box's front railing.

Just as he had to stand to turn and drop over the edge, Anna streaked toward him, spraying her remaining two bullets toward the opposite ring of boxes. She heard a thud on the stage as she ducked down behind the balcony's front lip and laid her gun down. She didn't think the gunman had fired but the noise from her own weapon might have masked the silenced bullets. She desperately hoped Nicholas had jumped and not fallen as she counted to five.

She half-rose, grabbed the railing firmly and swung herself over the side, checking for the edge of the stage floor as she hung for a split second. She had at least a five foot drop so she braced herself and let go, rolling the second she hit the stage. An enormous crash sounded behind her as she ducked into the tenuous shelter of a kettle drum. Another crash rang out and she scuttled behind the next kettle drum.

Nicholas was hunkered down behind the conductor's podium, systematically knocking down the music stands within his reach. Being metal, they clattered against each other with surprising volume. Anna made a short dash and came up beside him.

"Thanks," she said. "Now let's see if he's still shooting."

He stopped toppling the stands and they both held their breath, waiting for the betraying "pfft" of the shooter's weapon. For a moment the great hall held a heavy silence.

Then all hell broke loose as Mac's voice sounded from the stage door.

"Hold your fire!" he bellowed. "We have armed police officers on all floors. If you come out without your weapon, you will be detained peacefully. If you fire another shot, we will consider you armed and dangerous and will protect ourselves as necessary."

The sound of doors being banged open sounded through the auditorium as Mac's team took up positions to cover the two people on the stage.

Anna felt a wave of relief wash over her. Mac had come through as always. She locked her gaze on the open stage doors and sure enough, he slid into view behind the door frame, as an officer with a sniper rifle knelt at his feet. She watched the sniper scan the theatre with his high-powered sight before he spoke to her partner.

Mac waited until the sniper was back in ready position and then signaled Anna to make the run to safety.

"Okay, they've got us covered. Stay low and run like hell," Anna said.

"Ladies first," he said, giving her bottom a gentle shove.

Anna made an exasperated sound but took off. Sensing he was directly behind her, she sped into the welcoming shelter of the backstage area. Mac stepped out onto the stage for a split second and gave the watching officers a hand signal before ducking back into the shelter of the doorframe. Anna heard a lot more banging of doors and understood they had gone from protecting herself and Nicholas to searching for the gunman.

"You two okay?" Mac asked, turning to Anna.

"I'm fine. We need a medic for Nicholas," Anna said.

"Nonsense," the conductor said. "There's a first aid kit in the office. All I need is a bandage."

Mac took a look at the blood encrusted scarf wrapped around Nicholas' upper arm and waved a uniformed officer over to him.

"Teresa, take Mr. Vranos to the office and tell Juan we need him to look at a gunshot wound."

"Juan's an experienced EMT," Anna said. "He'll fix you up."

"You're going with him," Mac said. "I need you to watch the monitors since you've seen the chauffeur in person."

"I'm fine," she said again, looking him squarely in the eye.

"That's good," he said, looking right back at her. "Now go."

Nicholas had been watching the exchange. As Anna stalked past him, his eyes gleamed with amusement.

"Don't say it," Anna warned him as he came up beside her. "Mac's pissed at me and he's getting me out of the way. Damn, this floor's cold."

They had hit the cement steps, and Anna was barefoot.

"I'd be happy to carry you."

That reminded Anna of their hasty trip down his hallway and she flushed.

"Yeah, sure, I'm going to let a wounded man carry me down a flight of cement steps."

He laughed and Anna felt another surge of relief; he was going to be all right. Now that the adrenalin rush was fading, she couldn't help thinking about how much worse things might have been. She knew Mac was going to have a few things to say about her actions but she hoped catching the gunman would soften his attitude. She had every confidence that tonight they would get the murderer and crack the case. Her mood lifted again.

Nicholas submitted to Juan's ministrations with only minor protests and Anna went on to the security office. Two police officers and two Carnegie Hall guards were seated in front of the bank of video monitors.

"Hey, Lieutenant, good to see you in person," one policeman said. "Although you look real good on camera too. Lundqvist here spotted you on the screens."

Anna turned to the security guard and shook his hand.

"Thank you, Mr. Lundqvist. I was confident someone would see us and send help, but you must have done it at record speed."

Lundqvist, who was young and blond, blushed to the roots of his hair and mumbled something about just doing his job before he turned back to his screens.

The policeman shared a grin with Anna.

"You just visiting or you need a chair?" he asked.

"That depends," Anna said scanning the screens for signs the gunman had been captured. Her earpiece had fallen off when she rolled on the stage so she couldn't monitor the progress of the search. "Any sign of the shooter?"

"No, they're coming up empty."

"What?!" she said, leaning in closer. "That's not possible. We've got this place sealed up tight."

"We never saw the shooter at all from here but these cameras don't cover the whole building by a long shot," the policeman said.

Anna hissed in frustration.

"Mr. Lundqvist, I'm trusting you to watch every exit like a hawk," she said, before she wheeled and left in a flutter of blue chiffon.

The young security guard swallowed hard and hunched even closer to the screens, much to the cops' amusement.

Anna padded into the House Manager's office as Juan was wrapping a bandage around Nicholas' arm. The conductor was stripped down to his evening shirt and even that was missing the entire left sleeve. He looked up.

"They still haven't caught him," Anna said.

"I know. Juan's been keeping me up to date," he said. "Where the hell could he have gone?"

"They're doing a room by room search now," Juan said, winding an elastic strip around Nicholas' biceps.

"How's the wound?" Anna asked the officer.

"A deep graze but no stitches necessary. I cleaned it up and put some antibiotic ointment on it. It'll be sore for a few days but it'll heal good as new."

"Thank you, officer," Nicholas said. "I appreciate having the benefit of your expertise."

"No problem," Juan said, closing up the first aid kit and heading for the door. "My wife'll be real happy about those opera tickets."

"Opera tickets?" Anna asked, raising her eyebrows. "Bribing police officers again?"

"Merely expressing my gratitude for a job well done," the conductor said, touching his pristine bandage and then wincing.

"It hurts, doesn't it?" Anna said in a completely different tone.

"Like a son of a bitch," he admitted with a rueful smile.

"I'm sorry."

She wanted very badly to go over and lay her head against his chest so she could hear his heart beating with all the power of life but anyone could walk into the office at any time. She contented herself with a quick touch of his hand where he rested it on the desk.

"You kept it from being significantly worse," he said. "Remember that."

"I put you in danger."

"No, you formulated a very effective plan which worked, by the way."

"Yes, but you were my responsibility."

"Really?" Nicholas said. "Is that because of the case or because we're lovers?"

Anna stood silent for a moment.

"Both," she said.

An odd expression swept across his face.

"Wrong answer?" Anna asked.

"No, it was just startlingly honest, something I'm not entirely accustomed to." He looked away. "Does being shot officially remove me from the list of suspects?"

Anna sighed.

"No. It just means we stirred up the Archduke."

Nicholas looked at the clock on the office wall.

"I have to get to the next party. Billy and I are scheduled for an appearance there in twenty minutes."

"You're not going anywhere but to your apartment," Anna said.

"I beg to differ with you, Lieutenant," he said, standing up. "I have a commitment."

"I've heard that before," Anna muttered before making her voice very firm and official. "You can't go to another public event tonight unless we catch the shooter. I can't let you expose yourself that way."

"You already have security measures in place for the second party. It also seems likely the murderer's plan was to shoot me here so I should be quite safe at the next venue. He probably didn't expect to miss."

Anna and Nicholas locked gazes until Anna changed tactics.

"Well, you'd probably get a lot of sympathy looking like that but your dignity might suffer," she said.

"A valid point," he said. "I'll get a messenger to bring a tuxedo from my apartment."

"You can borrow mine," a deep voice with a Texas twang came from the doorway.

"Randall, Kate, what are you doing here?" Anna asked.

"We got sprung from the party room after they matched us up with our photos and persuaded one of the officers to tell us where you were," Randall said.

Kate was looking at the conductor's bandage.

"Oh dear, perhaps you shouldn't give him your tux," she said.

"It's only a graze," Nicholas said. "I'd appreciate the loan."

He and Randall exchanged one of those utterly male looks of perfect understanding, and Randall began to unbutton his jacket.

"What on earth happened?" Kate asked.

Anna gave them a very condensed version of the evening's events as Randall divested himself of the top half of his tuxedo. A policeman was dispatched to bring down a clean shirt and Nicholas' leather jacket from the Maestro's Suite. Anna had also requested the return of her shoes and her pistol when they retrieved them.

"That's not quite the whole story," Nicholas said as Anna concluded her barebones outline.

"I figured as much," Randall said, handing his diamond studs to his wife. "I'll buy you a drink and you can tell me the rest another time."

Nicholas had unfastened his own studs and was working his shirt off his shoulders. Anna saw him grimace and, after a moment's hesitation, went over to help him.

"This doesn't mean you're going to the other party," she said, easing the starched fabric over the bandage. "I just don't want you to start bleeding again."

Randall shrugged out of his shirt at the same time and Anna had to quell a gasp of admiration as the two big men stood facing each other, bared to the waist. Randall passed his shirt to Nicholas and Anna swallowed hard as muscles rippled under bare skin.

She tore her gaze away and saw Kate's eyes alight with the same unholy appreciation.

"I feel like I'm at Chippendale's," Kate said. "Anna, can I borrow a five?"

CHAPTER 25

Nicholas and Randall looked so identically appalled that Anna cracked up. Kate giggled when Randall gave her a look that promised retribution later.

Nicholas pulled on the borrowed shirt amazingly quickly for an injured man.

Sagging against the desk, Anna wrapped her arms around her aching ribcage. The release of laughter felt good.

"Want to share the joke? I could use a laugh right about now." Mac's voice killed the hilarity instantly.

Anna straightened as her partner walked into the office.

"We lost him," she said.

"Yeah," Mac said.

"Damn," she said. "Any idea how he slipped through our fingers?"

"We're pretty sure he went out a fire door and up to the roof. There's a tower of studios and offices up there with its own entrance onto the street. He probably got into the hall that way too. What the hell's going on here?" he asked, suddenly taking in the clothing exchange.

"Mr. Vranos insists on making his appearance at the next party," Anna said.

"My coat is slightly the worse for wear so Mr. Johnson very kindly offered me his."

"Well, I've heard of giving a guy the shirt off your back but never the tux jacket," Mac said, shaking his head. "You're making our life difficult, you know."

"My apologies," Nicholas said, sounding not in the least bit apologetic.

"Yeah, sure," Mac said.

"Thank you for chasing off the gunman," Nicholas continued. "I wasn't looking forward to covering the last twenty feet of open stage."

"No problem," Mac said.

Several people arrived at the door simultaneously, bearing clothing and other items. Anna strapped her silver sandals on, reloaded her gun and stashed it in her evening purse. Randall put on one of Nicholas' clean blue Oxford cloth shirts and his leather jacket. Billy Leon wanted to know what the f—k was going on and where was Nicholas.

"I had to make a wardrobe change," Nicholas said as he stabbed his own onyx cufflink through the starched buttonhole.

He winced as he raised his arms to drape Randall's bow tie around his neck and again Anna couldn't let him suffer. Although the act felt far too domestic and intimate to perform in front of all these people, she folded and tied the black silk for him.

As soon as she flipped the collar down, Nicholas lowered his chin and gave her a smile meant only for her.

"Thank you," he murmured. "I'm not sure I could have done that on my own."

Anna returned the briefest of nods and moved back into the controlled chaos of the police activities.

"So are we going to the effing party or not?" Billy demanded as soon as Nicholas was fully dressed.

"At your convenience," the conductor said.

"It's at the effing cops' convenience," Billy said. He pounced on Anna. "Can we get out of here now? We've got fans waiting for us."

"Yes, the limousines are outside," Anna said, since she and Mac had already consulted on some extra security precautions. "Yours is the first one, Mr. Leon, and Officer Cunningham will be your escort along with your own bodyguards. Mr. Vranos, we'll go in the second limo."

The plan was to make sure the shooter saw the flurry of activity that surrounded Billy Leon and the limo he entered. If the gunman was still waiting for his chance at Nicholas, they didn't want the rock star caught in the cross fire. They were actually going to put Nicholas into his limo in the loading bay and leave very quietly.

"Salazar," Mac said as the rock star was shepherded out the door. "I need to talk with you privately for a minute."

He led the way to a small empty office down a side corridor.

"What the hell were you thinking?" he asked the minute the door was closed. "Why didn't you just sit tight and wait for backup?"

"I couldn't. I didn't know where the shooter was. Vranos was bleeding. I couldn't make radio contact. I didn't want officers walking into gunfire unawares. I made a reasonable decision to try to get out."

Mac swiped his hand across his face wearily.

"Okay, I'll give you some of that. But we found a lot of bullet holes in the plaster. And all you had was that little pea-shooter of yours."

"Yeah, from now on I'm carrying an evening backpack so I can take my semi. I've never felt so incompetent at protecting someone."

"Hey, you brought him back with just a scratch," Mac said. "Don't beat yourself up."

"Right," Anna said, feeling a sudden prickle of tears in her eyes. "Thanks for riding to the rescue."

"No problem. Take Vranos to the party. I'll be right behind you this time."

No one shot at Nicholas Vranos either on the way to the party, while he and Billy were on stage, or as they circulated through the crowd. No one would even know he had been injured although Anna could see the muscles of his face tighten when a friendly party guest brushed against his left arm. Only after he had slid into the concealing interior of the limousine for the trip back to his apartment did he allow himself a grimace of pain.

Since she sat facing him, Anna caught the fleeting expression in the dim lights.

"Is it worse?" she asked, leaning forward. "I have the painkillers Officer Garcia gave you."

"I'll be fine."

Xavier Cunningham and a uniformed policeman joined them in the car and it surged into the late night traffic. Anna was too exhausted to make small talk herself so she said, "Xavier, what did you think of Billy Leon's symphony?"

Xavier took his cue and launched into a complimentary but knowledgeable monologue which required no input from any other party. After a few minutes of listening to Xavier's melodious tones, Nicholas' posture changed subtly and he interjected a comment. Soon the two music lovers were engaged in an increasingly technical discussion and Anna relaxed back against the leather seat, even as she kept watch through the window for anyone showing undue interest in their car.

After a thorough search of Nicholas' apartment, Xavier and the other officer departed for their outside posts.

Nicholas sprawled on the Biedermeier sofa with a crystal tumbler of Scotch in his hand. Taking a sip, he focused his blue gaze on Anna as she collapsed in a chair opposite him.

"Sorry it took so long to let you in but this place is huge," she said. She flipped the safety catch on and carefully placed the Glock she'd retrieved from her duffle bag on the occasional table.

"How often do you get shot at?" he asked.

"What?"

"How often does someone shoot at you? Once a week? Once a month? Once a year?"

"I don't know. I don't keep track," Anna said.

"So, too often to easily count," he said, putting down the Scotch and yanking loose the borrowed bow tie and flinging it on the coffee table.

"Well, no. I *could* count but I don't bother. It's just part of my job."

He stood abruptly, stalking around the coffee table to brace his arms on the armrests of her chair.

"When you stood there in that bright blue dress, making a target of yourself while bullets hit the plaster all around you, I wanted to kill you myself before the bullets did," he snapped, leaning down so his face was near hers. "I was furious that you would expose yourself that way."

"That makes no sense and I wasn't exposed," Anna said. "I was laying down covering fire."

He gave a muffled groan and shifted his hands to her shoulders, pulling her upright against him. He wrapped his right arm around her and pressed her cheek against his chest.

Anna slipped her arms around his waist, taking care not to jar his left arm.

"I know what I'm doing, Nicholas," she said to his chest. "I've had a lot of training and a lot of practice. I don't take stupid risks."

She wasn't sure if the sound he made was a laugh or another groan.

"Your idea of a risk and mine are worlds apart," he said, his grip tightening as he felt her relax into him. "I'd thank you for saving my life but I know what you'll say."

"I didn't save your life; I got you shot."

He threaded his hand under her hair and splayed his palm against her bare back.

"Let's go to bed," he said.

"I'm sleeping on the couch. I'm on duty."

"Since your duty is as my bodyguard, it would seem logical to stay as close to me as possible."

He reached down and took her hand. Tugging gently, he started toward his bedroom.

Anna stood firm.

"I'm staying where I can see the alarm panel and cover the entrances," she said. "I'm not letting anyone get close enough to shoot at you again."

"You humble me," he said, releasing her hand to trace a line from her temple to her chin with his fingertips. "No one else has ever been willing to throw themselves in front of a bullet for my sake."

"I'm trying to make sure that's not necessary."

"Will you at least help me undress?"

"You think that will change my mind, don't you?"

He laughed.

"I'd sound insufferable if I said 'yes' but a man can hope."

"You'd be insufferable if you weren't so close to being right," she said. "However, I have an iron will."

"There's no doubt about that," he said, in a tone as dry as the desert.

Anna had a few doubts on the topic but she couldn't let Nicholas endure more pain than was unavoidable so she let him interlace his fingers with hers as they strolled down the hall to his bedroom.

As soon as she had eased his borrowed tuxedo jacket off, he sat down on the bed and drew her between his thighs, raising his chin to give her access to the studs. When she gave him a dubious look, he said, "I thought it would be easier for you to reach this way."

Anna snorted as she started working the studs loose from the buttonholes. While both of her hands were occupied, he slid his right hand around to cup her bottom.

"Stop it or I'll make you do this yourself," she said. "For a man who claims to be in pain, you're pretty lively."

He gave her rear a quick squeeze and let his hand drop.

The back of Anna's fingers brushed against his bare chest as she worked another stud loose and she felt the contraction of his muscles as he went very still.

"This is worse torture than the gunshot wound," he said, seizing her hand and moving it away from his skin. "I'll finish."

"Don't be ridiculous," she said. "You don't want it to start bleeding again."

She pushed through the last stud and reached down to pull the tails of his shirt out of his waistband. She realized she would have to reach around him to finish the job and hesitated for a moment.

"Hoist in your own petard, my love," he said with a deep chuckle and a wicked gleam in his eye. "Please continue."

She gave him a bland look and stepped into full contact with his upper body, wrapping her arms around his ribcage and working the back of the shirt loose. She could feel his erection against her stomach. Stepping back slightly, she began to slide the cotton fabric down his shoulders, taking special care to lift it past the bandage that almost seemed to glow against his olive skin. When the shirt was finally shed, both of them were breathing faster than was normal.

For a long moment, neither one moved.

"May I return the favor," he said with a slight rasp. "My experience with evening dresses is that they're difficult to unfasten."

"Thanks. I'd hate to do any more damage to this outfit than I already have," Anna said, raising her arm to let him unhook and unzip the side opening of her dress. He did it so swiftly that the bodice almost slipped down to her waist before she caught it.

"I should have known you'd have fast reflexes," he said with a regretful sigh.

"I should have known not to trust a man who has experience with evening dresses," she said, hugging the chiffon firmly against her chest.

She leaned forward and brushed her lips against his.

"Sweet dreams," she said.

"'Sweet' is not the word I'd use to describe what I'm going to dream about," he said.

Anna laughed as she closed his bedroom door behind her and headed for the foyer. She grabbed her duffle bag from beside the entrance door and went into a spare bedroom to change into her black jeans and police tee shirt. Folding the slippery blue chiffon gown into some semblance of neatness proved impossible so she gave up and bundled it into the bag. Just as she had decided she could nap and keep watch from a handsome and well-stuffed chaise longue tucked into a corner of the immense space, her cell phone rang.

"Allo, allo? Lieutenant Salazar?"

The caller's accent was French.

"Yes, this is Salazar."

The caller was Paul Germain from Interpol.

"We have identified the man in the drawing you sent us. He is Viktor Ivanov, an ex-KGB officer who was working for organized crime in Russia when we last met up with him."

"He's Russian?"

"Latvian, actually," Monsieur Germain said.

"I thought he was Austrian or German," Anna explained.

"He speaks German, according to our records, along with four other languages. He has a long record which I'll fax to you. I knew it was late there, but I wanted to warn you directly. Be careful with this one, Lieutenant."

"I will. *Merci*," Anna said, using one third of her French vocabulary.

She looked at her watch and decided Mac would still be awake, so she speed-dialed his number.

"What is it?" he said, sounding tense.

"It's okay. I just have some new information," Anna reassured him.

"Jesus, you scared the hell out of me, calling at this hour."

"Were you asleep?"

"No."

"Then quit grousing. Interpol called. The Archduke's chauffeur is ex-KGB and current Russian mob."

"Shit," Mac said.

"Exactly. You know what bothers me the most? A KGB agent might have missed the first shot tonight but he wouldn't have missed the second or third."

"Yeah, but then who the hell shot at Vranos?"

"That's the multi-million dollar question. We're going to have to change some of our plans for tomorrow's, or rather, today's meeting."

"I'll get on it in the morning."

"And another thing, Mac."

"What's that?"

"You owe me three dollars for cursing." She started laughing as he added to his offenses. "Make that four. Now we're up to five."

CHAPTER 26

A chime sounded softly and Anna was on her feet with gun in hand before her brain caught up with her instincts. Sunlight streamed through the French doors so she could see the living room clearly as she half-crouched behind the big chaise. She heard movement in the hall and pivoted in that direction.

"Anna?" Nicholas' voice had a hint of early morning gravel in it which made her name sound incredibly sexy.

He walked into the room dressed in navy silk pajama bottoms and nothing else but the bandage. His hair was tousled from sleep but his blue eyes were brilliant and intense. When he saw the couch by the fireplace was empty he stopped and swung around.

"Good morning," Anna croaked as she put her gun on the chaise and stood up straight.

He smiled and she felt it right down to her bare toes.

"Good morning," he said. "I hope you got some sleep."

"You should hope I didn't sleep at all," Anna said.

"On the contrary, I want to make sure your dreams were as vivid and as frustrating as mine," he said, smiling in a way that made her knees wobble as he stalked toward her. He backed her up against the wall and trailed a line of kisses down the side of her neck.

"Mmmmm," Anna said before she stood on tiptoe and planted a kiss on the bare skin at the base of his throat. She couldn't resist using just the tip of her tongue to taste his skin.

He growled and started to bend down to her again but she braced her hands on the warm skin of his chest and said, "We're going to have company in an hour. How's your arm?"

He glanced dismissively down at the bandage.

"Fine."

"Mac's bringing a doctor with him to take a look and re-wrap it."

"It's fine," he repeated, looking annoyed.

"When do you have to conduct again?"

"This afternoon at a rehearsal."

"Then you want to make sure it's healing well before you start waving it around," Anna said.

"I'm going to make coffee," he said shortly. "How do you like yours?"

"I've died and gone to heaven. A man in silk pajamas is going to make me coffee. I like cream and sugar, please."

"Heaven is where we would have been last night if you hadn't been on duty," he said as he headed for the kitchen.

Anna pulled the toilette kit out of her duffle and did a quick morning cleanup in the guest bathroom. She longed for a shower, especially when she saw the array of expensive scented soaps and shampoos, but she couldn't afford the time.

In truth, she felt amazingly energized considering her sleep had in fact been very light and interrupted often by tension and the sounds of an unfamiliar environment. The *New York Times* delivery boy had been very surprised when she had yanked the door open with gun drawn as he stooped to lay the paper neatly on the marble floor.

Then there had been the dreams, feverish and highly sexual, in which Nicholas Vranos would somehow change into Viktor Ivanov as he made love to her. She had dreamt about cases before but never in such a disturbingly intimate way. Maybe her subconscious was sending her the same warning Mac was.

Anna wove her hair into a tight braid and wrapped an elastic band around the end, making sure it wouldn't come loose. It was going to be a long day.

As she opened the door, the delicious scent of coffee drew her inexorably to the kitchen, where a huge mug stood steaming beside a basket of croissants on a marble-topped island. Even more delicious was the sight of Nicholas Vranos leaning against the island with one ankle crossed over the other, a coffee mug in one hand and a folded section of the *New York Times* in the other.

"Now *this* is a good way to start off the morning," she said, letting her gaze sweep the length of his body.

"I can think of several better ways," he responded, "involving less clothing."

Anna laughed and seized her mug. She inhaled deeply before she took the first sip. "Just as good as the *Opus*."

"Blasphemer," Nicholas said. "Have a croissant. I just want to read the review of last night's concert."

Anna demolished one of the buttery rolls and washed it down with a swallow of the fresh coffee.

"Did it get a good review?" she asked when Nicholas dropped the folded paper on the counter.

"Mostly," he said. "You never know if the *Times* will side with the snobs who dismiss rock stars writing classical music as gimmicky and an affront to high art or if they'll decide to be counterculture cool."

"And?"

"They leaned toward cool with a few swift jabs at the weakest spots."

Anna picked up the paper and found the review. Nicholas had been too modest.

"Well, they might have criticized the symphony in places but they certainly have a high opinion of you. *Persuading Maestro Nicholas Vranos to conduct Mr. Leon's debut was a stroke of genius on the part of the rock star-turned-composer. Mr. Vranos' authority on the podium bestowed an imprimatur of legitimacy and his mere presence rendered the performance more significant. The conductor discovered heights and depths in the music that a lesser musician would have been unable to call forth, guiding his orchestra through the previously uncharted waters with a firm and inspired hand.*"

"That's from my press release."

His tone was so deadpan that Anna had to look closely to see the twitch at one corner of his lips. She chuckled.

"Well, *I* thought you were brilliant but I'm both biased and musically uneducated so my opinion doesn't count."

"On the contrary, your opinion counts double."

He smiled very slowly.

"I got some interesting news last night," she said, taking a gulp of her coffee. "The Archduke's henchman Karl is a former KGB agent and Russian mobster named Viktor Ivanov. That means we're going to have to make a few changes in the plans for your meeting today."

Nicholas put his mug down.

"Such as?"

"We won't put a wire on you because he might look for that. Listening equipment has been set up in the room next door to his. We've got a good angle on his suite windows from the building across the street so we can use a long-lens video camera from there. We'll see what other thoughts Mac has when he gets here."

"I'm just wondering," Nicholas said.

"About what?"

"About whether a highly trained KGB agent would have missed last night."

Anna looked at him over her coffee mug.

"I'm wondering about that too," she said. "He might have hired someone else to do the job."

"A professional who couldn't shoot?" Nicholas said, raising an eyebrow.

"Trust me, it happens a lot, which is lucky for the targets," Anna said. "You have to spend real money to get a competent pro."

The telephone rang.

"That will be Norman with a summary of the reviews," Nicholas said. "Excuse me."

Anna went back to the living room, strapped on her holster, and got out her cell phone to make some calls. By the time she finished, Nicholas was in his bedroom dressing and Mac and his team were on the way up in the elevator.

She opened the door for her partner, a police doctor whom she knew from being treated for an injury, and two plainclothes officers who would be shadowing Nicholas when he met with the Archduke in two hours. Xavier Cunningham was already on-site at The Pierre, setting up the surveillance equipment.

Anna escorted the doctor down the hall to Nicholas' bedroom. Much to her relief, the conductor allowed him in to examine the wound. She joined Mac in the kitchen where she had sent him for coffee.

"The only excitement last night was when I almost shot the *Times* delivery boy," Anna said, refilling her own mug.

One of the plainclothesmen choked on his drink.

"Don't encourage her," Mac said. "I brought the fax from Interpol. Some of the info is sketchy but Ivanov started as a field agent before he moved up to management."

"So he wouldn't have missed more than once," Anna said, scanning the papers Mac handed her. "Maybe he was just trying to scare Vranos?"

"It doesn't make sense. The Archduke wants Vranos at the meeting today so he can see where he stands, maybe try to persuade him the music is authentic. After getting shot at, the conductor would have every reason to cancel or at least postpone."

"I know. I've been thinking about it all night," Anna said. She wasn't going to share some of the other things she'd been thinking about.

"Good morning, gentlemen," Nicholas said as he strolled into the kitchen. "I see you found the coffee. Shall I make more?"

"No, thanks," Mac said. "With the size of these mugs, I'd get the caffeine shakes."

Anna had to give herself a moment to recover from Nicholas' entrance. The conductor was dressed in a navy blue suit that must have been custom-tailored. It made his shoulders look a mile wide and his legs look two miles long. A yellow paisley tie glowed against a pale blue Egyptian cotton shirt. His dark hair had been groomed into neat, gleaming waves and his early morning stubble had been erased. The amount of power he radiated was almost overwhelming. He was dressed to do battle with the Archduke.

The doctor had followed Nicholas into the room and Anna beckoned the medical officer into the far corner.

"How's his arm look?" Anna asked.

"Good," he said. "Excellent coagulation. No visible infection. No stitches necessary. All it needed was more ointment and a bandage change."

"You know he's a conductor so he uses his arms a great deal. Can he conduct today without doing any damage?"

"He asked me that and I told him if he could bear the pain, he could use the arm."

"So it's painful?"

"Wounds in that location always are because the skin is constantly being stretched and moved. I gave him some painkillers but I suspect he won't use them."

"Damned stubborn man," Anna muttered.

"If I remember correctly, you wouldn't even accept the painkillers I tried to give you," the doctor pointed out.

"I'm a cop."

"And a damned stubborn one," he repeated.

"Compliment taken," Anna said. "Thanks for coming, Doc."

"No problem. I'll let myself out."

Nicholas gave her a look that said he knew she was checking up on him but he said nothing as she joined the men seated around the kitchen table.

"Okay, let's go over the situation," Mac said. He spread out diagrams of the hotel, the streets around it, and the suite where the conductor was meeting the Archduke.

"It's very important that you refuse to change the venue of the meeting," Mac said. "Play the prima donna if you have to but keep it where we can see what's going down."

"My artistic temperament will be on full display," Nicholas said dryly.

Anna coughed.

Mac outlined all the protection that would be in place.

"No matter what we set up outside," he concluded, "you're going to be in there alone for however long the Archduke wants you to be. Be careful and don't do anything to make him think it's a set-up."

"I'll be the soul of discretion," Nicholas said, looking down to adjust the snowy cuff of his shirt.

"Mr. Vranos," Anna said in a warning tone.

He looked up at that.

"Viktor Ivanov is very dangerous. He probably murdered Alexei Savenkov and may have tried to shoot both of us last night. He torched two apartments. Don't go out of your way to provoke him."

The conductor's smile did not reassure her.

"I have full confidence in your ability to protect me," he said.

Now Anna was really worried but she just held his gaze for a long moment before saying, "I'm off to join Xavier now. Good luck, everyone."

Standing, she came around behind Nicholas' chair and gave his shoulder a brief squeeze.

"Don't push him," she bent down to say in a low voice before she left the room.

On her way to the car Mac had brought for her, she stopped to check in with Dirk Boland in the security office of Nicholas' building, making sure he was aware that extra vigilance would be necessary from now on. Boland had added security guards on every shift and made them all aware of the situation. Mac had also alerted the security chiefs at Carnegie Hall and the building on Madison Avenue where Allegro Productions had its headquarters.

Nicholas' apartment was almost directly across Central Park from the Pierre with its posh Fifth Avenue location. After negotiating the traffic, Anna parked her car on 62nd Street in a "No Parking" zone. Before getting out, she raided her duffle bag, stuffing her braid under a Yankees baseball cap, hiding her face behind a pair of oversized sunglasses and slinging an embroidered jean jacket over her holster. She was already wearing a pair of artistically ripped jeans and no one could see her leather boots held the subcompact pistol tucked in the holster. They didn't want the Archduke or Ivanov spooked by the presence of a police officer they recognized.

She followed Xavier's directions to the service entrance of an apartment building located just across 61st Street from the Pierre's corner. The place on the 16th floor had good sightlines into the Archduke's suite and the apartment's owners had been more than happy to cooperate with the police.

The apartment was small but expensively decorated. Fortunately, the owners were not there to see their Ming vases shoved aside to make room for laptop computers and electronic surveillance equipment or leaky Styrofoam coffee cups sitting on glossy wood tabletops.

"Hey, Xavier, everything ready to go?" she asked as she surveyed the controlled chaos surrounding the detective and two other cops.

Xavier looked different today. He was dressed in jeans and a dark blue tee shirt and his shoulder holster held a Glock semi-automatic. Without a suit to cover the whipcord muscles and counterbalance the strong bones of his face, he looked more than capable of handling himself in a fight.

"All set. Want to take a look?" he asked, swiveling away from the computer screen.

"Sure," Anna said.

She bent over his shoulder and whistled.

"Nice setup," she said, taking in the chintz-covered sofa, mahogany arm chairs, and heavily fringed window draperies of the suite's sitting room. Xavier hit a key and the view shifted to the bedroom's four-poster bed loaded with bolster pillows and layers of thick bedspreads and puffy comforters. The Archduke was standing in front of the dresser, arranging the white handkerchief in his pocket. He was dressed in a charcoal gray suit and sported a red tie.

"Shit," Anna said as another man walked into the camera's view. "That's Ivanov."

"Yeah, he arrived about twenty minutes ago," Xavier said. "He's staying a couple of floors down on the other side of the building. I'd turn up the sound but they've been speaking German the whole time. We're recording everything, and Herb over there's working on the translation."

Anna glanced across at the young man wearing a headset who was typing furiously on another laptop.

"We've got a man in the room next door with the listening equipment," Xavier said. "Ivanov swept the room for bugs but nothing's actually in the suite so he wouldn't find anything. Got anything to report, Herb?"

The young man looked up briefly to shake his head.

"I think they do all their serious talking in the limo," Xavier said. "They've said nothing of interest since we've been listening."

"Because the KGB listened to everyone," Anna said, watching the Archduke walk into the sitting room and close the door behind him, leaving his companion in the bedroom. Ivanov picked up a newspaper before he pulled a chair over near the door. He sat down and unfolded the paper, spreading it across his lap.

"He can pick up the paper and fake reading it if he needs to," Xavier commented, as he split the screen so they could watch both rooms simultaneously.

"Wow, you've done a great job," she said.

"Anything for Beethoven."

He went still as he listened to his earpiece.

"They're almost here," he said.

Grabbing a pair of binoculars, Anna went to the window to watch the black car pull up at the Pierre's cream-and-gold awning on Fifth Avenue. A uniformed doorman leapt forward to open the car door and Nicholas emerged. He nodded to the doorman and strode under the canopy as though he owned the place.

Xavier pointed to the third man who was also seated in front of a computer screen.

"Steven's got the feed from the hotel's security cameras so he can watch the public areas."

After a few minutes of watching the screen, Steven looked up.

"It's show time."

CHAPTER 27

Xavier hit a key on his computer keyboard and Nicholas' knock sounded loudly through the speakers. The Archduke stood in the middle of the sitting room's deep red carpeting, his hands folded behind his back.

"Is he ever going to answer the door?" Anna muttered.

"Maybe he forgot he didn't bring his butler," Xavier said.

A few more seconds elapsed before the Archduke strolled to the door, opening it without checking through the peephole.

"Ah, Dr. Vranos. Thank you so much for coming," he said, holding out his hand.

Nicholas shook it briefly.

"I understand from the *New York Times* that the concert last night was a great success," the Archduke continued.

"Thank you," Nicholas said, accepting the compliment with a condescending nod.

The Archduke looked irritated.

"Turn the charm on," Anna said to Nicholas' image on the screen. "Don't antagonize him."

"Please sit down," Habsburg-Lothringen said. "Would you like some coffee or something stronger?"

"No, thank you," the conductor said, settling on a Chippendale-style armchair. "I have to get to a rehearsal."

"Your dedication to your art is admirable but perhaps you're working too hard."

The older man sat in the matching chair which faced the musician.

"I don't consider conducting work," Nicholas said, with a slight smile. "It brings me great satisfaction to study a piece of music and to help an orchestra interpret its subtleties."

"That's better," Anna breathed. "Give him some encouragement."

"I'm sure it does," the nobleman said. "And that's why I wanted to talk with you today. I believe you're aware that a consortium of wealthy individuals headed by Randall Johnson is interested in purchasing the Tenth Symphony."

Nicholas' response was another superior nod and Anna made an incoherent sound of frustration.

"I understand Mr. Johnson contacted you for your opinion of the manuscript."

"He did. I wasn't able to say with conviction that it's authentic."

"What would it take to convince you?" the Archduke asked pleasantly.

"More concentrated time to study the original and to compare it with Beethoven's other work. I can think of two scholars whom I'd like to show it to for their evaluation of its authenticity. Unfortunately, my schedule is quite full for the next two months and I can't free up the time your discovery deserves."

"I dislike having this masterpiece languish in obscurity any longer than it already has," its owner said. "And I certainly would hate seeing its premiere conducted by a lesser musician than yourself."

Nicholas raised his eyebrows at the threat. Then he shrugged.

"My reputation was not built in a hurry. I won't compromise it in one. Leading the premiere of the Tenth Symphony would be a great honor for me if it *is* indeed Beethoven's work. However, I am sure you can find another equally capable conductor if you can't wait."

The Archduke threw him a look that said they both knew there was no one who equaled Nicholas Vranos' stature as an interpreter of Beethoven.

"I had thought to offer you a share in the sale price of the manuscript in return for your presence on the podium," the nobleman said.

"An unusual proposal," Nicholas said. "Why would you do that?"

"Because, as you say, your reputation is a valuable commodity. I would not want you to risk it without a suitable reward. Are you aware of what the consortium is willing to pay for the symphony?"

Nicholas nodded.

"Your share would make you a very wealthy man."

The conductor laughed.

"I'm already a wealthy man."

The Archduke looked disgruntled.

A flicker of movement on the other screen caught Anna's attention. Ivanov had stood up and now he crumpled the newspaper into a ball and hurled it across the room.

"Your Highness."

Nicholas' voice brought her back to the confrontation in the living room.

The conductor was leaning forward in his chair as he spoke with great sincerity.

"Nothing would give me more joy than to be able to say with utter certainty your manuscript is real. Every lover of music hopes to find another piece of Beethoven's genius, and an entire symphony is a boon beyond the wildest of dreams. However, I cannot let my desire overcome my reservations. Your manuscript could be Beethoven's or it could be a clever compilation of his 'sketches'. With the little time I've been able to devote to it, I can't advise Mr. Johnson and his partners that purchasing the symphony is a wise investment, especially considering the amount of money involved."

"Of course not," the Archduke said, standing. "I couldn't expect you to. I am very sorry your . . . commitments do not allow you to be involved with an event of such importance in your field."

"As am I," Nicholas said, also coming to his feet.

"I will make sure you receive a ticket to the premiere," the nobleman said.

Nicholas inclined his head without taking his eyes from Habsburg-Lothringen's face.

The Archduke seemed at a loss when the conductor made no move to approach him.

"Thank you for coming, Dr. Vranos," he said finally.

"You're welcome," Nicholas said before turning on his heel and striding toward the door.

As he stepped into the corridor, Anna let out her breath.

"Well, he certainly pissed them off royally," Xavier said as Ivanov wrenched open the bedroom door and broke into a torrent of angry German.

"We wanted them panicked, not furious," Anna said.

"Sometimes you can't have one without the other."

She walked over to Herb's workstation and peered at the translation he was typing at high speed. As expletive after expletive scrolled across, Anna started to smile and then chuckle. One particularly inventive stream even got a snort from Herb.

Suddenly, Ivanov's cursing ceased.

"Vranos cannot stop this sale," Herb typed. "We have to remove him from the plan."

"That's not good," Anna said.

"You will—" Herb translated from the Archduke.

"Yes," Ivanov cut him off. "We will go to lunch now."

"Damn," Anna said. "I thought we were going to get something."

"He's too cagey," Xavier said. "Even when he's foaming at the mouth."

Anna's cell phone rang. It was Nicholas.

"Lieutenant McKenzie tells me you were watching my little charade," he said. "I think I annoyed our noble friend adequately."

"Adequately? You practically hung a sign on your chest that says, 'Shoot me'."

"Since he's already tried to, that seems superfluous."

"Last night was a very halfhearted attempt. I don't think Ivanov will give up as easily after your prodding."

"That will give us a better opportunity to catch him, won't it?"

Anna wanted to shake him.

"I'll see you after your rehearsal," she said.

"Why don't you join me for lunch? I'm meeting Norman at *Molyvos* just south of Carnegie Hall," Nicholas said.

"Thanks but I've got to go back to the office. I'll be checking in with your surveillance team so don't do anything you don't want me to know about. Good-bye."

He was laughing as Anna hung up.

"The Archduke and Ivanov are leaving the hotel," Xavier said into his headset. "Who's tailing the limo? Sanchez, that you? Keep us informed."

He turned to Anna.

"We've got this apartment until tomorrow morning so we'll keep tabs on the Duke's digs until then."

"Thanks, Xavier. I wish we could get a camera on Ivanov's room."

"We tried but it faces directly onto the park so no dice. All we can do is listen, and he keeps the television on all day."

"Cagey is right," Anna said. "I'll talk to you later."

She waved to Herb and Steven and headed for the service entrance.

"Go home and catch a couple of hours of sleep," Mac said when he came in and caught Anna with her head down on her desk.

"I just needed to rest my eyes," she said, sitting up straight.

"Your boyfriend's at Carnegie Hall for the next three hours and I'll call you if anything breaks."

Anna clamped her jaw down on a yawn.

"Go," Mac said.

"Okay," she agreed. "I'll go straight to Carnegie at four o'clock and meet up with the team there."

"Stop worrying. Security's so tight a mouse can't sneak by."

"Yeah, but what about a rat?" Anna said on her way out the door.

Anna savored the ripple of muscles across Nicholas' bare back as he conducted one of Billy Leon's rock songs. But then blood began to pour from his left shoulder and drip onto the podium. He kept on waving the baton, directing the orchestra to play louder and louder. She shouted at him to stop but he couldn't hear her over the music as its volume swelled.

Anna groaned as she came awake. She groped around and found the "off" button on her blaring clock radio. She'd been dead asleep for two hours and it felt like two minutes. As she lay there trying to will herself to sit up, her cell phone took up where the radio had left off. She swiped it off the bedside table.

"Salazar," she croaked.

"Did I wake you? My apologies," Nicholas said in her ear.

Anna sat up instantly.

"No, my alarm had already gone off. Aren't you supposed to be in rehearsal?"

"We're ending early. Lieutenant McKenzie wants to send me back to my apartment but I have a better idea. Let me come to yours."

"What? No!"

"I need a change of scene and Ivanov will never look for me there."

He had a point. Anna made a quick survey of the condition of her home, deciding it could be made presentable in twenty minutes if Nicholas didn't open any closet doors.

"All right." She gave him the address on Sixth Avenue. "Tell your driver it's between Prince and Spring Streets. And Nicholas, don't expect any Biedermeier furniture."

"I don't notice furniture when you're in the room."

Anna snorted but she was grinning as she went through the apartment like a reverse whirlwind, leaving order in her wake.

Thirty minutes later, she buzzed Nicholas Vranos into her building. She opened the door and listened as his footsteps echoed up the three floors of the oval stairwell. Her building was old, with settled floors that slanted noticeably and architectural moldings blurred by multiple coats of paint, but therein lay its charm for her. However, looking at the scarred wood of the steps and the dings in the paint where furniture had been banged against the wall as it was moved in or out, Anna wondered whether Nicholas would see the good bones of the place.

As he came into sight around the last turn, he looked up at her and her breath caught in her throat. He wore his black leather jacket over a black shirt and jeans. His eyes had the incandescent glow that always enthralled her but the effect was magnified. Until now, she had seen him in his milieu where he fit like the keystone in a perfect arch. Out of context, he blazed like a bolt of lightning on a moonless night. He didn't belong here.

But he kept walking, a smile tugging at the corners of his mouth as though he couldn't help himself.

"So this is how you stay in shape," he said, taking the last two steps in a single stride. Then his arms went around her and he kissed her so she forgot everything but the feel of his body against hers. After he had explored her mouth to his satisfaction, he lifted his head.

"I've been thinking about doing that all through rehearsal."

"I hope you were conducting Ravel's 'Bolero'," Anna said.

Nicholas threw back his head and laughed.

"You aren't the musical illiterate you pretend to be."

"Oh, come on," Anna scoffed, pushing off from his chest so she could close the door before one of her neighbors saw them. "Everyone knows it's the world's longest piece of foreplay."

Nicholas walked into the middle of her living room and pivoted, surveying the room closely. Anna tried to see her home through his eyes: would he find the combination of her favorite grandmother's Art Deco furniture and her own flea market finds whimsical or strange? She had tried to highlight the curving lines of the antique pieces by keeping the background simple with warm cream paint and light sheer curtains.

He ran his fingers over the wooden back of her favorite chair.

"It suits you. Unfussy, intelligent, and sensual."

"Thanks," Anna said, enjoying the double compliment, "but I thought you didn't notice furniture when I was in the room."

He shot her a glance from under his brows.

"It looks so normal. There are no bars on the windows or booby traps over the doors," he said.

"It's just like every other regular New Yorker's apartment."

"You have an alarm though," he said, spotting the keypad. His eyebrows went up as he read the name on it. "And a rather expensive one since I see it's from the same company as mine."

"I get a professional discount," Anna said. "Let me take your coat and I'll get you something to drink. My cellar doesn't run to 'Opus One' though."

"A beer would be fine," he said, wincing slightly as he slipped out of the soft leather jacket.

"Your arm hurts," she said. "Let me look at it."

"It's fine. It just pulls when I move a certain way."

"I'm going to look at it," she said, tossing the jacket over a chair and rolling his sleeve up to expose the bandage. She sighed in relief when no blood showed through the white gauze. "Didn't it hurt when you were conducting? You have to wave your arms around a lot."

"Fortunately, I have two arms," he said.

She unrolled the sleeve, her fingers lingering on the swell of muscle as it flexed under her touch. She didn't dare look up at him; he was too close and she was too aware of his presence in her own private space.

Picking up the discarded jacket, she couldn't resist sliding her hands inside to feel the warmth his body had imparted to the smooth satin lining before she hung it on a hook by the door. Shaking her head at herself, she went into the galley kitchen and opened a bottle of *Stella Artois*, pouring it down the side of the glass to kill the foam.

She went back into the living room and found her guest scanning the titles on her bookshelf.

"Locks, Safes, and Security: An International Police Reference. The Social Ecology of Crime. Investigating Murder: Detective Work and the Police Response to Criminal Homicide." He turned to take the tall glass from her. "I'm trying to come to terms with the fact that you get shot at so often you don't bother to keep track."

"It's not that I'm casual about it," Anna said, struggling to explain. "Mostly, there are shots fired when I'm in the area. They don't generally come that close to me because I know how to assess the situation and protect myself, and I've got the best partner on the force."

Nicholas shook his head and took a deep swallow of beer so Anna tried again.

"You take a risk every time you get up on the podium. You put yourself out there for the critics and the audience to judge. I just take a different kind of risk."

"The worst that could happen to me is getting hit by a rotten tomato," he said. "You could end up dead."

"You could get hit by a bus walking to Carnegie Hall. So could I. At least if someone's going to shoot at me, I get to wear a bulletproof vest."

"You weren't wearing a vest last night," he said, his voice taking on a husky note. "I'm quite sure of that."

Anna remembered his hands cupping her breasts through the gossamer chiffon and felt her nipples harden.

"Ultra-thin Kevlar," she joked, "developed especially for female detectives."

He put his glass down on the bookcase and took her by the shoulders, leaning forward to rest his forehead against hers.

"Ah, Anna, how can I do this?"

"Do what?"

"Love a woman who throws herself in front of bullets."

"I don't throw myself—" Anna stopped abruptly as the beginning of his sentence sank in. She stepped back from Nicholas so she could see his face.

His lips were curved in a rueful half smile but he watched her with an intensity that made it hard to meet his gaze.

She shoved her hands in her back pockets and looked at the ceiling. The monosyllable "love", spoken in his deep, cultured voice, kept ricocheting around in her mind, making it impossible to think of any other words. Love could mean so many things. It could be shorthand for "making love" or it could be something a man says to make a woman happy for awhile. But she didn't think Nicholas would use it in either of those ways and the possibility took her breath away and scared the hell out of her.

"I don't know what to say," she finally managed.

"I noticed. Ordinarily, I'd be pleased that I'd struck you speechless but not at this particular time."

His tone was dry but when she risked a quick peek at his face, the half smile was still there, much to her relief. She wanted to ask him to explain more fully what he meant but she was afraid of what she'd hear. Something of her indecision must have shown in her face because he drew her against him, tucking her head under his chin.

She pulled her hands out of her pockets and wrapped her arms around his waist, hiding her face against the soft weave of his tee-shirt and savoring the rise and fall of his chest against her cheek. She was embarrassed to feel tears welling up in her eyes.

"A positive sign," he said, his voice seeming louder and deeper because it rumbled through his chest. He took a deep breath before saying, "Anna, I won't deny I've made love to women without feeling more than a physical attraction to them but I don't make a habit of it."

"Well, that's a relief," she said.

After a moment, he said, "I suspect you don't make a habit of it either."

"No," she said, smiling because he felt the need for her to tell him so.

His arms tightened and his posture relaxed at the same time.

"I'm going to take that as another positive sign," he said, shifting his hand around to pry her face away from his chest and tilt her chin upward. "Are you crying?"

"Not really," she said. "I'm just surprised and I don't know what's going to happen next. We're so different, from such different worlds."

"Not so different. You seek justice and I seek beauty. Both require truth. That's important to both of us."

"Justice and truth. It sounds very grand but I'm just a cop, Nicholas. You're a scholar and an artist and a damned *genius*."

"You're taking Norman's press releases too seriously."

"No, I've been interviewing a lot of people who know what they're talking about and that's what *they* say."

"I need you, Anna," he said, all laughter gone from his voice. "When I saw Lexi slumped over the piano, I felt as though the world had been emptied of everything except anger and grief. Now I don't."

"But I haven't even caught his killer!"

"It doesn't matter as much anymore. Even if Ivanov never gets arrested, you've restored me."

"That's giving me a lot of credit I don't deserve."

He took her by the shoulders.

"You walked into the rehearsal room at Carnegie Hall to
interview me, and I knew you were as angry about Lexi's death
as I was. Yet you had never met him when he was alive.
You're an extraordinary person, Anna. I'm just a musician."

She took a deep breath.

"All right, I'll give you parity between a cop and a genius
for the sake of argument but you're filthy rich too."

"It's only money," he said.

"Spoken like a rich man."

He shook her very slightly.

"Don't accuse me of not knowing what it is to struggle."

"I'm sorry. The way you are now, it's hard to remember
where you came from," she said, touching his cheek in apology.

"Let me love you, Anna," he said.

She still didn't understand exactly what he was asking of
her but she decided to take it at face value for now and simply
nodded. She couldn't stop a smile as all her doubts and
reservations were swamped by the sheer delight of knowing
this magnificent man was worried about her feelings for him.
Nicholas Vranos had said he loved her! It was incredible and
unthinkable, yet at this moment she believed him, especially
when he slid his arms around her back and brought his lips
down on the curve of her throat, tasting her skin with his
tongue.

"Oh yes, Nicholas," she said, leaning back to give him
better access.

He took full advantage, bending lower to reach her left
breast, using his teeth to pull lightly on the nipple through her
thin tank top and bra. Her nipple hardened and sent a streak of
heat zinging down through the center of her body to melt
between her legs.

The first few notes of a cell phone's ring sounded and
both of them went still. As the sound resolved itself into a tune
Anna didn't recognize, she relaxed back into his arms. He
hesitated a moment before he moved to her other breast,
laughing with satisfaction when she fisted her hands in his hair

and pushed herself against him. He drew the already taut tip into his mouth, wetting the fabric so the scrape of his teeth was joined by the heat and motion of his tongue.

All Anna could do was hold on as bolt after bolt of sensation jolted through her.

"I want more of you," he said, straightening and cupping her bottom to lift her feet off the ground. Anna wrapped her legs around his waist and he groaned deeply as she pressed against his erection.

The same electronic tones issued from the pocket of his jeans. Anna could feel the phone vibrating against the inside of her thigh.

"That's Kathy Gromyko's ring. Again," he muttered.

Anna rested her forehead against his shoulder and heaved a long sigh before saying, "Answer it. If it were Mac, I would."

CHAPTER 28

Anna unhooked her legs and slid slowly down his body to the floor. Nicholas jerked the phone out of his pocket.

"Yes, Kathy," he snapped.

Anna was grinning until she saw his face grow taut with concern.

"Stay calm, it may not be as bad as you think," he said. "I'll come right out and you can show me. Yes, as soon as I can."

"What's wrong?" Anna asked, as he flipped the phone shut.

He looked down at the device in his hand before lifting his eyes to hers.

"Kathy doesn't want the police involved."

"Involved with what?"

"She thinks Lexi was involved in something illegal. She's found some kind of proof that the artifacts he brought back to this country were not obtained through legitimate channels. She doesn't want this to dirty Lexi's name now that he's dead."

"And you think she might be wrong?"

"She was on the verge of hysteria. I could barely make sense of what she was saying."

"You can't go anywhere without me," Anna said. "However, I won't come inside the house unless you ask me to. I'll trust your judgment on whether I need to know."

She locked her gaze with his and waited.

"You have my word your trust is not misplaced," he said.

She nodded, reassured that he understood what she had just offered him.

"I have a bulletproof vest in the trunk of my car," she said, starting toward her bedroom to get her own gear. "You'll be wearing it under your jacket. And I'll be covering the house myself. Mac will know where we are and have backup standing by."

Nicholas followed her, halting in the doorway to lean against the wooden molding.

"I feel as though I'm going into battle," he said, his gaze turning wolfish as she stripped off her tank top.

"You may be," she said, grabbing a black tee shirt out of a drawer. She pulled a bulletproof vest from the closet and fastened it over her shirt before she buckled on her holster. Drawing her Glock, she double-checked the magazine and inventoried the vest's pockets for backup ammunition. Then she did the same for the subcompact in her boot holster.

The wolfish gleam faded from his eyes as he watched her.

"Would you consider applying for a desk job?" he asked.

"Would you consider giving piano lessons to first graders?"

He shoved away from the door and stalked back into her living room.

Anna went on with her preparations but she felt tears prickle behind her eyelids. Annoyed with herself and Nicholas, she yanked a black windbreaker out of her closet and slammed the door before walking into the living room herself.

"Love me, love my job," she said.

He turned from staring out the window.

"I won't apologize for wanting you out of the way of flying bullets," he said. "However, I'll try to accept that it comes with the territory."

Tears surged again and she swallowed hard.

"Thank you," she managed to choke out. "It's not easy being with a cop. Mac's wife Letitia has the same problems."

"But the rewards are vast," he said, breaking the tension with a smile that socked her in the gut.

"Yes, well, here's the plan," she said. "I'm going to get the unmarked car and drive around to the fire escape in the back alley to pick you up. I'll call your cell phone when I want you to come down but it may be a few minutes because I want to see if I'm being followed first. When I call, go out the window in my bedroom and close it behind you. Get in the back seat so it looks as though I'm your driver if anyone picks us up en route. You do take hired cars around the city, don't you?"

"Often enough."

"I'll put the bulletproof vest in the back seat so you can put it on while we're driving."

"You're enjoying this," he said.

"No, it's just what I know how to do," she said.

He came over to her and bent his head close.

"Be careful," he whispered against her lips before he kissed her hard.

"No one's trying to shoot me. It's you I'm worried about." She kissed him back and headed for the door.

"What about the alarm?" he asked.

"I can set it from the car."

His eyebrows shot up.

"My system doesn't have that feature."

"I've got better toys than you do, I guess," she said, slipping out of the door with a grin.

Anna didn't see any sign of a tail on their way out to Queens. While she drove, she asked Nicholas to describe the layout of Kathy Gromyko's house. Then she notified Mac of where they were headed and put two teams of local cops on alert for backup, just in case.

As Anna turned the corner three blocks away from their destination, she laid her Glock on the seat beside her and said, "When I pull up in front of the house, I'll start to get out as though I'm going to come around and open your door. Do a nice sweeping gesture—you're good at those—telling me to stay put and get out quickly by yourself. That will keep my face turned away from anyone who might be watching from inside."

"Being a conductor has some practical uses, I see," he said.

Anna grinned at him in the rear view mirror before she continued. "I'm going to park out of sight. In five minutes,

call me on my cell phone. If I don't hear from you, I'll assume
something's wrong and act accordingly."

"Which means?"

"Whatever I think is necessary," Anna said. "What time
do you have?"

"Five twenty-one," he said, glancing at his watch
impatiently. "Don't you think you're overreacting?"

"Not when you have a bullet wound in your arm."

He made a gesture so eloquent Anna laughed.

"You are *really* good at that."

Nicholas didn't share her amusement.

"I'll calm Kathy down and find out what she thinks will
damage Lexi's name and I'll call you," he said.

Anna nodded as she came to a smooth stop at the curb.
They enacted their planned charade. Anna held her gun
cradled on her lap and watched Nicholas walk up the short
sidewalk in the side-view mirror. She held her breath until the
door opened to show Kathy Gromyko standing inside. Putting
the car in gear, she drove a few blocks to a mini-mart parking
lot and slid into an inconspicuous space.

Nicholas leaned down to kiss the distraught woman on her
tear-stained cheek. Something of Anna's worry had infected
him so he deliberately left the front door slightly ajar behind
him.

"What is it, Kathy? What's upset you?" he asked, holding
her gently at arm's length so he could see her face.

She tried to speak but all that came out were great gulping
sobs.

Suddenly, a man's voice called from the back of the house.

"Bring him in here."

Nicholas let go of Kathy and spun around but there was
no one in the central hallway.

"He's—he's in the family room," she finally managed to
whisper.

"Who?" Nicholas asked in a low voice.

She shook her head and tugged on his wrist.

Nicholas didn't move.

"Please," she begged. "He's got Vera and Peter."

The conductor bit off a curse.

"Here?"

"No, a woman took them away right before I called you."

"Bring him here *now*," the man commanded, a faint accent sounding through the impatient tone.

Nicholas pushed Kathy behind him and walked down the hall, stepping through the second door on his left.

Viktor Ivanov stood in the dim light filtering through the closed slat of the shades, a gun gleaming in his hand.

"Come in, Dr. Vranos," he said. "And Mrs. Gromyko as well. Sit down on the couch."

The gun pointed unwaveringly in Nicholas' direction as the conductor reluctantly sat. As his eyes adjusted to the dimness, he noted the Russian was wearing gloves, a detail that sent a chill through his blood.

"You should have taken the bribe the Archduke offered you," Ivanov said. "Then you would have been useful. Now you are an obstacle. Just to let you know, Mrs. Gromyko's children are being held unharmed at the moment. However, if I do not call my assistant at certain set times, you will never see them again."

"He's going to shoot us both, Nicholas," Kathy suddenly said. "He made me write a suicide note, accusing you of murdering Lexi."

"Enough," Ivanov snapped.

"I'll support the manuscript's authenticity," Nicholas said, his eyes locked on Ivanov's face. "If you kill me, I won't be able to tell anyone I've changed my opinion so there will still be doubt."

"I thought of that, but it's too difficult to guarantee your ongoing complicity," the ex-KGB agent said. "We've found another Beethoven scholar who's more easily convinced of the

symphony's genuineness. If you are not here to contradict
him—" Ivanov shrugged.

"The police will still have the proof Lexi found showing
the symphony is a fraud," Nicholas said. "The offer from
Randall Johnson was a setup."

Ivanov said something in Russian that made Kathy gasp.

"Savenkov had nothing," Ivanov continued in English.
"Otherwise he wouldn't have carried the manuscript here."

"He wasn't sure exactly what he had which is why he
gave it to me," Nicholas said.

"Savenkov lied and you're lying. Nothing left the
Archduke's palace except the manuscript," Ivanov said.

"And the sketchbooks," Nicholas said. "It was in one of
those."

"*What* was in the sketchbook?"

"A piece of paper with fingerprints on it. They belonged
to a hit-and-run victim named Franz Gadde, a brilliant young
student of composition."

Nicholas was drawing out the revelation, hoping to fill
Anna's five minutes and then some.

"I know who Franz Gadde is. He worked for the
Archduke," Ivanov said. "What was on the paper?"

"Five staves of music, filled with musical experimentation.
Some of it was from the sketchbook, modified to fit between
two passages in the symphony. One of the experiments found
its way into the symphony itself."

"That means nothing. He could have simply been
copying from the original and playing with it."

"That would be possible except the phrase he chose to use
was not from the sketchbooks. It was his signature."

"Signature? What does that mean?" Despite Ivanov's
increasing agitation, the gun never moved.

"It's a combination of the notes F, G, A, D, D, and E with
a sharp inserted on the G."

The spate of Russian was furious until a cell phone's ring interrupted him. He touched a button on the earpiece he was wearing and spoke in the same language into it.

"What's he saying?" Nicholas asked Kathy under his breath.

"He's saying there's a delay and to call him back at the next scheduled time," she whispered back.

Ivanov touched the button again and said, "*Zwei.*" As he waited for the phone to dial the programmed number, he gave Nicholas a hard look.

"We will check part of your story," he said, before breaking into German.

Nicholas had a rudimentary knowledge of the language and could follow most of the conversation. Ivanov was telling the person on the other side of the conversation to get the copy of the symphony. Triumph surged through Nicholas' body; his delaying tactics had worked. Now all he had to worry about was Anna getting shot. Fury instantly replaced triumph.

"Where is the so-called signature?" Ivanov asked Nicholas in English.

"In the fourth movement, about six pages from the end. There are twelve measures of the theme with variations."

Ivanov went back to his conversation, explaining the sequence of notes and where it was located.

"What's going on?" Nicholas asked when Ivanov touched the earpiece again.

"Someone is checking the manuscript."

"The Archduke?"

Ivanov ignored his question.

"Take off your jacket," he commanded instead. "Slowly and without touching the pockets."

Nicholas drew the zipper down as deliberately as he could, trying to delay the moment when Ivanov discovered he was wearing a police-issue bulletproof vest. Easing his arms out of the sleeves, he kept his eyes on their captor, waiting for the right moment to tender a plausible explanation. He knew the moment Ivanov recognized his unusual accessory.

"Where the f--k did you get that?" Ivanov said, taking three steps closer so he could examine the vest more closely.

"The police gave it to me after you shot at me last night."

"If I'd shot at you, you wouldn't still be alive," the ex-KGB agent said flatly. "Take the vest off."

"It's not easy to hit a moving target across Isaac Stern Auditorium," Nicholas said, as he started to unfasten the vest. He paused and rolled up his sleeve slowly to show the bandage. "You did wing me."

The Russian seemed about to smile at the sight of the injury but the expression was gone the next instant.

"Take it off," he said again.

Nicholas went back to the fastenings and shrugged out of the heavy garment, letting it fall behind him on the couch on top of his leather jacket.

Kathy put her head in her hands and began to shake silently.

"May I?" Nicholas asked sardonically, holding his arm out behind her shoulders but not touching her until Ivanov nodded.

The conductor wrapped his arm around her and pulled her against him, shifting sideways so the bulletproof vest was closer to Kathy. He started to whisper words of comfort but Ivanov barked, "No talking."

Nicholas tightened his grip on the weeping woman and gave the Russian's cold stare right back to him. There was no sound in the room except an occasional stifled whimper from Kathy and the sound of a passing car. The tension in the room wound tighter and tighter. The sudden chitter of a fussing squirrel made Kathy flinch against Nicholas' side and drop her hands.

When the cell phone rang, Nicholas saw the gun jerk in Ivanov's hand, and the conductor's lips curved into a savage smile. Taking advantage of the Russian's divided attention,

Nicholas took one of Kathy's hands and made her grip the edge of the bulletproof vest behind their backs, hoping she understood she should use it if possible.

Their captor spent most of the conversation listening, so Nicholas couldn't guess what the Archduke was saying on the other end.

"F--king egomaniac composer," he muttered after he disconnected. "I should have burned him alive in his apartment."

Ivanov adjusted the angle of his gun so it was pointed directly at Nicholas' heart.

"Stand up," he ordered.

CHAPTER 29

Anna froze with her back against the left wall of Kathy Gromyko's hallway as a chill ran down her spine. The tone in Viktor Ivanov's voice made her decide she couldn't wait for backup.

Taking a deep breath, she steadied her gun in both hands and spun around the doorjamb, shouting, "Police! You're under arrest."

"Ivanov has a gun," Nicholas' voice rang out.

"Don't shoot him! They'll kill my children!" a woman shrieked at the same time.

Her brain registered Nicholas standing in front of a sofa to her left even as she brought the muzzle of her Glock to bear on Ivanov to her right.

"I'm not going to shoot anyone," she said calmly, although she wanted to very badly when she saw the Russian aiming at Nicholas' chest. Ivanov glanced briefly at Anna before returning his attention to the man standing in front of him. Nicholas' stance radiated frustrated fury, and Anna worried he was about to do something foolhardy.

"A cop?" Ivanov said, having read the white lettering on her jacket. "I thought you were FBI."

"Does it matter?" Anna said, sliding farther to the right so the Russian couldn't see her without turning his head.

"I might have been a little more careful," he said. "Move back to where you were or I'll shoot Vranos."

Anna moved back.

"Drop your gun," the Russian said.

"No!" Nicholas said. "He'll just shoot all of us."

"Drop your gun or I will have Mrs. Gromyko's children killed."

"I have no intention of dropping my gun," Anna said calmly, as a voice in her earphone confirmed the local police had arrived and silently surrounded the house as per her instructions. She hoped they followed the rest of her directions and stayed in place until she called them. "You don't want to kill babies, Ivanov. You're already facing two murder charges in this case. Don't add to your problems."

She'd read all of Interpol's file on the ex-KGB agent. While his orders had sent many people to their deaths, he hadn't done any killing himself in recent years. That didn't mean he had a conscience but at least he didn't seem to get a thrill from the act itself, as some agents did.

"I heard the woman who took them say something about a room key," Kathy Gromyko said suddenly. "They must be at a motel."

"Shut up," Ivanov said. Anna could see a sheen of sweat gleaming on his forehead. He was not as imperturbable as he pretended. "We seem to be at a standoff."

"Not at all," Anna said, her voice as steady as her gun. "The house is surrounded by cops. We can start scouring the area for a woman and two children in a motel but it would be a lot easier for you if you simply told us where they are."

"Easier for *you*," Ivanov said. Suddenly, his face contorted with rage and he swung the gun around to point it at Anna. "Do you know how much time and money I invested in this f--king symphony?" He swiveled back to aim at Nicholas' head. "Do you know how many millions of dollars your f--king interference has cost me?"

Anna saw the muscles of Nicholas' thighs flex and tighten and she wanted to yell at him as she realized he was going to attack an armed man. She adjusted her aim slightly and, with a heartfelt prayer, squeezed the trigger. Nicholas sprang at Ivanov just as her bullet smashed the gun out of the Russian's hand and shattered the glass of the window beyond. Ivanov screamed and the two men crashed to the floor in a writhing mass of limbs.

"Hold your fire," Anna yelled into her earpiece as she heard the front door slam open.

She ran closer to the struggling fighters just as Nicholas rolled Ivanov onto his back and locked his long fingers around the Russian's throat.

"Tell me where the children are or I will crush your throat like an eggshell," he snarled into Ivanov's purpling face. He must have tightened his grip further because the other man's mouth gaped open as he tried to draw in air.

"You'll have to let him breathe so he can talk," Anna said, as she bent down to pick up the Russian's gun. She wasn't going to underestimate his KGB training.

After a moment, Nicholas' fingers relaxed slightly although he kept them wrapped around Ivanov's neck.

"Where are they?" he growled again.

The Russian tried to swallow and breathe at the same time, bringing on a coughing fit. Anna saw Nicholas' shoulders tense again.

"Give him more time," she said. "He's trying to tell you."

"C-c-come On In Motel," Ivanov rasped. "Room 312."

Anna turned to the police officers who had come through the door while Nicholas was literally squeezing the information out of Ivanov.

"You know where that motel is?" The officers nodded. "A woman and two children named Vera and Peter, ages four and two years," she said before turning back to Ivanov. "Is the woman armed?"

He didn't try to speak through his bruised throat, just nodded an affirmative.

"Mrs. Gromyko," she said to the woman still huddled behind Nicholas' bulletproof vest. "Can you confirm that?"

"I didn't see any weapon," she said lowering the vest, "but she had a big handbag and he said she'd kill them if I didn't get Nicholas to come here alone. I believed him."

"I would have too," Anna said before looking back at the officers. "Be careful."

They left and three other policemen approached Nicholas and Ivanov.

"We'll take him now," one said to the musician.

Nicholas straightened his fingers and rose to his feet as the cops rolled Ivanov over and cuffed his hands behind his back.

Anna wanted to throw her arms around Nicholas and sob her relief that he was alive and unharmed. She also wanted to scream at him for endangering himself.

"Are you all right?" she asked quietly, mindful of the many cops milling around in the room.

He looked at her, and she felt a punch of shock at the fury still burning in his eyes.

"Except for the fact that I didn't get to kill the son of a bitch, I'm fine," he said.

An electronic tone sounded from Ivanov's pocket and the room went still.

"Answer it," Anna said. "Tell her the police are on the way, and she and the children should go with them. Speak only in English."

One of the cops reached into Ivanov's jacket and brought the phone to his ear.

The look of hatred the Russian sent her way made Anna wonder if he would cooperate or if he would have Vera and Peter killed out of sheer spite. However, he followed her orders and, after some tense minutes, the cops reported they had all three in custody.

Kathy Gromyko let out a cry of pure relief and collapsed on the couch sobbing. Anna was tempted to join her. She felt her customary pang of envy when Nicholas strode across the room to cradle the hysterical woman against his chest. He seemed to sense her yearning because his gaze met hers over Kathy's head in a look that made the air whoosh out of Anna's lungs. His arms might be wrapped around Kathy Gromyko but his eyes made it very clear he wanted Anna there instead.

She had to turn away before she did something stupid. She put Ivanov's gun down on the computer desk by the door.

"Who fired the shot?" the Queens police lieutenant asked.

"I did," Anna said.

"At?"

"I shot the gun out of Ivanov's hand."

"Nice work," the man said with a low whistle, "but risky."

"He had two hostages and one of them was about to go straight for him. I didn't want to chance killing Ivanov until we knew where the children were," Anna said, but the lieutenant was right. It had been a calculated risk, made possible partly because the Russian had such a steady hand that she could count on his gun's position. She had taken it when she realized she was too far away to throw herself between Nicholas and the gun.

"What the hell is going on here?" Mac said, almost knocking over Anna as he barreled into the room.

"Thank God!" she muttered under her breath before speaking to her partner. "Ivanov set a trap. He was planning to kill Vranos and Mrs. Gromyko, making it look like a murder/suicide triggered by Lexi's murder. He used Mrs. Gromyko's children as leverage."

"Everyone okay?" Mac asked, scanning the controlled chaos behind her.

Anna nodded, and Mac looked at Ivanov where he stood penned between two policemen.

"You got the bastard," he said with satisfaction.

"You want us to bring him to your precinct house in a cruiser with a cage?" the lieutenant asked.

"And a couple of escort cars too," Anna said, nodding. "With his KGB background, I'm not taking any chances on losing him in transit."

"You got it." He turned to his men. "Let's get him locked up."

"I need medical attention," Ivanov managed to croak as the cops pushed him into motion. "My hand's broken and I can barely swallow."

"Ask for a doctor when you get to jail," Anna said with an utter lack of concern.

Ivanov stopped dead in front of her and gave her a cold smile.

"You think you've solved your case," he rasped out, "but I didn't kill Savenkov."

"Right," Anna said. "So tell me who did."

"You want me to do your job for you? It should be obvious." He looked long and deliberately at Nicholas before shifting his gaze back to Anna.

"Get this piece of dirt out of here," she snapped.

The cops jerked Ivanov forward and out of the room.

"Will you mop up?" Anna said to Mac. "I'm beat."

"Sure thing," he agreed, giving her a searching look before he stepped further into the room.

Anna walked out of the family room, down the hall and into the kitchen. She braced her forearm against the cool steel of the refrigerator door, dropped her head against her arm, and gave in to a serious case of the shakes.

When Ivanov had lost it and raised his pistol toward Nicholas' head, she'd been terrified to the marrow of her bones. Terrified the Russian would really pull the trigger. Terrified her aim would be off. But most of all, terrified by the vision of how utterly empty her world would be without Nicholas in it.

That was what made her shake so hard her teeth clicked together.

She heard footsteps on the linoleum floor and then she was lifted away from the refrigerator and engulfed in Nicholas' arms.

"Anna, Anna, are you all right?" he asked.

She could feel the dampness where Kathy's tears had soaked into his shirt and smell the sharp tang of adrenalin-induced sweat. She tried to nod in answer to his question but he seemed to be trying to merge the two of them into one entity so she just wrapped her arms around his waist and squeezed.

"As soon as you came through the door, I cursed myself for stalling until you could arrive with the cavalry," he said.

"If Kathy and her children hadn't been involved, I would have dealt with the bastard myself."

Anna managed to wedge her arms between them so she could look up at his face.

"You did the right thing. He was armed. You weren't."

He cradled her head in his hands, his gaze devouring her face before his mouth came down on hers with a fierceness that would have scared Anna two hours ago. Now she kissed him back with equal intensity.

After a long time, she tilted her head away from his.

"I've never been afraid before," she said. "I've been angry at the perp or worried about a bystander's safety or even ticked at Mac for putting himself in danger but I've never felt terror until I saw Ivanov point a gun at your head. I actually prayed. It's been years since I've done that."

She felt his chest rise and fall as he took in a long breath.

"Now you can understand my position," he said.

"Lieutenant Salazar!" someone called from the hallway.

Nicholas dropped his arms and stepped back.

"On my way," Anna called back, wishing he hadn't been so quick to release her. "We'll have to go to the station and do paperwork. It would be easier if you came with us."

"Of course."

Something about his manner made her uneasy. He suddenly looked every inch the impresario, magnificent and untouchable.

"Nicholas—"

"Salazar, let's get moving," Mac said, walking into the kitchen.

Nicholas gestured for her to go in front of him and they were swallowed up in the swirl of activity outside.

CHAPTER 30

Hidden behind the two-way mirror, Anna watched as Mac made a gesture of exasperation and stalked out of the interrogation room. Ignoring the two policemen standing in the room, Viktor Ivanov turned to stare straight at the mirror and repeated yet again, "Savenkov was dead when I walked into that room. You can't prove I committed a crime I'm innocent of."

Anna put her hand to her head and massaged her aching temples. They'd gotten a lot of information about the forged Tenth Symphony out of the Russian, especially after they brought in the Archduke and he tried to disavow all knowledge of the scheme. Furthermore, the ex-KGB agent admitted Lexi had insisted Ivanov come to Carnegie Hall to meet him, saying he had an important question about the Tenth Symphony. The Russian was the one who had gone through Lexi's pockets after he was dead, desperately searching for anything that might be connected with the manuscript. He admitted he had worn a disguise because he knew there would be video cameras and he didn't want to be identified. His description of his encounter with Jessica Strauss matched hers. He had been so furious at being thwarted in his meeting with Savenkov that he'd been careless when he encountered the young woman.

However, the Russian continued to maintain he hadn't murdered Lexi Savenkov. Or run down Franz Gadde.

Of course, a murder charge was much more serious than the white collar crime of forgery so it made sense for Ivanov to deny his guilt.

Unfortunately, the ballistics report on Ivanov's gun came back as matching neither the bullet that killed Lexi nor the one that wounded Nicholas. Ivanov had predicted this would be the case but he could easily have used and disposed of a different pistol or two; he had all the necessary contacts to obtain firearms.

The observation room door swung open and Mac dropped into a chair beside her.

"He's been on the other side of an interrogation too often. We're not going to get anything out of him he doesn't want to tell us," he said. "The woman's useless, just a hired hand with no prior connection to Ivanov."

Anna grimaced in agreement.

"The Archduke's the weak link," she said.

"Yeah, but he didn't do the dirty work."

"All he has to do is implicate Ivanov."

Mac shook his head.

"Ain't gonna happen. All we've got them on is trying to sell a document they knew was a fake, and maybe even creating it."

"I think we need to get in touch with Interpol about dead forgers," Anna said. "If Ivanov killed Gadde, he probably killed the poor schmuck who copied Beethoven's handwriting onto the antique paper."

"Good idea. I'm hoping we can connect Ivanov with the fire in Savenkov's apartment based on the arson in Gadde's place in Vienna since Ivanov basically admitted to setting that. And the cops in Vienna are re-opening Gadde's hit-and-run case to see if they can shake something loose there. They want Ivanov either in jail or out of their country."

"I'm looking for the former myself," Anna said.

"You're such a hard-ass," Mac said, giving her shoulder an affectionate squeeze. "Why don't you take a break? I'll keep an eye on our friend."

"Thanks. I'll be in our office if you need me," Anna said, standing up and stretching.

As she passed through the precinct house, she took some ribbing about bringing in a former KGB agent. By the time she got to her office door, she was looking forward to putting her head down on her desk and closing her eyes for a few minutes.

"Hello, Anna," Nicholas said from the same chair he'd occupied on his last visit.

She pulled the door closed behind her.

"You didn't have to stay," she said, leaning down to kiss him.

He cupped his hands around her head and held her lips against his for a long moment before he released her.

"Did you get anything from Ivanov?" he asked.

"Not about Lexi," she said, collapsing into her desk chair. "Ivanov swears he was dead already."

Nicholas slammed his fist onto the arm of his chair.

"It's hard because he's an experienced interrogator himself," Anna said. "But we're working on other angles too. We'll get him somehow, trust me."

"I agreed to do that the day we met," Nicholas said.

His tone was almost nostalgic, as though he was reminiscing about something fond but distant. Anna couldn't put her finger on why that bothered her; she was just too tired.

"What will happen to the forged document?" he asked.

"It'll be kept for evidence until any legal proceedings are finished. Then I guess it will be destroyed so no one else tries to pass it off as real."

"Would I be able to buy it? It's an interesting composition, and I'd hate to have Franz Gadde's work be completely lost."

"I'll see what I can do," Anna said. "You'd probably have to sign a million disclaimers and bonds and things but the Department always needs extra cash."

"So a contribution would be . . . useful," he said.

"It would undoubtedly grease the wheels," Anna said, disturbed by the cynicism in his voice. "You know, as much as I'd like to curl up in your lap right now, you should go home."

For a moment, the strain on his face eased. Then the frown lines returned and he ran his fingers through his hair, leaving it even more rumpled than before. He pushed up out of his chair and Anna did the same.

"Shall I come to your apartment tonight if it's not too late?" she asked, wanting to obliterate the terror of the day in his bed.

"Come whenever you can get away. I don't care how late it is."

They met halfway around Anna's desk. He looked down at her with the intensity she found both unnerving and thrilling. Then he bent to kiss her deeply. When he released her, he picked up his jacket and walked out the door without another word.

Sometime after midnight, Mac looked at Anna across their paperwork-strewn desks and said, "I'm turning into a stinking pumpkin. We're calling it a day."

"And night," Anna said, tossing her pen down with a sigh of relief. "God, I'm tired."

Yet the anticipation of seeing Nicholas sent a sweet jolt of adrenalin through her blood.

"What are you smiling about?" Mac asked as he shut down his computer.

"The thought of Ivanov stewing in a holding cell," she lied.

"And they call women the gentler sex," Mac said.

Anna picked up her holster off the back of her chair and started to slide it onto her shoulder. She stopped and thought for a moment before shrugging it back off and locking it in her desk drawer.

Mac raised an eyebrow but said nothing.

The two detectives grabbed their jackets and walked out of the building together, arguing about who got to drive the next day.

"Don't forget, breakfast at my place tomorrow," Mac said. "Tish'll have my head if she doesn't get to stuff you with a proper Scottish meal."

"Got it," Anna said, setting the alarm on her digital wristwatch. She didn't trust herself to remember anything at all once she walked into Nicholas' arms.

By the time Anna got to the front door of Nicholas' building she was practically humming with anticipation.

"Evening, Lieutenant," the doorman said as he swung open the heavy door before she could identify herself. "I guess you worked late."

She smiled and thanked him before jogging to the elevator. Using the polished brass panel for a mirror, she loosened her hair from its braid and brushed it into smooth waves over her shoulders. Then she decided to take off the NYPD windbreaker which left her in jeans and a black tee shirt, the best she could do.

The doorman must have called ahead because Nicholas stood in his open door, looking so elegant in a black silk shirt and crisply pressed black slacks that she instantly felt rumpled and dirty. However, a shower and shave hadn't expunged the grim lines that had settled around his mouth. She closed the distance between them, pulling his head down for a kiss that held all her terror, longing, frustration, and triumph in it. A tendril of confusion snaked through her mind when he seemed to hesitate before responding, but once his arms tightened around her, she lost herself in the feel of his silky hair sliding against her fingers, the sharp fragrance of soap mixed with his own warm, male scent, and the sound of his breathing growing more ragged as she entwined her legs with his to pull herself closer to his body. He wove his hands into the fall of her hair and groaned into her mouth.

"Anna, you drive every rational thought out of my mind," he said.

She tilted her head back, both to laugh and to offer him her neck.

"It's a gift," she said, purring as his lips brushed the sensitive triangle at the base of her throat. "And you're giving it back to me. The last thing I want to do right now is think."

At that, he shifted, resting his forehead against hers before he carefully untangled his hands from her hair.

"Where's the gun?" he asked, touching her holster-less shoulder.

"Locked in a drawer in my office. I decided to leave my job behind for the night."

She waited for some acknowledgement of her concession but he made no comment.

"I have wine waiting," he said, taking her arm and leading her to the bar in the living room. One of the French doors to the terrace stood open and the hum of an occasional car passing on the street drifted in, softened by its flight upward through fourteen stories of dense New York air.

Nicholas handed her a balloon glass of deep red wine and touched it with his own goblet.

"To capturing Lexi's murderer," he said.

"To convicting Lexi's murderer," Anna corrected before she took a sip.

The complex flavors of the wine flooded her palate and she closed her eyes to savor them. She didn't lift her eyelids again until the liquid was sliding down her throat, leaving a trail of pleasure in its wake.

She caught Nicholas watching her, the incandescent blue of his eyes adding heat to the effect of the wine. Then he looked away.

"Let's go outside," he said.

"Wow!" Anna said as she preceded him through the door. The tile-paved terrace seemed almost as vast as Nicholas' living room since it swept across the front and around the sides of the building. Between anchoring brick pillars, the ornate polished steel railing glinted in the myriad lights of the great city. Trees and plants in massive terra cotta pots created "rooms" for several groupings of wrought iron chairs and stone-topped tables.

Anna looked beyond the terrace itself to survey the dimly lit treetops and lawns of Central Park spread before her like an enormous garden.

"Wow," she said again.

As she moved away from the shelter of the building, the wind played with her hair, sending stray tendrils trailing across her face.

She started to lift her hand to pull them away but Nicholas was faster, his long fingers deftly gathering the strands and smoothing them to the back of her head.

"It's always windier up here than at street level," he said.

"Thanks," Anna murmured, still enjoying the ripple of pleasure his touch always created.

She took another swallow of wine as she contemplated the differences between Nicholas' home and hers. None of them made her happy.

"Anna."

She jumped slightly and turned toward him as his deep voice interrupted her cataloging.

"How far north can you see on a clear day?" she asked.

"To the Bronx," he said.

"From my place, I can see the McDonald's three blocks away," she said.

He didn't smile.

"Anna, I learned something today."

"Something bad, evidently," Anna said, noting the rigidity of his shoulders.

He turned his blue gaze on her full force.

"You're an extraordinary person," he said. "I admire your integrity, your courage, your willingness to put your life at risk for the safety of others." His attempt at a smile twisted painfully. "I admire your beauty and I crave your body. Today when Viktor Ivanov turned his gun toward you and I thought he was going to pull the trigger, I—" he stopped as his hand traced despair and denial in the air. "I realized I couldn't stop him and it nearly destroyed me."

He brought the wine glass to his lips, and Anna watched the muscles of his throat work as he swallowed.

"I'm a selfish man. I want you safe. However, I can't ask you to stop doing what you feel most passionately about, any more than you would ask me to stop conducting. That would poison everything between us."

Anna wrapped her arms around her waist.

He started to reach for her but thrust his hand into his pocket and drew in a deep breath before he continued.

"In my life, there have been very few people whom I've loved without reservation. All of them are dead except you. I don't think I could survive your addition to that list."

The lights of Manhattan seemed to flicker and dim around them as Anna stood silent. She knew he was waiting for her to say something but she couldn't speak.

"Lexi always said I needed to control people and that's why I chose conducting as a profession." Nicholas' laugh was short and bitter. "Once again I've proved he knew me better than I know myself."

Anna stared at him, standing dark against the artificial glow of the city sky, his hair teased by the same breeze that rippled the black silk of his shirt, a study in light and shadow except for the deep red of the wine.

The distance between them seemed to expand despite their motionlessness. A car's horn sounded, and the noise jabbed at Anna's eardrums like a scalpel.

"What are you saying?" she finally asked.

He turned his gaze out toward the park.

"I love you too much to bear what you are," he said. "I love you too much to ask you to be less than what you are. That leaves me with only one choice. To let you go on being what you are without me."

Anna tried to stifle the sob that forced itself out of her throat but he heard it.

"Oh God, Anna!" he said, starting toward her.

She held her hand out to stop him.

"Please, I understand. Not everyone can handle being with a cop."

It was true. She'd seen too many divorces in the department because a spouse couldn't withstand the constant anxiety that on any given day a cop might not come home. At least Nicholas had figured it out before their relationship progressed any further and the pain of separation grew even worse.

Although she couldn't imagine anything worse than the fingers of despair ripping at her gut right this minute.

Until she thought of something else. *Maybe Mac had been right and Nicholas had just used her to feed him information on the case. He wasn't the murderer but he was focused on bringing Lexi's killer to justice.*

She shoved the idea away as fast as she thought it. She couldn't believe that of Nicholas.

"It's better we find out now," she added just to fill the silence. She couldn't manage anything more because her throat was closed tight against the tears she was trying not to shed.

She started toward the open door, before realizing she still held the glass of wine. Veering toward a table, she put the goblet down so clumsily that the slender stem snapped and the fragile bowl shattered on the stone top.

"Damn it!" she said as the wine spread like a bloodstain.

The accident seemed to release Nicholas from his immobility. In two strides he was beside Anna, pulling her into his arms.

"It's nothing," he said. "Forget it."

His touch broke her. She wrapped her fists in the silk of his shirt as great racking sobs shook her.

Nicholas knew she wasn't weeping over the spilled wine and he held her, stroking her hair until her emotion was spent. Had she been able to see the desolation in his eyes, Anna might have tried to argue him out of his decision but her tear-streaked face was pressed hard against his chest. She wanted to memorize the feel and smell of him before he let her go for the last time.

"I've never regretted being a cop before," she said as she stepped back and he dropped his arms.

"You shouldn't regret it now."

He pulled a handkerchief out of his back pocket and handed it to her.

"So you don't use these just for dress-up," she said, unfolding the fine white cotton square and swiping it across her cheeks.

"One of Paul's legacies," he said, following her lead into meaningless small talk. "He hated paper tissues."

In a moment of truly pathetic weakness, Anna blew her nose on the handkerchief.

"I'll wash this and return it to you," she said, tucking it into her jeans pocket.

"Keep it," he said, as she had known he would when she soiled it. It would give her one small memento to cling to.

"I'll make sure you're kept up-to-date on the case," Anna said, starting to back toward the door. "And I'll pass on your request for the forged symphony."

"Thank you," Nicholas said, following her.

Anna turned and strode into the brilliantly lit living room, trying to ignore the fact that she could feel Nicholas behind her at every step. She kept going until she reached the foyer. The scent of lilies saturated the air to the point of suffocation and she reached for the door handle.

"Anna," he said, stopping her with his voice.

She stood staring at the grain of the oak panels.

He walked around her and cupped her face in his long fingers.

"Remember the music," he said.

Anna stood absolutely still under his caress and he released her.

"I don't think I'll be listening to Beethoven for a while," she said, before turning on her heel and slipping out the door.

Somehow she smiled at the doorman as he once again held the entrance door for her. She walked out into the artificial glare of the city night and stopped on the sidewalk.

Then Anna did something no sane New Yorker would ever do: she walked into Central Park at 2 A.M.

CHAPTER 31

"Anna, come in, come in," Letitia said, opening the glossy green front door of a brownstone in Brooklyn. Her elegant silver hair was pulled back in a bun and she exuded the scents of warm bread and lavender. "I've got a proper Scottish break—what's wrong, lass?"

The older woman stepped back to let Anna inside, then closed the door and wrapped her arms around her, saying, "What's happened to my poor wee lassie? Tell Tisha."

Anna realized she must look like hell because for all the warmth of her generous heart, Letitia was not given to hugging. A quick peck on the cheek was her usual style.

"N-nothing. I didn't sleep much," Anna said. She'd walked in the park for a long time, almost hoping someone would try to mug her so she could find a physical release for all the anguish pent up inside her. When she finally returned to her apartment, she'd fallen on the bed fully clothed and slept like a corpse for the few hours left of the night.

"Don't try to fool me," Letitia said. "You look as though you've lost every friend you ever had in the world."

Mac walked in from the kitchen, and Anna fought off her desire to collapse into Letitia's arms and sob.

"Hey, Mac," she said over Letitia's shoulder.

"Ach, Kevin," the Scotswoman said, turning to her husband while keeping her arm around Anna's waist. "Anna and I are going to have some girl talk in the bedroom. Will you watch the scones in the oven for me? And no sneaking a sausage, mind you."

"I never touch the stuff," Mac said with a smirk at his partner. "But I might borrow a scone."

"Be off with you, man," Letitia said, leading Anna back to the couple's bedroom.

It was furnished with a matched furniture suite in heavy dark wood. A puffy plaid quilt covered the bed and a set of bagpipes decorated one wall. Another was adorned with crossed golf clubs over a painting of a field of heather.

Anna couldn't even muster her usual quip about Letitia being from France.

Letitia pulled her over to the bed and plunked them both down on the quilt.

"I'm just tired," Anna said. "It's been a rough case."

Letitia gave her a look that spoke volumes of disbelief.

"You've got despair in your eyes," she said. "Is it the conductor?"

Anna swallowed and nodded.

"What's the bampot done to my lass?"

"What's a bampot?"

Letitia waved a hand in dismissal.

"Ach, it's not a nice thing to call someone," she said.

"Good."

"I'm glad you've got some spirit left," Letitia said. "Now tell me what's fashing you."

"He can't handle my being a cop," Anna said. "He doesn't want me getting shot at."

"You can't blame him for that. I don't want you getting shot at either."

"Yes, or no, or whatever, but he doesn't want to have a-a relationship with me. He says he's lost too many people he loves and he can't do it again."

"I see," Letitia said. "He was orphaned when he was young, wasn't he?"

Anna nodded again.

"And his adoptive father died not long ago."

"That's right."

"And his best friend was just murdered."

"Just because I understand doesn't make it hurt any less," Anna said.

"Of course not," Letitia agreed. "I'm just thinking he needs more time for the wounds to heal. He must be a strong man to have gotten to where he is and he'll find the strength to love you."

"I don't know," Anna said in a low voice. "Mac said all along Nicholas was using me to get information on the case. What if that's true?"

"Do *you* believe it, lass? In your heart of hearts?"

Anna shook her head.

"But I'm not the most unbiased judge."

"Well, no more do I. Mac says the man was mad for you the moment he saw you."

"This may be better in the long run," Anna said. "We're from different worlds. He's, well, you know what he is: a musical genius who hangs out with royalty and presidents and lives in an enormous place on the Upper West Side furnished with priceless antiques. I'm just a cop who can barely afford the payments on her little apartment that's not even quite in Soho."

"Don't you go running yourself down. He came from nothing."

"Exactly, and look where he is now," Anna said.

"And look where you are: the youngest detective ever to make the homicide squad of a proud police force in one of the most famous cities in the world. Lift your chin, lass, and look me in the eye. Now tell me you don't believe you're as good as any man."

Anna followed her instructions and found herself held in Letitia's fierce gaze.

"You're right," Anna said. "I didn't mean that other crap."

"Language!" Letitia tsked.

"Garbage," Anna corrected. "But I can't see our paths crossing again once this case is finished. He'll forget about me."

"And that's a bit of garbage itself. He'll no more forget you than you'll forget him. But I'm not going to brangle with you about that." Letitia's eyes and voice softened. "I know your heart is breaking, lass, but don't give up hope. And I'm here anytime you need to talk so don't keep it all bottled up inside."

Tears spilled down Anna's cheeks and she reached out and hugged the older woman.

"Thank you so much," she choked out.

Letitia patted her on the back.

"There, there, lass. Tisha's here."

For a few blessed moments, Anna let the tears flow. Then she pulled herself together and let go of her comforter.

"I'll be all right. It's just so fresh," she said.

"Do you want me to tell Kevin about this so you don't have to?"

"No, I'll do it," Anna said.

"You don't have to be a martyr, you know."

"No, he'll want the chance to say 'I told you so'," Anna joked weakly.

"And I'll bash him one on the head if he does."

Letitia sent Anna into the bathroom to wash her face while she bustled into the kitchen.

Mac had evidently been briefed enough not to ask any questions when Anna sat down at the kitchen table because all he said was, "We'll go see what's shaken loose at the precinct. Then we're taking the rest of the day off."

"No way," Anna said, regarding a long stretch of hours empty of the distraction of work with horror. "I've got to do the rest of the interviews for the Levine case."

"You'll make me look bad," Mac said.

"You have a wife. I've got an empty apartment."

Letitia put a basket of gently steaming scones in the middle of the table.

"They're hot," Letitia warned.

"They're carbs," Anna said, reaching for comfort.

"Ivanov's lawyer is trying to get him out on bail," the desk officer told Anna and Mac when they walked into the precinct house.

Anna snorted.

"Yeah, an ex-KGB agent is not a flight risk," she said.

"He's still denying any involvement in Savenkov's death."

"What else?"

"The conductor, Vranos, called to say he's going to be tied up in auditions all morning but he'll be checking his voice mail regularly. Claims he tried to reach you on your cell but couldn't," the officer continued, looking at Anna.

She pulled her phone out of her pocket and swore. She'd forgotten to turn it back on when she woke up. Sure enough there were three missed calls and one number was Nicholas'.

The desk officer gave them the rest of their messages and they proceeded to their office to deal with them.

Anna dialed into her voice mail and found Nicholas' message. As the dark, rich tones of his voice poured into her ear, she found herself hoping he had called to say he was a fool and had reversed his shattering decision.

"Anna, I'll be in auditions at Carnegie Hall all morning but leave me a message if anything happens. I'll check my voice mail whenever possible."

He paused and now she heard pain in his voice.

"I'm sorry, Anna. Truly sorry."

The call was over. She pushed the "save" key and turned to Mac.

"You want to observe while I go at Ivanov again?"

Mac took in her expression and said, "Yeah, but just to make sure you don't get accused of police brutality."

CHAPTER 32

An hour later, they were once again facing each other over their desks.

"Okay, we've got the logistics of the forgery nailed down now," Anna said. "The Archduke found a stash of Beethoven's sketchbooks when he was renovating his music room, went looking for a black market buyer, and found Ivanov. The Russian saw the potential for a much bigger payday and came up with the forgery scheme."

"You gotta give Ivanov credit for keeping the story near the truth. He's a pro."

"Yeah, and he's almost got me convinced he didn't kill Savenkov," Anna said, sighing.

"He killed Savenkov," Mac said flatly.

"Probably, but let's assume for the sake of argument he didn't," Anna said. "Who else might have?"

"Bostridge has motive but he's also got an alibi," Mac said.

"Unless he sent someone to do his dirty work for him. What about Jessica Strauss? She was at the scene of the crime."

"She can't handle an audition without having a nervous breakdown. I can't see her being able to plan killing someone. Remember she had to get the gun in and out of Carnegie Hall. And what's her motive?"

Anna sighed again.

"Got me, but maybe we didn't dig deeply enough. Maybe she and Bostridge are lovers."

"If they are, it's the best-kept secret in New York," Mac said.

Anna idly keyed their names into an Internet search engine. There were no joint entries, just their professional websites and a few reviews. She clicked on Bostridge's website. It featured a dramatically lit black-and-white head shot.

"That picture's got to be about fifteen years old," Anna muttered as she switched to Jessica Strauss' homepage.

The young woman's professional portrait was more recent. Also done in black-and-white, it showed her long hair pulled back into a bun and utilized the same side-lighting as Bostridge's.

"I'd say she's at least twenty years younger than he is," Mac added.

"Like that's ever stopped anyone from having sex," Anna said, scanning through Strauss' resume without finding anything of interest. She pushed back in her chair. "Mac, there's something you should know. Nicholas and I aren't, um, together anymore."

"I figured something had happened," Mac said, looking uncomfortable. "Tish doesn't have 'girl talks' unless it's serious."

"Just don't say it."

"What? What am I not supposed to say?"

"'I told you so.'"

"Why state the obvious?" Mac said.

"Right. I don't want to talk about it again."

"Good. I don't either."

Silence hung between them.

"How about we go do the Levine interviews?" Mac said.

Anna unlocked her desk drawer to pull out her gun and shrug into her holster. The feeling of the leather hugging her shoulder was so right she almost cried.

"Okay, next stop 446 East 78th Street," Mac said, squinting at his notes.

Anna pulled out of the illegal parking space without responding. A nebulous anxiety had been hovering at the edges of her brain all morning and she was determined to wrestle it to the ground.

"Hey, we're going uptown," Mac protested as she turned the wrong way.

"Oh, sorry," she said, swinging into an illegal U-turn that made three taxis slam on their brakes and lean on their horns.

"You've got to get some sleep," her partner said.

"Holy shit," Anna said, whipping the car over to the curb as the anxiety took on a frightening shape. "You drive. I've got to make a couple of phone calls."

It was a measure of the strength of their working relationship that Mac switched places without further discussion.

"Where to?" he asked as he moved the driver's seat back to accommodate his longer legs.

"Carnegie Hall."

Anna was already speed-dialing the office there.

"This is Lieutenant Detective Salazar with the NYPD. I need you to check the schedules for the rehearsal rooms immediately. Right. Is there a Brian Bostridge or a Jessica Strauss listed anywhere? No? What about Nicholas Vranos? Where's that room?"

She listened intently and Mac drove.

"Could you transfer me to Security?"

"This is Detective Lieutenant Salazar with the—oh good Frank, it's you. Listen, do you know Brian Bostridge or Jessica Strauss? Yeah, Bostridge is a jerk all right. Have you seen him today? Are you sure? Jessica Strauss is about twenty-eight, tall, and has very long, very red hair. I'm going to get her photo faxed to you right away. Will you check the tapes and see if she's come in? Call me if you find either one of them. Thanks."

Anna made a quick call to the precinct to arrange the fax transmission. She dialed Nicholas' cell phone number and swore when it went straight to voice mail.

"Nicholas, if you get this message, go directly to Security and stay there. Especially avoid Brian Bostridge or Jessica Strauss if you see them."

"What'd you figure out?" Mac said when she flipped her phone closed.

"They look alike," Anna said. "Bostridge and Strauss. I was looking at the head shots on their websites. Bostridge's was taken when he was a lot closer to Jessica's age now and it just clicked that they look enough alike to be related, maybe even father and daughter. It could give us a connection and a motive."

"We did a background check and that didn't come up," Mac said. "Bostridge has never been married."

Anna had her eyes closed, trying to visualize the biographical information on Bostridge and Strauss. "She could be illegitimate, adopted by a stepfather. Damn! I can't remember what it said about her parents, if anything."

"Doesn't matter," Mac said.

As the lights turned red for five blocks in front of them, he pulled out the magnetic flasher and slapped it on the roof of the car.

"Thanks," Anna said as the wail of the siren filled the car and Mac edged into the intersection. "I'm probably crazy but I just have a bad feeling about this."

"Practice rooms, Jessica Strauss, Carnegie Hall," Mac said, hitting the gas pedal as they cleared the cross traffic. "I'm thinking it's déjà vu all over again."

"Idiot cab driver coming up on the right," Anna warned as a taxi ignored their siren and pulled out in front of them.

Mac dodged it and sped up.

"You know, you're the world's best partner," Anna said.

"Don't make me cry when I'm driving."

The radio bleeped.

"Mac? Salazar? You there?" a voice came through the speaker.

"Yeah, we're both here," Anna said.

"We got a 9-1-1 call from Carnegie Hall. Unidentified female caller says someone's been shot in a rehearsal room. We've dispatched a squad car and an ambulance."

"Who's been shot? Is the vic still alive?" Anna barked. "Which rehearsal room?"

"The caller hung up before we could get more details but she said the name of the vic was Vranos."

"We're almost there," Anna said. "Thanks for the call."

Mac glanced briefly over at his partner before he sped up.

"Put your head between your legs and breathe," he said. "You're white as a sheet."

"Just drive," Anna said but she took a deep breath and reached under her jacket to pull out her Glock. She checked the ammunition and left the gun resting on her lap.

"Easy, partner," Mac said.

"I'm not going to lose him this time."

Mac didn't ask her if she meant Vranos or the person who had shot him.

CHAPTER 33

"Thank you so much for agreeing to hear me play," Jessica Strauss said, setting her violin case carefully on the piano.

"Don't mention it," Nicholas said, as he sat down on a chair and crossed his legs. He checked his cell phone for messages but the signal strength was too weak to receive any sort of transmission. He stowed it back in his pocket.

Jessica Strauss had been waiting outside the door of the audition room when he finished his last scheduled appointment. Ordinarily, he would have politely but firmly directed her to the orchestra manager, but he felt a sense of obligation to her for helping catch Viktor Ivanov. In fact, he welcomed the distraction since his thoughts had an unfortunate tendency to turn toward Anna when he wasn't otherwise occupied.

However, irritation began to surface when Jessica insisted on traipsing up to a distant rehearsal room, saying she had reserved it to ensure they wouldn't be disturbed. She seemed nervous and he recalled her fragility the day Lexi was killed, so he followed her to the inconvenient location.

As she laid out her music with her back to him, he frowned, thinking she seemed less attractive than he remembered her. She was wearing a long, shapeless sack of a dress, and what he vaguely recalled as a rather abundant head of red hair was completely covered by some strange sort of turban.

When she turned around holding a pistol instead of the violin he expected, it struck him as absurd and he laughed.

"Put that down. I've had one too many guns pointed at me in the last few days," he said, starting to stand up.

"Sit down. I'm not ready to kill you yet," Jessica said.

Her voice held the steel of determination and the quaver of madness. She held the gun without apparent effort, the strength of her violinist's arms apparent in the steadiness of her grip.

Nicholas slowly sank back into the chair.

"I want you to know why you're going to die," she said.

"Good, because I'm rather curious about it myself," he said, crossing his arms.

"I killed Lexi Savenkov," she said. "I tried to kill you after the Billy Leon concert. I'm just as glad I missed now."

Nicholas' eyes narrowed.

"There's an ex-KGB agent in jail for killing Lexi," he said.

"He's lying. *I* killed him. For my father."

"Your father?"

"Brian Bostridge. His brilliance would be recognized if it weren't for Lexi Savenkov. And now *you*," she said, her gun hand wavering slightly for the first time as she glared at Nicholas.

"I have nothing to do with Bostridge's talent being recognized or not. Neither did Lexi."

"Yes, you do. You won't hire him to play in your orchestra. You're protecting your friend's reputation by not letting my father prove he's better."

"I didn't know Brian Bostridge was your father," Nicholas said, trying to redirect her anger. "He's never acknowledged you in any way."

"He's my biological father," she said, as tears started to run down her cheeks. "He gave me my musical talent and I want to give him something in return, something that will tell the world I'm his daughter."

"Does he know what you've done?"

"He doesn't believe me. After all my planning, tricking Savenkov into meeting me, sneaking the gun in, and then hiding it so the police couldn't find it." She smiled. "I had to improvise that part after that stupid electrician scared me. He claims he killed Lexi but I did it. I told my father everything but he says I made it up. He doesn't think I'm clever enough to have fooled the police. When I kill you, he'll believe me."

"Why would he believe you this time?"

"Because I've called the police and told them you're dead. They'll find me here with your body and the murder weapon. And you're going to sign this."

Without taking her eyes off Nicholas she swiped a piece of paper off the piano and held it out.

"Take it," she said, leaning far enough forward so he could just reach the paper. She released the paper and straightened the moment it touched his fingertips.

"Here's a pen."

She reached behind her back again and came up with a ballpoint pen, tossing it to him. He caught it with his left hand and slid it into his breast pocket.

"May I read my death warrant?"

"Do it quickly."

Nicholas scanned slowly over the handwritten lines, not really absorbing what he read, as he mentally sorted through his options. They were limited. Jessica Strauss was insane but her mind seemed to be functioning with unfortunate clarity. She wouldn't come close enough to give him a real chance to use his superior height or strength to take the gun away. She wasn't easily distracted. Even worse, she had already demonstrated she had the nerve to go through with a cold-blooded murder.

"By the way," she said, "I'm very good with a gun. My stepfather made me go hunting with him so I can hit a moving target without any problem."

"Your stepfather?" Nicholas asked, stalling.

"He was a hog farmer," Jessica practically spat. "The only music he listened to was grunting and squealing. Do you know what it was like growing up without music when your soul craves it?"

"Yes."

"You? How would you know?"

"I grew up in a foster family who considered music sinful. I ran away when I was fourteen years old."

"And got taken in by a millionaire," Jessica said. "You never suffered like I did. I thought I was the daughter of a pig farmer. I didn't know my father was a musical genius until my mother was dying two years ago and she finally told me the truth."

Nicholas' eyebrows rose when she referred to Bostridge as a genius.

"Why didn't she tell you before?" he asked.

For the first time, Jessica seemed to hesitate.

"She claimed when she told my father she was pregnant he refused to marry her. But that was because he didn't know he had passed his talent on to me. I may never be as great as he is but at least I can help him get the recognition he deserves. I got Lexi out of his way and I'll get you out of his way. Then he'll be proud of me. He'll tell the world I'm his daughter," she said, before holding up her hand for silence. "What's that?"

Nicholas had heard the quiet footsteps already. Someone was coming down the hall with frequent pauses and the occasional sound of a door opening.

Jessica smiled and leveled the gun at Nicholas' heart.

"I think the police have arrived."

CHAPTER 34

"Where's the shooter?" Anna yelled at Frank in the security window as she raced through the stage door.

"What shooter?" Frank asked.

"The 9-1-1 call," Mac said, coming up behind Anna. "Who made it?"

"I don't know about a 9-1-1 call or a shooter," Frank said, "but I found a woman who might be Jessica Strauss on the security video."

Anna swore and took off up the stairs that led to the backstage area. Mac pounded up the steps behind her, his gun also drawn.

When she reached the second level, she hesitated for a moment to get her bearings, then turned and ran down a hall to find the rehearsal room where the office manager had told her Nicholas was holding auditions. She edged around the door frame only to find it empty.

"Damn!" she said, dropping her gun to her side. "We're going to have to go room to room. You take this floor. I'm going to go up another level."

"Be careful," Mac said, as he started for the next doorway with his gun ready.

"You too," Anna said over her shoulder as she headed back to the staircase.

After taking the steps two at a time, Anna paused at the top to get her breathing under control and to listen. The corridor was silent so she went to the first open door. Another empty room. She worked her way down the hallway, quickly checking through open doorways and moving on. Only four doors were closed. The first three revealed nothing more than a closet and two deserted dressing rooms. The fourth closed door was the last on the corridor. As she approached it, she steadied her gun and kept her footsteps as quiet as she could.

Her gut sensed tension emanating from the room. She put her hand on the knob and eased it to the right. It wasn't locked.

As she braced herself to open the door, a gunshot sounded from inside.

Anna threw the door open and went in fast with her knees bent. Jessica Strauss and Nicholas stood locked chest to chest, their hands held high above their heads as they struggled for possession of a pistol.

"Drop it, Jessica," Anna commanded. "You can't escape."

"She doesn't want to," Nicholas ground out as he tried to wrench the gun from the woman's grasp. "She wants you to know she killed me."

He was moving awkwardly, and Anna spotted a dark stain spreading across the side of his shirt.

Her vision went red around the edges before she could tamp down the rage.

"Hold onto her," Anna said, as she swiftly worked her way around behind Jessica.

Reversing the gun in her grasp, she slammed the butt into the back of Jessica's head. The woman crumpled to the floor, dragging Nicholas down with her.

"Nicholas, how bad is it?" Anna said, dropping to her knees beside him.

With an obvious effort, he pulled the gun from the unconscious woman's fingers and shoved it away under the piano before he groaned, "Ribs. Hurt like hell."

Anna rolled him away from Jessica's inert figure and yanked open the blood-soaked shirt. A sob welled up in her throat and, for a moment, she couldn't see through the tears. She swiped her sleeve across her eyes and tried to gauge the seriousness of his injury. Blood was pumping out of his side so she tore a piece off the hem of Jessica's long dress and pressed it hard against the wound.

"Nicholas, stay with me," she said as his eyelids fluttered closed.

He actually smiled faintly and said, "Oh, I intend to. For a very long time."

Then he went limp.

"Anna! You all right?" Mac came around the doorframe, his gun trained on Jessica Strauss' inert form. "How's Vranos?"

"Still alive, but hit. Where's the damned ambulance?" Anna said, fighting tears again.

"Coming. What about her?" He jerked his head toward the unconscious woman lying beside Anna.

"I knocked her out with my gun butt. She should come around soon. Her gun's under the piano."

"What happened?" Mac asked as he bent to retrieve the weapon.

"Nicholas said she wanted us to know she'd killed him."

Mac spotted the letter lying on the floor beside an overturned chair and picked it up.

"You're not going to believe this," he said as he read it. "She confesses to killing Savenkov and Vranos because they were blocking her father's career. And guess who her father is?"

"Brian Bostridge," Anna said, checking Nicholas' pulse and finding it reassuringly strong before she asked again, "Where's the damned ambulance?"

Voices and footsteps echoed down the hall and Mac shouted, "Last door on the left."

"About time," Anna said and let the tears fall.

"The bullet cracked a rib and then ricocheted back out," the doctor explained as Anna stood in the hallway outside Nicholas' hospital room. "That's why he was in so much pain. But the blood loss was stopped quickly enough so he'll be able to go home much sooner than he really should."

"Thanks, Dr. Stern," Anna said. "Can I talk to him now?"

"If he's still awake. I prescribed a pretty strong painkiller so he could sleep."

Anna tiptoed into the antiseptic white room. Sunlight forced its way around the edges of the drawn window shade and fell on the man lying propped up against the pristine hospital linens. His broad chest was bare except for the swath of bandages wrapped around him halfway up to his armpits. A neat sling held his left arm immobilized and she could see the bandage from his first wound still wrapped around his biceps. His eyes were closed, the lashes fanning dramatically across his high cheekbones, and his dark hair rioted in tousled waves across the pillow.

"Nicholas," Anna whispered, as she quietly approached the bed.

His eyelids flew open and his blue gaze hit her squarely in the heart. For a split second, she thought the blue flame might be joy before he closed his eyes and muttered, "I'm such a fool."

Swallowing the pain his greeting caused her, Anna said in her most professional voice, "I need to ask you a few questions. Are you up to answering them?"

He tried to take a deep breath but the cracked rib evidently stopped him because he gasped and grimaced.

"Yes, although I'm a bit fuzzy. I think the doctor gave me something to lessen the pain."

"Can you tell me what happened at Carnegie Hall?"

With a bit of prodding for details, Nicholas described the events in the rehearsal room. As Jessica leveled the gun at his chest, Nicholas realized he had to move or die so he stood and leapt straight at her. She fired but her aim had been for a man sitting down so the bullet hit below his heart. However, the pain from the cracked rib had been powerful enough to impair his ability to wrest the gun from her. Her determined insanity had lent power to the muscles of her musician's hands.

"If you hadn't come through the door just then, I'm not sure I could have stopped her from shooting again," he said. "And I don't think she would have missed the second time. Thank you. Again."

"Just doing my job," Anna said, then wished she hadn't as his expression went dark. "Not very well either. You got shot twice."

"I'm alive, thanks to you," he said.

Anna was torn between a desire to throw herself on his bare chest, sobbing with love and relief, and a need to get out of the room before his distant manner drove any more knives into her gut.

"I'm curious about a few things," Nicholas said. "How did Jessica get Lexi to meet her at Carnegie Hall the day she killed him?"

"It was simple. She made an appointment with him, claiming she wanted to get his advice about interpreting a particular piece of music."

"Lexi was always willing to help a young musician out with that sort of question. Jessica would have known that, God damn her," Nicholas said. "Where did she hide the gun though? You never found it."

"She'd planned to carry it out in her violin case but after she ran into the electrician and got spooked, she decided to hide it," Anna explained. "We discovered she's very familiar with Carnegie Hall. As a teenager, she took ballet lessons in the south tower and she and her friends would sneak out a window onto the roof to smoke. They explored quite a lot of the exterior of the building—-that's how she got away after shooting at us the night of the Billy Leon concert. At any rate, Jessica hid the gun on an exterior cornice of one of the practice room windows and came back to retrieve it three days later."

"Amazing for a woman who seems incapable of hailing a taxi," Nicholas said.

"She was focused on one thing only: getting her father's attention," she said. "We have to talk to Bostridge about not coming to us with Jessica's confession."

"He didn't believe her. He also may have been afraid of being implicated in Lexi's murder somehow." Nicholas' voice took on a harsh edge. "What kind of bastard doesn't acknowledge his own daughter when she wants him to? She was a grown woman. She wanted nothing from him except some recognition of their relationship."

"If it makes you feel any better, he's in trouble," Anna said.

"In more ways than one. I'll make sure the complaint he filed with the union has a basis in reality from now on. If he thought I was obstructing his career before . . ." Nicholas stopped and looked at her for a long moment, and Anna held her breath but all he said was, "How did you get there so fast?"

"Mac and I were on our way already. I happened to notice a resemblance between Bostridge and Strauss in their professional photos and it gave me a bad feeling. Then we heard about the 9-1-1 call and—" she stopped and swallowed, "I was afraid you were dead already."

He closed his eyes as though he couldn't bear to see the pain written on her face, and she pivoted toward the door.

"Anna," he said.

She turned back to find him holding out his good hand to her, palm up.

"Can you forgive me for being a coward?"

"Coward?" she said, putting her hand in his and feeling the exquisite pleasure of his long fingers closing firmly around hers. "You tackled two armed killers barehanded. I don't see how that makes you a coward."

He shook his head against the pillow.

"Not that. I was a coward about loving you." He drew her hand to his lips and kissed it ever so gently. "Do you know when Jessica turned around with the gun in her hand I laughed? It struck me as funny that I was being threatened with a gun for the third time in as many days. But it made me understand something. How having a gun pointed at you can become almost commonplace but it doesn't make you take it any less seriously."

He rubbed the back of her hand against his cheek, the slight stubble rasping against her skin.

"I also realized I'm just as mortal as you are," he said. "I can die as easily as you can. Yet you weren't afraid to love me."

"Yes, I was. I was terrified, for different reasons," Anna said, turning her hand to cup his face, "but I couldn't stop myself."

"What about now?" he asked, his fingers tightening around hers. "Can you still not stop yourself?"

"No. I mean, yes," Anna said, a laugh of relief bubbling up. "I mean, I love you."

The blue of his eyes went incandescent and he pulled her down against him, as something between a laugh and a groan was wrenched from his throat.

"Don't hurt yourself," Anna said, trying to shift her weight off his injured side.

"Hold still and let me kiss you," he said, sliding his hand around the back of her head and tilting her face to his.

Anna tried to brace herself away from his cracked rib but Nicholas' good arm tightened around her like a steel band, crushing her against him, bandages and all. He kissed her with a ferocity that took her breath away, as though he was trying to overwhelm any doubts she might have about the strength of his passion.

His grip loosened as he changed the angle of his mouth against hers, and Anna managed to pull her head an inch away.

"You don't want to start bleeding again," she said, tenderly smoothing his dark hair back from his face.

"I've been bleeding since you walked out the door of my apartment last night," he said. "A gunshot wound is nothing compared to that."

"Are you sure about loving me?" Anna whispered. "About loving a cop? I know it's not easy."

"You're wrong," Nicholas said. "It's the easiest thing in the world."

He took hold of her braid and tugged her head back down to him, and Anna stopped worrying about anything except how to find a way to breathe.

EPILOGUE
A Year Later

Nicholas' baton slashed downward and the last note died. Silence filled the concert hall as the audience took a moment to absorb the fact that the glorious sound had come to an end. Suddenly, applause poured from all corners of the auditorium and people rose to their feet like a wave, shouting, "Bravo! Bravo!"

Nicholas turned and bowed, causing a near frenzy of cheering and clapping. In the center box, Anna stood and clapped as well, letting the tears stream unabashedly down her face. Karin Gadde stood beside her but she was unable to applaud. Her face was buried in her hands as her shoulders shook with sobs. Finally her brother's "Ghost Symphony" had been heard by the world.

The printed program dedicated this performance to the memory of Alexei Savenkov while it credited two composers with the symphony's authorship: Ludwig von Beethoven and Franz Gadde. Nicholas had titled the piece, saying it was a collaboration between two ghosts. The blank measures in the second movement were left blank; Nicholas had instructed the orchestra to remain silent for those beats so the audience could pay tribute in their thoughts to the men who had created the music.

The original announcement of the performance had created an immense stir in the media since it allowed the dark history of the symphony to be dredged up and dissected again. The music critics were alternately fascinated and dismissive.

Nicholas had ignored all the hoopla. He simply felt Franz Gadde's work should not be allowed to disappear without ever being performed. And of course, the concert was standing room only.

It had taken a lot of string-pulling to get the manuscript released to Nicholas, even after Ivanov and the Archduke were convicted. Anna took a moment to relish the knowledge that

Ivanov had gotten nailed for vehicular homicide in Vienna, thanks to an eyewitness who came forward when the Austrian police reopened Franz Gadde's case.

The young composer's murder had not gone unavenged.

Anna, Mac, and Letitia slipped unobtrusively through the door of the Rohatyn Room, where the small, private post-concert reception was being held, catered by *Vranos*, of course. Anna knew Nicholas hadn't arrived yet; she had always been able to sense his presence in a room instantly.

Kelly Sinclair spotted them and raced over.

"You look fabulous," she said, looking Anna over from head to toe.

"Isn't that somewhat self-congratulatory since it's Rafael's design and you picked it out for me?" Anna teased, as the layers of rose chiffon swirled around her knees.

"I meant you wear it well. Not everyone can handle a dress that feminine," Kelly said. "Did you really put your Glock in the purse?"

"Are you kidding?" Mac said. "No cop would come near Carnegie Hall without a weapon. It's got a bad reputation nowadays."

Letitia elbowed him.

"Have you got something you want to share with us?" Kelly said, eyeing a rather conspicuous diamond ring on Anna's left hand.

"Anna, how wonderful to see you!" Kate Johnson interrupted, strolling up with her husband Randall.

"Kate, Randall, I'm so glad you're here," Anna said with a sigh of relief as she hid her hand behind her back.

"I just heard the most shocking story," Kate said. "That toad Brian Bostridge is writing a book about his insane daughter and is making some outrageous amount of money from it."

"Yeah, he started visiting Jessica in prison and taking notes on their conversations," Anna said. "She finally got him to pay attention to her so I guess she's happy now."

Just then the entrance door swung open, and Nicholas strode into the room, wearing his tails. A spontaneous round of applause broke out. He stopped and gave the crowd a slightly ironic bow. As he straightened, his gaze skimmed over the faces of the guests until he found Anna. His brilliant smile was entirely for her.

Anna's heart started the little dance it always did when he came into her view.

Still holding Anna's eyes with his, Nicholas swept a glass of champagne from a passing waiter's tray and leapt onto a chair.

"Ladies and gentlemen," he said in the voice which commanded the attention of entire orchestras.

All conversation ceased.

"This is both a memorial and a celebration," he said. "Tonight I feel our ghosts have been laid to rest at last. I'd like to drink to the spirits of Lexi Savenkov, Franz Gadde, and Ludwig von Beethoven, men of great genius whose absence has made the world a poorer place."

He lowered the glass to take a generous swallow and the crowd followed suit, murmuring their approval with a scattered "Hear! Hear!" or "To Lexi, Franz, and Ludwig".

"Not a dry eye in the place," Mac muttered beside her as he raised his beer in a salute. "Your boyfriend is playing this crowd like a fine Stradivarius."

"That's why he went into conducting," Anna murmured back.

Nicholas wasn't finished.

"Fortunately for us, they've left behind their music," he continued, "some of which we had the privilege to hear tonight. Only time, and the critics, will determine if the "Ghost Symphony" will become part of the musical canon or if it will be viewed as merely a curiosity. It doesn't matter as long as it is heard. I regret only that Lexi could not play his part in the orchestra. He would have loved the drama."

For a moment, Nicholas' expression became somber and Anna longed to erase the shadows from his eyes. Then he smiled directly at her again and the room fell away, leaving only the two of them.

"Now I would like to turn to the future and a more personal note. You all know Detective Lieutenant Anna Salazar was instrumental in solving the mystery around this symphony and my friend's death. She also saved my life, in more ways than one."

As attention began to shift from Nicholas to Anna, she tried to edge her way behind Mac's broad shoulders.

Nicholas held out his hand with that unassailable leader's authority, saying, "Anna, come join me."

"I'm not standing on a chair," she muttered, as Mac stepped aside and gave her a gentle shove in Nicholas' direction.

The guests smiled and moved out of her path as she walked forward. Nicholas descended from his perch and slid his arm around her waist, looking down into her eyes with a love that still overwhelmed her. Then he turned to the room.

"This morning I succeeded at a Herculean task, one I have been pursuing diligently over the past year. I finally persuaded Anna to marry me. Please—"

Whatever else Nicholas had been planning to say was drowned in the cheers of the guests. Glasses were emptied in a single gulp and people surged forward to congratulate the bride- and groom-to-be.

Between well-wishers, Anna growled out of the corner of her mouth, "You didn't need to make such a public spectacle out of it."

Nicholas' laugh was that of a man who'd found and claimed his soul mate.

"Great music should be heard," he said. "Great love should be shouted from the rooftops. However, I can think of one way to keep me quiet."

"Impossible," Anna said.

To prove her wrong, he bent her over his arm and brought his mouth down on hers.

The crowd went wild.

Printed in the United States
128708LV00014B/10/A